The Higher Education of
Geetika Mehendiratta

Anuradha Marwah is a professor, playwright and novelist. Her wide-ranging publications also include poems, essays, articles and reviews. *Aunties of Vasant Kunj*, her fourth novel, was published in 2024 to immense acclaim.

Her first novel, *The Higher Education of Geetika Mehendiratta*, published three decades ago, was among India's earliest campus novels.

Anuradha lives in Vasant Kunj, Delhi, surrounded by a community of trees and cats.

You can reach out to her at:
Instagram: @author_anuradhamarwah
Website: anuradhamarwah.com

'Humour is the surprise in Anuradha's novel. It has a female protagonist writing in the first person in gleeful abandon.'

—India Today

'Anuradha's remarkable novel is intelligently crafted, touchingly told. Free from stylistic affectations, her fluent prose is devoid of the subverting impact of pleonastic frills.'

—The Sunday Times of India

'What is not to be taken for granted are the clear flashes of insight into character, the incisive use of dialogue to pad out the even tone of the narrative style, so that Geetika becomes unforgettable not just for her polysyllabic name (which she hates), but because she has been so believably and recognizably put together.'

—The Metropolis on Saturday

'The book is wholly modern and yet Indian enough, [and] is fluently written and easily read.'

—Hindustan Times

'It is a charming story […] about growing up. The style is reminiscent of Sue Townsend's *Adrian Mole* series.'

—Sunday Magazine

'Not many Indian writers have dared to use the M-word and one appreciates the candid talk, especially because it is almost impossible for women writers in India to tear away the straitjacket of social-prudery and feminine grace imposed on them, more so when the narration is in the first person.'

—The Indian Express

'[The book] point[s] to an indigenous state of good literary health.'
—Professor Meenakshi Mukherjee

The Higher Education of
Geetika Mehendiratta

Anuradha Marwah

RUPA

Published by
Rupa Publications India Pvt. Ltd 2025
161-B/4, Gulmohar House,
Yusuf Sarai Community Centre,
New Delhi 110049

Sales centres:
Bengaluru Chennai
Hyderabad Kolkata Mumbai

First published in 1993

This is a work of fiction. Names, characters, places and incidents
are either the product of the author's imagination or are used fictitiously
and any resemblance to any actual person, living or dead, events or
locales is entirely coincidental.

P-ISBN: 978-93-7003-094-7
E-ISBN: 978-93-7003-266-8

First impression 2025

10 9 8 7 6 5 4 3 2 1

The moral right of the author has been asserted.

Printed in India

Author's Note

More than thirty years after this novel first appeared, it feels like a gift to be able to bring it back into the public realm. On a recent journey to the town of my birth aboard a superfast train, I was reminded of the steam-hauled, metre-gauge train that used to ply between Delhi and Ajmer in Geetika's time, and especially its quaint ladies' compartment.

My novel, however, does not invite readers into a sepia-tinted past, even though so much appears to have changed since it was written. Geetika, my outspoken protagonist, questioned and challenged, and the issues she grappled with are by no means resolved till date. Young people, I find, continue to face similar dilemmas: career or family, feminism or femininity, love or rebellion. I am excited to present Geetika once again—contemporaneous, relevant and adding the heft of history to present-day conversations on marriage and partnership.

—**Anuradha Marwah**
2025

Part One

....

MA

❧ Desertvadi ❧

It was morning. I didn't have to go to college till 10.30 a.m. There was nothing to do except cry, make a phone call or masturbate—I didn't want to do any of those. My eyes would be bleary, and excesses were not compatible with my thin face.

From my window I could see the distant Aravallis that ringed this little town, Desertvadi. Desertvadi is a real town in Rajasthan, like many other towns that are and aren't. Even though it doesn't matter what one calls them, Desertvadi is singularly inaptly named. It is not quite a desert, and is called a *vadi* (valley) only because it is surrounded by hills.

This inappropriateness would dawn on the bureaucrats whenever a dignitary visited the place, or whenever there was a proposal to attract more tourists. Once, the Municipal Council had all the rooftops neighbouring the railway station painted a dirty salmon pink. But Desertvadi could never be called 'pink city', since that name had been claimed by Jaipur, which was far more exotic and attracted far more foreign currency than Desertvadi could ever hope to. Another time, they built fountains in the centre of the marketplace so that in conjunction with the few lakes the town had, the 'valley' aspect of the town could be accentuated. That very year, severe water shortage hit Desertvadi. Not only did all the taps run dry, the lakes also evaporated. Nevertheless, the dry lakes continued to fascinate the few impecunious tourists (mostly foreigners), but that is another matter. More on that later.

In this town of indeterminate character, I had done nothing this morning but lounge on the string bed, wondering what to do. The morning air was already beginning to turn hot and dry. Time was running out. I had to bathe, lock up the house and reach college—all within the hour. Purposeful at last, I set about planning my look: a loose pink shirt to complement my fair complexion and slight figure, with tight jeans. It was just another day, not a special one. When Anirudh—Andy—was in town, days became special and required special planning. I was in love with Andy. He was my boyfriend.

The moped I rode to college was a black and bulky Hero Majestic. I hummed the ad jingle as I unlocked the chain: Hero Majestic moped, for comfort and economy, is the best. As I weaved through tongas, rickshaws, cycles, motorcycles, scooter, three-wheelers and the occasional stray cow- and bullock-cart, I tried to look like the girl in the ad. Her long hair was all over her boyfriend, who sat pillion. It could have been Andy and me on the moped. Andy was in love with me. Andy was my life.

I drew up in front of Desertvadi Government College, where I was doing an MA in English Literature. The college auditorium was the biggest and grandest in Desertvadi, and the parking was right opposite it. Tony was sitting on the steps of the auditorium. Andy and I had sat there soon after we started dating. Did Tony know about Andy and me? How stupid I was! How would he?

Tony was the only boy in our MA English class who could speak English. He was from that high-and-mighty public school for boys, Macaulay College. Very few from Desertvadi could afford that elite residential school. His father taught there, so his education had been free. Tony was very uncomfortable in the government college, where Jats and Rajputs duelled in the corridors. All his friends from Macaulay were at places like The College in Lutyenabad, the capital city.

The College was so named because it did not need a name. Everyone in Lutyenabad—and the whole country—knew it was the best. People said Tony had not been able to make it to The College or anywhere because he was on drugs. So, he had remained in Government College as an anomaly. In truth, our college had very few interesting boys at the graduate level. Interesting boys—boys who could speak English, boys who had learnt English at missionary day schools in Desertvadi—were all either in medical and engineering colleges or doing things like business management. My brother, for example, was out learning to collect income tax and Andy was out learning to be an executive. Tony shone among the municipal school boys in our class. The girls, who were all from English-medium missionary schools, often remarked on the dearth of interesting boys in our college. We all hated the government college, but since we had not opted for any professional training, this was our only option for MA.

I did not have to make Tony fall in love with me. I was secure. I had a boy who was in love with me. Still, I longed to dangle Andy before Tony to make him jealous.

'Hello Tony!'

'Hello Geetika!'

He did not call me Geeti, marking a formal distance from me. His voice was gruff. What should I say next? 'Maha bore class.'

'Whose?'

'Mrs Sharma's. Let's do something.'

'Like?'

My imagination was running out. The indifferent Tony was actually listening to me. I had to sustain his interest, had to be outrageous—outrageously funny, brilliant.

'Let's make her uncomfortable… Ask questions about Wallace Stevens—'

'I don't know a thing about Wallace Stevens. Anyway, who will ask the questions?'

'Let's ask about his life…' I was desperate to show off. Twentieth-Century American Literature had been inexplicably introduced into the course this very year. Nobody knew anything about Wallace Stevens or Ezra Pound. The university that had designed the syllabus was miles away. None of the lecturers were familiar with these writers. I had found a book in the library of another college that said Stevens was a successful executive besides being a poet.

'Don't get me involved in all this,' said Tony, looking bored.

My friend Vinita was passing by. She was tall and slender with a lovely bosom. I hated her. I knew I could hold Tony's attention if I invoked Vinita.

'Vini, suggest something to bug Sharma, no!'

'Faint... Fall down...'

Tony's interest piqued. 'Looks like you were a hell of a kid in school, Vini.'

'Who will faint?' I chimed in, trying to highlight the impracticality of it all.

'I will do it,' Tony answered.

We sat in class with bated breath. It was a lovely room—high ceiling, big windows. The college building was old and gracious, a fine example of British colonial architecture. The inmates were examples, too, of something similar. The boys, carefully groomed to hide the poverty of their origins, smiled desperately to avoid conversation in the language in which they were supposedly earning a master's degree. The girls, lovely like the building, were waiting for the doctors and engineers to declare their worth.

But of course, I was different. I was beyond all this. I was going to be famous. I was going to ace the exams, get into the civil services. I was going to become a famous writer. I had a boyfriend—did Tony even realize how different I was from Vinita, who had a pert bosom and was going to marry the man her mother chose?

Sharma entered the class.

'There is not a single book available on Wallace Stevens,' she fumed, defeated by his poetry. 'Have you found anything on him, Geetika Mehendiratta?'

I flinched. I hated being called by my full name. Nevertheless, now was my chance. 'Not really. But I remember reading somewhere that he was...is...a successful execu—'

There was a crash from the backbench. Tony was on the floor, eyes shut, beads of perspiration glistening on his amazingly ugly face. The girls buzzed around him in a swirl of colourful dupattas, clucking excitedly, grinning uncontrollably—they were all in the know. Usha held his wrist, pretending to feel his pulse;

Gayatri took off his shoes. Vinita—God!—she actually had his head in her lap.

The boys hovered at the periphery of this charmed circle of English speakers whose language and culture they longed to emulate. They were gaping at this unfamiliar norm of dealing with a sick person. One of them—nicknamed Pigeon by us—had confessed his ambition to me a few days back while attempting to borrow my notes. He wanted to become a primary school teacher and, to that end, was painstakingly studying Shakespeare and Milton. The teacher recruitment exam actually had a paper on General English, in which candidates were expected to write 200 words on esoteric topics like 'If I were the Chief Minister of…'.

Pigeon had round, bird-like eyes, now fixed on the spectacle Vinita was making of herself. I was suddenly angry—with her, with myself, with Tony. Suddenly, becoming a school teacher seemed important, and I felt Pigeon ought to be included in all this.

'Tony hasn't fainted,' I whispered to him. 'Get a jug of water…'

Pigeon always did as he was told. Besides, he wanted my notes.

While Sharma gaped in stunned silence, Pigeon got a jug of water and proceeded to pour it over Tony's face.

Tony got up, spluttering. 'You, son of a—'

Sharma walked out of the class with a terse, 'Tony, see me in the staff room.'

'What an ass Pigeon is,' said Vinita.

⊰ Shame ⊱

Pigeon came to see me the next day. College was closed but he had run into Tony in the library.

'Why you make throw me water? Tony ji anger very much at me. I not like to get into politics. I only come to read English in college.'

I replied in Hindi, hoping he would follow suit. 'Did you tell Tony that I asked you to do it?'

'Of course. He anger so much,' Pigeon replied, still persisting with English.'

I wondered what Tony must think of me now.

'He anger very much at you. He say you plan the trick. Why you do these things? You are the studying kind,' he complained.

'Vinita planned it, not me. She is the naughty one.'

'Vinita is a nice girl. So beautiful. So many boys after her but she not give lift to anyone. Everyone say she is good girl, though smart.'

What would they say about me if they found out about Andy? There had already been some talk about us during the play rehearsals. But it was hard for people to believe such things about me. I *was* the *studying kind*, after all.

'I will tell Vinita what you said about her,' I teased Pigeon. 'She will be delighted.'

'What is the use?' replied Pigeon. 'She not care for boy like me.'

I promised him I would intercede on his behalf and make it known to everyone, even to the angered Tony, how apolitical he really was.

In the evening, I found my parents reading a letter from my maternal grandfather. My mother smiled indulgently as she read.

'Would you like to marry a doctor settled in America?' she asked me.

'No, of course not,' I said—perhaps too quickly. It must be fun living in America—people speaking in that different accent, boys and girls kissing on the streets, women in bikinis...

'Why not?'

'I don't want to marry for the sake of marrying,' I said. I didn't. I really didn't. How could I get excited at the thought of marrying a stranger? No, it wasn't marriage that excited me—it was the idea of living in a foreign country.

'That's what I thought,' my mother said, turning to my father.

'No daughter of mine can be satisfied with mere marriage. Our Geetika has always done so well in studies. I am sure she will clear the civil services exam easily.'

'She must choose the Rajasthan cadre and come as a collector to Desertvadi,' replied my father.

My parents were really unconventional. In Desertvadi, they were recognized as social workers of repute. They ran vocational centres in the poorer parts of town and taught in local colleges. They had no time for anything else. Our house was always brimming with official files and people employed by the government for the upliftment of the downtrodden. I hated those people for ringing the bell just as we were sitting down to tea. I hated them for their worn-out clothes. I hated them for the long conversations they had with my parents. I hated having tea on my own. My brother, who was years older, was always away.

'I have not got any jewellery made for her. My colleagues in college are surprised that I am not saving up for the dowry of a daughter who is almost twenty-one,' continued my mother, who taught at a women's college where lecturers knitted sweaters in their spare time.

'The whole concept of not spending every extra rupee on jewellery must be alien to them,' I commented.

Vinita often showed off the jewellery her mother had gotten made for her. I particularly liked the armlet. It had a dancing peacock motif, studded with tiny green and blue gems. Emeralds and sapphires, Vinita had informed me. She also had a *navratna*, which was a necklace set with nine different kinds of precious stones. All of it was stored in a bank locker, but Vinita was allowed to wear these to family weddings, so everybody could see how much jewellery she had. Her family was from Desertvadi, so there were many family weddings to attend.

My relatives all lived far away. Ours was not a close-knit family at all. We did not belong to any place, actually. As children and adolescents, my parents had lived in what was now Pakistan. Then they became refugees. But they worked in the poor Muslim locality of Desertvadi. They did not hate the Muslims like some refugees did. They loved Desertvadi. They said it was a beautiful place.

I would have preferred to live in Lutyenabad and study at The College, which was a very elite institution, indeed. My father said it was not necessary to study at places like Macaulay and The College to do well. After all, weren't my brother and I as good as anybody else in the country?

I didn't know about the country, but I had certainly done very well up till now by Desertvadi standards. I used to tell my father that the government college was unchallenging. And yet here I was, lusting after jewellery...and boys...

But there was nothing wrong with having boys as friends. Andy could be called a friend. I was not behaving like Booba and Sangeeta, after all.

❧ *Blood* ❧

Booba—I think that was her name. Perhaps short for Mehbooba. I was young back then, too young to know for sure. She told me I had sharp features, which was a compliment. I accepted it reverently. She told me boys found her sexy, but that she loved Sam. We giggled a lot at that. I asked her whether I was sexy. She said no, of course not—I had no boobs. I asked her whether anybody, any boy, would ever fall in love with me. She said she didn't think so; not yet anyway. She confirmed my worst fears.

Booba was having an affair with her cousin, Sam, in whose home she was living. At the time, I was also living in that house, but only as the tenant's daughter—not as an impoverished, fatherless relative. So he did not have an affair with me. Besides, I was seven years old and breasts-less. I took his lack of interest in me as a personal affront. After all, I *did* have sharp features. I took to jiggling my bottom at him. He told Booba he thought I had a problem with my feet—were they flat? Booba made me walk barefoot, with wet feet, across the floor. Then she told me I was flat-footed.

They were found out one day by the landlady, Sam's mother. The landlord was, after all, just eighteen. His father had died, leaving him two adjoining houses. Sam's mother was a large, commanding woman, who slapped him hard when she found him with his hands under Booba's skirt. She also confiscated our lawnmower. She scolded me for plucking raw mangoes from her tree. She sent Booba packing. I cried a lot when Booba left, sobbing into a green kerchief. There was now no one who would tell me about boys.

I already knew a lot. Booba had told me about blood. Boys did things to one that made one bleed. I did not like that. I preferred the Hindi film version—films I watched with my parents. They had intellectual discussions about them later. I liked to express my opinion about films too but, of course, I did not mention scenes that left me breathless and excited. I knew my parents would be shocked if I told them that I liked it when the villain ripped off the heroine's clothes, she screamed and the hero jumped in to save her and beat the blackguard. I preferred such scenes to the ones in which the hero treated her similarly and she only laughed and sang. Anyway, there was no blood anywhere in either and I was quite upset by Booba's insistence that there invariably was.

Booba had not been the studying kind.

Sangeeta was not the studying kind either. She used to fail most examinations. She was seventeen and still in tenth standard. Most of us were fifteen. Sangeeta was a bad girl, or so everybody said. She was having an affair with a boy from the medical college. She used to spend nights at the medical college hostel. She had a slim waist and a whole lot of pimples. That, the girls said, was because she was on the pill.

Before him, she had been friendly with a shopkeeper, who, it was rumoured, gave her a lot of money. She had had an abortion because of him. Her parents were very conservative. They had seven children. They were Jains. Jains were strict vegetarians and were not even supposed to kill flies. But Sangeeta used to have kebabs with her low-caste lover. She was a very bad girl.

When we went to Madras on a school trip, Sangeeta was also supposed to come with us. But instead, she went to Kashmir with her boyfriend. Everybody found out about her affair. She was expelled from school. We never saw her again. People said her parents were keeping her under lock and key. But what was the use? Who would marry her?

◄ *Anglo-Indians* ►

The Hindi films that I used to watch with my parents always had a vamp to set off the virtues of the heroine. My favourite vamp was an Anglo-Indian—Helen. Later, I discovered she was Anglo-Burmese, which was not quite the same thing. I loved her dances. They were called 'cabaret dances' in Desertvadi parlance. In one film, Helen wore huge plumes and not much else. I also wanted a dress like that. My mother told me only bad women wore such clothes.

My teacher in third standard was also an Anglo-Indian, Miss Gema. She wore short skirts and stockings, and sometimes no stockings. She went dancing with boys. I asked my mother if that made her a bad woman. My mother said Anglo-Indians were different.

There were so many Anglo-Indians in school. They had dance parties. I didn't know what went on at these parties, but my mother said it was not the 'Indian way of life'. I asked her if Kiran, whose father was a doctor and whose mother did not go out at all, was living the Indian way. My mother said yes, but they were much more traditional in their thinking than we were. We were not traditional because she worked—not only in a college but also as a social worker. There were hardly any women social workers in Desertvadi. Other lecturers from Mummy's college went right back to their homes after their four hours of teaching. I knew Mummy was different.

I met Sheila when I was eleven years old and in the seventh standard. She was thirteen, already buxom. I told my mother that Sheila, an Anglo-Indian, was my best friend. But I knew I couldn't go to parties with her because we were different. And anyway, where did I have the time? I had to study so much to maintain my position in class. Sheila, because of her family environment—Anglos, you know—couldn't be bothered.

'You must call her over for Diwali,' my mother said.

Sheila told me she was a teenager. I loved the sound of it and asked her whether I could be taken for one too. She said no, that I looked so young; it would be ages before I wore a bra.

Sheila did not wear a chemise like me. I always thought 'chemise' was a Hindi word until I grew up and learnt it was French. In Desertvadi, it referred to the hand-embroidered cotton shifts little girls wore under their dresses. Sheila wore only nylon, lacy slips under her skirt. The lace of her bra was always visible through her terrycot blouse. She plucked her eyebrows thin, very thin. The teachers were very nasty to her. They were nasty to me too, but that was because I always prepared my lessons too well and asked too many questions. They told me not to be so proud of my knowledge. I got higher marks than the others only because both my parents were in the teaching profession and helped me with my lessons. Other girls were so much brighter but didn't have enough opportunity.

Sheila told me not to mind all that. The teachers were frustrated—so many of them didn't have husbands. 'Spinsters are always frustrated,' she said.

I asked her whether all the nuns in school were frustrated. She said yes, yes; couldn't I see the way they behaved whenever the only good-looking priest in Desertvadi came to the convent for a visit?

'But you are a Catholic,' I said.

'So what?' she asked. 'Everyone knows nuns are frustrated. Last year a young novice ran away with the school bus driver's son—and he wasn't even Christian!'

I asked whom she would marry.

'The man I fall in love with,' Sheila replied, 'will be rich.'

She would meet him at a party. He would be captivated by her dancing, Sheila would say.

Sheila got new clothes stitched for every party. Her mother stitched them. She also baked cakes. They spoke only English at home. Her father was a Major in the army.

The Colonel's daughter in our class used to cut Sheila dead.

'These Hindus are so conservative,' Sheila would say. 'These officers' families, so snobbish.'

'We are not conservative,' I would tell her.

I could never go to her house because the cantonment area was too far. No question of spending the night there, my mother had told me. By the time I was old enough to disobey, Sheila had left Desertvadi.

Justine was also an Anglo-Indian. A swimmer. She had brown eyes, tanned brown skin and hair bleached brown by the chlorine in the pool. Her father was the physical training instructor at the high and mighty Macaulay College. She lived on the Macaulay campus and swam in the school pool. There were not many pools in Desertvadi. At fifteen, she was the best female swimmer in town. Everyone from my school loved her; they said she was a good girl despite being Anglo-Indian.

She loved a prince. The prince studied at Macaulay. There are no princes in independent India, our Civics book said in tenth standard. Yet, everyone in Desertvadi knew princes studied in Macaulay College. Princesses studied with us, in the convent school, and lived in the school hostel under strict surveillance by the nuns. Girls who stayed in the hostel were much richer than us day scholars. My father used to say convent schools survived because of the hostellers. If they took only day scholars, they would shut down. Nobody could pay a lot of fees in Desertvadi, especially since people didn't really believe in spending on education.

Mahima Kumari of Deogarh, a hosteller at my school, got married when she was in eleventh standard, to Virbhadra Singh of Roopgarh. Her father was a member of Parliament. Nobody said she was underage. The nuns even gave her a wedding present.

Mahima used to wear tank tops and hot pants in the hostel. Her sister Sushma was in my class. She said her Jija-sa was very upset about having to cover her face for the wedding. She did not like the heavy veil she had to drape around her, and she did not even like the priceless lehenga sent by Jijo-sa's family.

Sushma said her Jijo-sa was very handsome. We found all this Jija-sa–Jijo-sa business very funny. All Rajput girls—whether princesses or not—addressed their relatives in the same way. Instead of 'yes', they would say 'hukum'. My mother said it was their court culture.

I asked Sushma whether Mahima could still wear hot pants. She said, 'Yes, of course'; after all, they were honeymooning in Europe—did I expect her to wear saris and lehengas there?

I asked her whether her Jija-sa had met Virbhadra before the wedding.

'Yes, of course,' she replied. 'They went out dancing at a discotheque in Lutyenabad after the marriage was settled.'

'But what if Mahima had refused to marry him?' I asked. 'What would your parents have done then?'

She told me to stop asking stupid questions—Jijo-sa was so handsome, from Macaulay *and* settled abroad.

Everybody said the prince from Macaulay would never marry Justine. Rajputs are very conservative, they said. So why was she wasting her time? She should have been looking for a nice Anglo-Indian boy.

But Justine really loved the prince. For his birthday, she baked eighteen cakes. Justine used to read a lot of Mills and

Boon novels. I was an intellectual so I read only Thomas Hardy and Agatha Christie. Teachers at school said that was good—but only expected from a daughter of lecturers. They themselves read Barbara Cartland and Mills and Boon.

⊰ Honour ⊱

At Desertvadi Government College, there were hardly any royal Rajputs. The interesting boys either attended The College or had gone abroad or were managing what was left of their ancestral financial empires. The girls had left too—either to study at exclusive women's colleges or to get married, like Mahima Kumari had, in eleventh standard. But other Rajputs remained—those who came from the villages the royalty used in their surnames. They fought duels with rusted swords and, along with the Jats, brought shame to the once-famous name of the Desertvadi Government College.

'The college is closed today'—we were told at the gate.

Bad luck! I thought. I won't get to know the fallout of the fainting affair. But Vinita won't get to meet Tony either. Just as well!

There had been a fight between the two communities again. A Jat boy had 'teased' a girl. This girl was the *rakhi*-sister of a Rajput boy. Lots of girls had rakhi-brothers. This was better than having boyfriends. They could have coffee together in the canteen and nobody would whistle. They could even touch each other in public. The rakhi-brother would swear to protect the honour of his sister.

The custom of rakhi-brothers had originated somewhere near Desertvadi. A certain Rajput queen had sent a rakhi to a powerful Mughal ruler, asking him to protect her honour—and her husband's empire. Such was the glorious history relived time and again at the government college.

The rakhi-brother saw red when the lissom figure of the sister was remarked upon, and attacked the erring Jat. It so happened that the Jat was several inches taller and some kilos heavier than the gallant Rajput. The Rajput's black eye ultimately led to communal warfare.

Hockey sticks were the conventional weapons in such skirmishes. But some boys had used swords this time. They had brought them from their villages and had kept them in their hostel rooms for such eventualities. According to eyewitnesses, both sides had been too inebriated to know who they were hitting. But six boys—two Rajputs and four Jats—sustained injuries. The college was closed to prevent further violence. The Jats had sworn to even out the number of injuries.

I decided to go to Vinita's home and boast about the rose petals I had received in a letter from Andy. They had fluttered out when I excitedly tore the envelope open in front of my parents. Mummy had wondered aloud why my pen friend, Anita, wrote so often, or sent dried flowers with her letter.

I would have to give Andy another address, I decided, as Mummy was suspicious. But Andy was being weird. He had written to say he had told his parents about us. They had said he was grown-up enough to know his own mind. Andy had written it would be a good idea if I went and met them before his next monthly visit.

Was he mad? What would I tell them? 'I am your son's girlfriend. I hope you approve of us kissing behind the bushes'?

Besides, they had already met me. They had seen me on stage, acting with Andy. We were the leads—a middle-aged couple. It was an English play about marital boredom, set in London.

Neither of us had been to London, but I knew about British boredom. I had read about old ladies with cats. Andy was enthusiastic about the fireplace—'Peat, a kind of coal, is what they use!'

My dress was most inappropriate, I had thought. A nylon gown bought from Hong Kong. A friend had lent it to me. I told the director that my costume was wrong. A middle-aged woman should wear a skirt. He said if I showed my legs on stage, there would be too much whistling. I said it didn't matter, but he was adamant.

We rehearsed for fifteen days. We were most careful about our pronunciation. Nobody except Andy and me could pronounce 'photographer' correctly. Obviously, we fell in love.

This play was being sponsored by the Lions' Club. Members of this club called each other 'Loins' and their wives 'Loinesses'. My father, who taught English, always said the standard of English in Desertvadi was appalling.

'It's a foreign language,' my mother, who taught Hindi, would say.

The Lion's Club had a lot of money. That year, they were promoting arts and aesthetics in Desertvadi.

I had been quite shocked by Andy's mother. On the day of the performance, she came backstage and abused him in chaste Punjabi. We were Punjabis too, but we spoke Hindi at home. Not only had Andy taken all her imported lamps—she had five—for the stage setting, he had also skipped breakfast and lunch. She was very particular about his diet, as he'd had typhoid when he was four.

Andy was short and thin. She caught him by his collar and made him eat two egg sandwiches. We had all laughed uproariously. I had said, 'All the best, mama's boy,' to him before the performance.

I had asked Vinita how I looked on stage.

'Too thin,' she said, 'and you forgot to put talcum powder in your hair—you were supposed to be middle-aged, weren't you?'

Vini was in the kitchen. Her mother was very particular about teaching her how to cook. After some giggling in the kitchen, we sat down in the verandah. That was the only place to escape her mother's vigilant ears. It was too hot and dusty for her to tiptoe silently behind the bamboo blinds to eavesdrop.

Instead of talking about the rose petals, I found myself telling Vinita about Andy's unreasonable desire to make me meet his parents.

'What is so unreasonable about it, Geetika?' she replied. 'You will have to meet his parents eventually. You told me you are going to marry him.'

'Not in the near future.'

'Why not? You are twenty already, aren't you? You can't wait till you are thirty!'

'But…'

'Come on, Geeti, go and charm them. They will be so glad their son has chosen such a fair-complexioned *bahu* and one so intelligent… Besides, you are a Punjabi, too… Where is the problem?'

Unreasonably, I felt close to tears. Andy would be here in a week. I didn't want to meet his parents. I wanted to go home and masturbate. I wanted to watch a clothes-tearing routine from a Hindi film. I wanted to cry.

'What would your parents say if you were to insist on marrying Tony, Vinita?' I asked her, just to be difficult.

'Kick me out of the house. He doesn't even have a proper job. But why would I want to do that?'

'He is attracted to you. You even had his head in your lap that day.'

'So what, Geeti? Since when have you become so narrow-minded?'

'But what if my parents say they don't want me to marry Andy? My mother says girls ought to marry late, after choosing a career.'

'Oh, come on, you can manage all that.'

I could. Ours was a liberal household. My parents would merely be shocked and disappointed to hear that their daughter wanted to marry at twenty-one. But I didn't want to tell them about Andy's Punjabi-speaking household. I just wanted to cry.

'I know you are attracted to Tony, Vinita,' I persisted.

'So what?'

'Then why don't you admit it?'

'Look, Geeti, I'm not going to get into these hassles. My family is quite conservative.'

'Tony is not a hippie or something. He will get a job after his MA.'

'He is on drugs. And what kind of a job can he get after an MA? It is not a professional degree.'

'He can become a lecturer or get into the civil services...'

'Lectureship is good for women. You know, the hours away from home are not too long. I wouldn't mind being a lecturer, but catch me marrying one.'

I didn't want to remind Vini that my father was a lecturer. But even Papa didn't want either Bhaiya or me to get into teaching. He said money wasn't important; what mattered was one's position in society. And ours was a feudal society. Lecturers had no power over anybody—not even over their students, not even to pass or fail them in exams held by the university—and were never taken seriously by anyone. A clerk in the post office has more power, my father would say.

⊰ *Tears* ⊱

There was no hurry to get back home from school. I would find the door locked. The key would be with the neighbours. The teacher had scolded me in class even though I was the only one who had done the General Science assignment.

I had been giggling with Sheila. I was telling her that as the teacher was a vegetarian, she probably had teeth like those of herbivorous animals. Sheila said yes, she even looks like a goat. I asked her whether nuns were herbivorous or carnivorous. She said they were all wolves in sheep's clothing. We had learnt that phrase in English class that very day. That was the only class that interested Sheila.

The General Science teacher noticed us sniggering and said I should know better than to associate with girls like Sheila. I replied defiantly that Sheila was my friend, so she asked me to get out of the class. She told me pride always suffers a fall, and the eighth class exams would prove I was not as good as I thought myself to be.

'Why would you mind what the old goat says,' Sheila had remarked after class.

I wanted to tell my mother all this. I didn't want to go home, open the lock, light the gas stove and heat up my lunch. I was very clumsy with matches anyway. There was nowhere else to go. All the neighbours slept in the afternoon. All of Desertvadi seemed to sleep on hot afternoons but I couldn't sleep in the empty house. My mother said I had a tendency towards insomnia, like my father. Actually, I was too scared to close my eyes. There were ghosts everywhere, in every corner of the house.

The maidservant, Shugni Bai, who did our washing and cleaning, had told me all about ghosts. I knew my mother would only laugh if I told her about the woman with her feet facing backwards. She might even get angry. I had myself told the maid not to talk such nonsense. But often, in the silent afternoons, I heard the tread of strange feet...

There were also those psychopath killers who looked perfectly charming until they were ready to kill. Then they would get that mad glint in their eyes. I couldn't read Agatha Christie unless there was someone in the house. I had bought one of her novels. *I must try to overcome this fear.* My mother often said only cowards are scared.

I suddenly remembered the teacher prophesying my downfall in the exams. Perhaps she had already planned to fail me. I wanted to cry.

There was cold dal in the cooker. I hated dal. I was hungry.

Why couldn't it be different? Why couldn't my mother be there with hot food? Why couldn't I tell her to cook what I liked? Why were we so different from everybody else?

Shugni Bai said there was no need for my mother to work. But what would she know—she was not educated, and her husband beat her. I asked her why she worked. She said her husband spent his entire salary on drinks, but my father was a godlike man who made tea for everyone in the morning. My mother was so lucky.

⋅⊰ Cows ⊱⋅

What would Mummy say if she came to know about Andy? I didn't want to talk about him to her. She was sure to ask too many questions.

Did I love Andy? It was terrible of me to start questioning the relationship as soon as…

But nothing had happened; he had only asked me to meet his parents. There was no need to tell Mummy, not yet. He was coming today. College was also reopening today after the December break. I would slip away to his home from college on my Hero Majestic moped.

What should I wear? It has been a month since I met Andy. As soon as we realized we were in love—which was after the incident of pronouncing 'photographer' correctly—he had joined a company in Kota as an executive trainee and left Desertvadi. After that, there had been just two visits and many, many letters.

How romantic was he! He had told me he knew I was too good for him. In fact, he had called me his goddess. He said he wanted to kiss my feet. But he had kissed my mouth instead. His lips had been cold and wet and soft. Weren't men supposed to have hard, demanding lips? Perhaps he was effeminate. He certainly wasn't tall and broad. But were looks everything?

He had proposed so beautifully. 'Would you consider holding my hand?'

I was confused about what he meant. Wasn't that desi-English, or a literal translation from the source language, as my father would say? I had asked him in a sophisticated way whether he was proposing. He had gone down on his knees and kissed my fingers to drive home his point. We had laughed a lot after that.

It would be fun to laugh with him again. We could go for a ride on his scooter, the wind catching our hair. We could have ice cream together.

The phone rang just as my parents were leaving for work.

'Who is it, Geeti?' asked my mother.

'Vini,' I lied.

I told Andy I would be at his house at twelve-thirty sharp. How could I have doubted my feelings for Andy? What a traitor I was to think of all the fun I could have in America just by marrying a stranger.

Andy's house was big—an old colonial bungalow. His father worked for the Railways. In small towns, even second-class government officials were treated like princes.

'Think of the respect a collector commands,' my father would say. 'You could be collector even before you are thirty-five.'

Andy's house even had a cowshed with two cows near the kitchen garden.

'What do you do with all the milk? Who milks the cows?' I asked him. 'What do you do with all these vegetables?'

'My mother handles all that,' he replied. 'She is very particular about our diet.'

Andy's mother was short and plump and had a very loud voice. She was very welcoming.

'Come, come, *beta*. I have been waiting to meet you. My Annu has told me so much about you. This is your last year in college, isn't it?'

Why does she want to know? I told her it was.

'Just as well,' she said.

Inside, the house was spotless; the floors shone and smelled heavily of disinfectant.

'What is this stink?' I asked Andy as soon as we were alone.

'Oh, the floors are mopped everyday with phenyl.'

'Whatever for?'

'My mother has this penchant for cleanliness.'

I thought of my own house, which always had books and papers strewn all over the floor.

'Let's go for a ride on your scooter, Andy.'

'It's so hot outside. Besides lunch is at one-thirty sharp—that's when my father comes back from office.'

'Do we have to eat here?'

'Yes, of course. You have hardly spoken to my parents.'

Conversation was easy at the table. Andy's mother, who I addressed as Aunty, kept piling my plate with food. Uncle, his father, kept repeating how skinny I was and how I didn't look like a Punjabi at all. When I confessed to not knowing any Punjabi, they were horrified and said I must learn at once. It was past two-thirty when we were able to be alone again.

'You were quite a hit with my parents,' Andy said.

'Was I? I don't speak Punjabi...'

'How long will it take you to learn? I will teach you. My mother is very affectionate, Geeti... And she is captivated by your complexion. She has a thing for fair complexions, as she herself is so dark...'

I digested this. It had felt so domestic to sit together for lunch. And there had been so much to eat: three types of vegetables, dal and after that, a sweet dish. We hardly ever had lunch like this at home. Bhaiya, even when he was home, preferred to eat by himself.

In another thirty minutes, I would have to leave. I was just about to reach for Andy when his mother came in again. After a while he said, 'You wanted to see the cowshed, didn't you?'

'No, of course not,' I replied, perplexed.

'She loves cows,' he told his mother and whisked me away to the smelly place. 'Idiot,' he said, drawing me into his arms. He smelled nice, of cologne and talcum powder.

❧ Trophies ❧

There was a rumour in college that the exams were being postponed again. These decisions were taken at the far-off university. My preparations were already complete, except for the Wallace Stevens paper. In the previous year of my MA, I had stood first—not only in Desertvadi but in the whole of Rajasthan. There were so many colleges like the government college. An amazing number of students—300—were doing their master's in English. My college accounted for thirty of them, Pigeon being one. Yet, my father had been so pleased with my position in the first year, though my brother said that coming first didn't mean much.

'How is Sanjay? Still at Mussoorie?' asked Mishra sir, spotting me in the corridor on his way to class. I began telling him about Bhaiya's first posting in Bombay. My brother was well-known and liked at the government college. I knew the lecturers were rather proud of the fact that he had qualified for the civil services, though not in the top rung. He was thin like me and breathtakingly handsome. He had light brown eyes. I had brown eyes too, though not as light as his, my mother used to say. He was also a basketball star. Basketball was a popular sport in Desertvadi.

Taking the roll call diligently, Mishra sir said the exams would now be held only in June. This year, it was being said, the university was not going to waive the minimum requirement of sixty per cent attendance as a prerequisite for taking the exams. Everybody groaned, except me. I didn't want college days to end.

'We will have to come to college in the heat,' said Vinita.

'With all those power cuts,' grumbled Tony.

'At least some of you will have a chance of passing the exams,' Mishra sir said, looking very hard at poor Pigeon. Pigeon had told him in the last class that Wordsworth used to take long walks in his garden and was particularly partial to daffodils. Also, nature poetry became fashionable only because of him, and that others like 'Tennyon' and 'Berowning' began to write about lakes and hills after reading his *Lyrical Ballads*.

Mishra sir was a very sarcastic man. He wore only khadi and spoke only Hindi outside class hours. But then, people said he was a communist and they were always strange. He was usually on leave from college. He used to hold various *kavi sammelan*s to improve people's minds in Desertvadi. He would invite only Hindi poets to them. The only English poet in Desertvadi, who taught in another college, was never invited. Mishra sir would assert that it was against his principles to promote an alien literature. Due to that, perhaps, he would never finish the course in class.

In fact, before he came into class, Tony had written on the blackboard: 'In today's kavi sammelan, Coleridge, Keats and Shelley have to be read aloud with notes and annotations.' This was to remind Mishra about the portion that still had to be covered. It was the end of April and we had discussed only Wordsworth. This did not bother me. I had already prepared the Romantics.

'Oh Geeti, these people are coming from America to see me in June. I will be so distracted,' wailed Vinita after class.

'Terrific, what does the boy do?' asked Usha.

The boy Vini's parents wanted her to marry was an MBA. He was earning a fabulous salary in Los Angeles. Usha's parents were also trying to get her married, but she was dark and had pimples. Her father fell ill every time a boy's family rejected her.

'It's better to be like Geeti,' Usha said. 'No hurry to get married.'

'How do you know I don't want to marry?' I asked her.

'Your parents are so broad-minded, and you are so intelligent.'

Intelligent? I didn't want to be only intelligent. Intelligence was not everything. In the final year of school, there had been a prize for the best student. It was also called the All-Rounders' Trophy. I had thought I would get it. The Minister of Agriculture had been invited to give away the prizes. The prize went to another girl. She got it because she used to do folk dance very well. She also played table tennis.

The teachers liked her because she was polite and well-behaved. Her father was a Brigadier. 'Breeding shows,' they had said. 'Army children are brought up in a disciplined way.'

I could have got it, but I was not so disciplined or well-behaved. Also I was too proud... Besides, I had the advantage of having parents in academics and studies, after all, are only a part of one's personality...

I wanted to dance too, but I was too awkward.

'You have no grace, you can only become the boy in the dance,' the dance teacher would say whenever I tried to participate in school performances.

My mother had been very keen on me learning to dance. She employed a teacher to teach me when I was fourteen, but that was way past the age I should have begun. I did not like Manak sir. He would never come at the designated time. He would come when I was out playing badminton with my friends. My mother would send the gardener's son to fetch me.

Manak sir was reputed to be 'half-mad' in Desertvadi. He had shoulder-length hair that he would toss around while playing the tabla. He told me I should feel beautiful while dancing. I would giggle at that. He had tried to teach me the *panihari* dance, in which Krishna flirts with the woman fetching water from the river.

'Move your waist in circles,' he told me. 'You have a pitcher on your head; now look at Krishna with love and anger.'

I glowered at him and tried to jiggle my waist at the same time.

'Not like this,' he said, and enacted the scene.

Manak sir had protruding teeth. He looked at me from under his eyelids. 'Like this,' he said and danced in between our worn-out sofas, swaying his hips.

There was a peal of laughter from Shugni Bai, who was bringing in the tea. 'Is he a hijrah?' she asked me afterwards. 'I can teach you better dance,' she told me.

She was surprisingly agile.

'I used to dance so well,' she said, 'this damned husband has beaten the spirit out of me.'

⊰ *Blyton* ⊱

'Now that you are in fifth standard, you will have to devote a lot of time to essay writing,' Miss Priscilla had said, crossing her long dark legs.

She then told me to stop fidgeting when I tried to sit like her in the narrow space between the desk and the chair. 'Geetika Mehendiratta, what are you doing?'

I flinched—what an awful name I had!

'The best way to improve your language,' she continued, 'is to read good books. Not *Chandamama*, etc., but good books like Enid Blyton's novels.'

I had been reading Blyton for over a year.

'Your essay assignment for tomorrow is to write two pages on "weekend at a farm" Now what does "weekend" mean? Who will tell me? Put up your hands.'

I told her what weekend meant. It would be awful if everyone started reading Blyton. Trust Miss Priscilla to give away the secret.

'Yes, that's right,' she said. 'And also think of a name for the farm.'

The only name I could think of, while returning home in the school bus, was Green Meadows. But if other girls also read Blyton, they would know where the name was from. My farm should be different from everybody else's. It ought to be better than everybody else's. After all, I read so much more than the others.

I loved Enid Blyton's mystery novels about the Five Find-Outers and the Secret Seven, also the school series, St Clare's. My favourite was *Claudine at St Clare's*, where the quaint French girl Claudine comes in contact with the tomboyish English schoolgirls. The French were very different from the English. They preferred needlework to sports.

I was quite a tomboy myself; I had got my hair cut very short. I had even asked my mother to get me a pair of shorts. All the naughty girls in Blyton wore shorts. My mother said she didn't know what they were, but I could explain to the tailor what I wanted. I took a novel of Blyton's to Sukhdev, our old tailor. The Five Find-Outers were all wearing shorts and standing on a hill. The dog was also there, wagging his tail.

Sukhdev said they were all wearing knickers and girls don't wear knickers—was I mad? he asked. I told him to make them anyway for me because I liked dressing up like a boy.

A week later, after returning from the market, Mummy said to me, 'Sukhdev has stitched your shorts.'

Excitedly, I tried them on. They were loose and baggy. They flopped down to my knees. My brother said I looked like a member of the RSS. Even my father laughed at that, as khaki shorts was the men's division uniform. He used to say that most Hindiwallahs in Desertvadi had RSS leanings.

Mummy asked me why I wanted to dress so queerly. 'Why can't you wear pretty dresses like Kiran?'

I said I was different, that's why. Kiran didn't read as much as I did; she didn't even come first in her class.

Mummy said I was a difficult child. God alone knew why I was always crying, and what was the point of getting dresses stitched when I would never wear them.

I couldn't wear pretty dresses like Kiran. Anyway, only stuffy, snobbish girls in Blyton wore pretty dresses.

Kiran was the girl next door. She had rosy cheeks and a

round face. My face was long. I had a beautiful red dress that I had worn to her birthday. My uncle had sent it from Japan.

'It is a wonder that he remembered us,' my mother had said when we received the packet.

Kiran liked the dress very much, but said it didn't suit me. Even her mother said I was too thin. The sleeveless dress hung on me.

'My liver is bad, that's why,' I had told her.

Kiran asked me whether I felt very weak. Next day, she told me her mother had said I must have a lot of sugarcane juice since it is good for the liver.

I had to snap out of my reverie as my bus stop had come. Perhaps I should write about an Indian farm for Miss Priscilla's assignment. But I had never been to a village. I should ask Mummy, since she worked in villages.

Mummy said farms around Desertvadi grew jowar and bajra, but how could I spend a weekend in a place like that? I asked her whether cows and pigs lived on these farms. She said how could they live on farms—what would they eat? Only bullocks who pulled the plough lived there, and there was never enough to feed them. Anyway, why should there be pigs; what use were they?

Mummy had never read Enid Blyton. In fact, she had read very few English books. When my parents were young, girls learnt Hindi and a bit of English, and boys learnt English and Urdu. This was in the Punjab that was now a part of Pakistan. Mummy spoke English hesitatingly. I felt very embarrassed when she spoke in English.

My father said, 'Rajasthan is so poor, perhaps you should write about Punjab, where there are tractors and wheat is grown.'

I didn't want to write about the Green Revolution, though Papa said it was very important. I wrote an essay about a farm called Honeydew instead, where there were honey bees, a cow called Daisy and a hollow oak in which I could hide; cheese was made on that farm and I slept in my shorts—I was having so much fun.

Miss Priscilla said my essay was good—very good—but I have to pay more attention to my punctuation.

⊰ Dada ⊱

It was just as well that the exams had been postponed. I still had to put in some work for the Twentieth-Century American Literature paper. I decided to scout around in the college library once more. There was nothing on the shelves that would help me. I decided to get a Wodehouse instead.

In the feverish exam preparation days, I liked to relax with P.G. Wodehouse—Bertie Wooster and Jeeves, French chefs and English butlers and all those whimsical, cheeky women. My father used to say that one could appreciate Wodehouse only if one understood the British way of life. But Mummy was against such anglicization.

I also read novels by Premchand, Jaishanker Prasad and Mannu Bhandari that she taught. I understood why she was so serious, always. Even Papa said Hindiwallahs had precious little humour.

In the Popular Fiction cupboard, I spotted a hardbound book titled *Modern American Poets*. I looked at the index... Wallace Stevens and even Ezra Pound. It had everything. Oh good! Somebody must have hidden it in the wrong shelf on purpose; students often did that. I got it issued on my card and almost danced out with it. That was one problem solved. One book was better than none.

According to the index, it had nine pages on Stevens. But if for five pages it discussed his biography, it would be of no use to me. Let me see.

God! All nine pages had been neatly torn out. What a fool I was not to have checked it before borrowing it on my card. The six pages on Pound were also missing. This was a common practice in Desertvadi colleges—an alternative to tedious note-making. I had to return this book and look for another one; there might be others in the same cupboard.

The Assistant Librarian was quite surprised to see me back. 'Why do you want to return the book so soon?' he asked.

'The pages I wanted to read have all been torn out.'

He looked very surprised, even though this was not an uncommon occurrence.

'Let me see,' he said, and began to turn the pages. 'This is a new book. It is very expensive. You should have checked it before borrowing it. You will have to pay the fine.'

'Why should I pay—' I began.

'You will have to. I will see to it… I will go to the Principal.'

'But I haven't torn the pages!'

'You may have; otherwise, why should you come back in ten minutes with the book?'

'But I told you myself that the pages are missing.'

'That was very clever of you.'

The Assistant Librarian was rude. Suddenly, I had tears in my eyes. I stormed out of the library, tears flowing, clutching the book. It was all wrong! Andy, exams and the future. I was sobbing. I didn't even have a handkerchief.

There was nobody in the classroom. I sat down at a desk, prepared for a good cry. Lakhan Singh came into the room. He was not in my class. In fact, very few people knew what Lakhan Singh did in college, academically. He was very active in student politics. He was a dada.

In Desertvadi parlance, 'dadas' were boys who could get things done. They had huge followings. Last year, he was elected College President. Rumour was that he had contacts even in the Parliament. He was a Rajput. Students said that in the last Jat–Rajput fracas, he had hurt two Jats with a big rusted sword. The two Jats had to take anti-tetanus shots. Otherwise, the injuries were minor.

'What happened?' he asked me abruptly.

I told him.

'Oh,' he said, sounding disappointed. 'I thought somebody had said something to you.'

He meant eve-teasing. He was muscular and tall. I felt very small, very protected beside him. I was almost sorry to disappoint him. He handed me a surprisingly crisp, clean handkerchief.

'What a baby you are,' he said. 'I will see this librarian fellow.'

'Thank you so much,' I said.

'You are Sanjay's sister, after all. I have played in the same basketball team. We are both the *chela*s of the same *guru*.'

I was a bit disappointed that this was the only reason for Lakhan to come to my rescue.

The Assistant Librarian was deferential to me when I went to return the book the next day. 'I didn't recognize you. How was I to know that you're a position holder? Lakhanji told me I had made a mistake.'

I wondered how Lakhan had told him that. Once, a traffic policeman had tried to fine me just outside the college for overtaking a bullock-cart from the left. Lakhan dada had been standing at the gate, smoking a cigarette. He had yelled at the policeman, telling him to mind his own business. Did the people who frame the traffic rules know about the existence of bullock-carts? I had felt very looked-after even then.

The policeman had grinned and said, 'Whatever you say, Lakhan-sa.'

◁ Dreams ▷

In seventh standard, we had a poetry competition. The topic we had to write on was 'My School'. I got the third prize, but Father William, who had judged the competition, asked to meet me. We used to call Father William 'Jesus Christ'. He resembled the calendar representations of Christ. Everybody in Desertvadi knew him, but very few knew that he had no Indian blood in his veins.

'He is fibbing,' said Sheila when I told her. 'All Anglo-Indians who look like that say the same thing.'

I asked Father William whether I had not got the first prize because 'blue sweater' did not really rhyme with 'alma mater'. He said I shouldn't try to use rhyme schemes anyway, and also I needn't use 'thou' and 'thee'. He didn't say my poems were great but for three hours, he discussed all eight that I had taken with me in great detail.

In between, he closed his eyes and took a short nap. His mouth fell open. Then he opened his eyes after five minutes and continued with the discussion. He said he got up at five every day to pray. He also converted Bhil tribals who lived near Desertvadi. Father William said he loved Desertvadi. I asked him how much of a Britisher he was. He said he didn't feel English anymore. I wrote all my poems to him after that. I knew I wasn't in love with him, but it didn't matter. He was grandfather, *dada*, because even my father called him Father.

Not many people knew that I wrote poems and short stories in a dog-eared little diary that I kept under my pillow. I wrote of love and death, and of loneliness and insomnia—but mainly of death.

Father William had wondered why I should write about death so much. 'Are you afraid?' he had asked me.

I was afraid of being abandoned, of living while everybody around me was dead. He asked me to pray. I prayed to God to keep everybody alive... Mummy, Papa, Bhaiya. But I knew I could keep them alive by writing about death; death wouldn't come if I kept shedding tears at night in dread of it.

During the day, my dreams were different. On my way back from school, I always looked for the window seat in the bus. I was thirteen. It would be years before I could be loved—three years or even more. By then I would be a famous writer.

He, the tall and handsome 'He', would come to know of me through my writing. In fact, he would fall in love with my writing. He would love me even more upon meeting me; I would be so beautiful. My hair would be long and thick and I would leave it loose.

I went go on to imagine that he would fall in love with another girl, Kiran. Then, I would pine and pine for him and write a poem that would get the State Award. He would read it and think I was in love with someone else; then there would be an accident and I would almost lose my life in it. I would be unconscious for three days and he would be there by my bedside. I would regain consciousness just as he would bend to kiss me and then—

My eyes were wet as the driver irritably asked me to get down from the bus, my stop had come.

Now I was doing an MA and had stopped daydreaming. Andy had not come to know of me through my writing, though he had liked the poems I showed him. He had even copied them out neatly in a notebook for me, since my handwriting was so bad. But I had not shown him anything for a long time.

Somehow, there was hardly any time to talk when he came to Desertvadi. We usually met at his home and his mother would be in and out of the room all the time. Then there were the long family lunches. Andy kept asking me to talk more to his parents. I didn't know what to say to them. They never really listened to what I said anyway.

I had tried to talk about the library incident at the table one day.

'It is terrible the way the college is being run by dadas these days.'

'Take some more curd,' said Andy's mother to his father.

'It is rather bad,' said Andy, 'No, Mummy, I don't want potatoes.'

'Lakhan seems to have clout even with the Principal.'

'Have some potatoes and you will start looking healthier; you look half-starved. Doesn't he, Geetika?'

'Yes…'

'He needs a wife to look after him.'

I gave up. Any mention of marriage served to lock up my mouth.

⊰ Wolf ⊱

'No, don't kiss me. I want to talk,' I said, pushing Andy away. This was the one time I had managed to get away in the evening, and we were sitting on the grass behind the mehendi bush in the backyard.

'What about? You have such lovely ears, Geeti.'

'They are too big.'

'All the better to hear me with. I am the wolf, let me eat you.'

'Aren't you getting hopelessly confused?'

'You are confusing...mmmm...delicious,' he said, nibbling at my ear.

We heard the crunch of gravel. Andy sprang away from me. 'That Sharma is, of course, a calculating...'

I half-wished he hadn't. Why did he feel so guilty about me? His mother had no business sneaking up on us like this. I knew I was being unreasonable. After all, I didn't expect him to kiss me in front of his parents. Yet, I hated the sheepish look on his face. His mother came and settled down beside us.

'It is cool here,' she said.

'I was just about to call you,' said Andy. 'We must sit out more often.'

'You seem to think of this only when Geetika is around,' she said with a pout. 'It has been a day since you came, and you haven't even told me about that man, Sharma.'

She reached out a hand to flick a fly off his forehead. I recoiled. Just two minutes ago, he had been kissing me.

Andy obliged with a long and boring tale about how Sharma exploited the 'dealers', taking things like cold drinks free of charge from them. My attention began to wander. It wasn't any good trying to demand Andy's attention; there were other claims on him.

Mother and son, how alike they looked—except for her girth. The same eyes and nose. That body had carried him in its womb. Did his grown-up body still belong to her? Hers to flick flies off?

What was I doing here? I shuffled my feet and told Andy I should be leaving.

'Oh, Geetika doesn't want to talk to me,' his mother said. 'She comes here only for Andy.'

'Of course not, Mummy,' said Andy.

'You know, she is very sensitive,' he said to me after she had gone back inside the house. 'We should be very careful not to hurt her feelings.'

'But it gets so difficult to talk...'

'Come on, Geeti, we get so much time together... Don't be unfair... After all, she belongs to an older generation. I am surprised by her broad-mindedness in allowing us so much freedom.'

I felt slightly sick. The resemblance between the two of them was nauseating. I didn't want to talk anymore. I wanted to get back to my room. I wanted to write something in my little diary. I told Andy it was late and that I should be going home.

We continued to meet only in his or my home because we didn't want rumours circulating about both of us in Desertvadi. Andy kept asking me to talk to my parents, but I didn't know what to tell them.

I couldn't tell them that I was in love; I wasn't even sure whether I was. I liked Andy kissing me, though I didn't like the stench of cowshed that accompanied it. I didn't like him fumbling with my bra because I was scared somebody would come.

What I loved was him telling me how lovely I was. When I masturbated, I thought only of that.

Andy's mother never missed an opportunity to exclaim how thin I was. Andy was thin too. Perhaps she meant I had small breasts. She herself was remarkably buxom. Her sari could never cover her properly. She was always touching Andy, smoothening his hair, hugging him, drawing him close to her pillow-like breasts.

I did not like that and asked Andy why she didn't leave him alone. He said she was very affectionate. She hardly ever left us alone either. She was in and out of the room, often carrying on a conversation with her Annu over my head. Andy said she did that to make me feel like one of the family—wasn't it lovely that she had accepted me so readily?

◁ Prayers ▷

Andy rang up just after my parents left for work. I wondered how he timed his calls so well.

'Hello, resigned from your job yet?' I asked him. It was his fourth day in Desertvadi.

'No,' he replied. 'I wish I could. My life is here. Want to go to Pushkar today?'

'Just the two of us?'

'No, no. This colleague of mine, Ratan, is here. His mother is here too. They are staying with us. They want to go... They have heard so much about Pushkar.'

Pushkar was one of the twin gems of Desertvadi. The other was the Dargah. The first was holy to the Hindus, the second to the Muslims. Severe water shortage and epidemics hit Desertvadi whenever the two held their respective fairs. People said that the absence of communal riots in the city showed the secular spirit of the people. Everybody also said that the area around Dargah, the Khadim Mohalla, was so dirty because Muslims were naturally dirty. They bathed only on *jumma*, which was Friday.

When Shugni Bai was on leave, Mummy employed a Muslim woman to clean the utensils. Lots of social workers stopped having tea in our house as a result. I was very happy I didn't have to make it for them, but Mummy was very angry and said they didn't deserve to be called social workers and that Desertvadi was so conservative. Hajra Bibi was really dirty—she peed in the garden. Kiran told me that her mother had said we were strange people.

I didn't want to meet Andy's friend or his mother, but it would be nice to go out with Andy. We hardly ever got a chance to go out together. Besides, I rather liked Pushkar. It had small shops that sold jewellery made out of cowrie shells and silk thread. I also liked to eat the sweet malpuas, which were supposed to be the specialty of the halwais there.

Pushkar was changing fast, everybody complained. It was so full of foreigners that all the sleazy hotels had signboards in French and German along with English. But this did not qualify as tourist trade because foreigners came there in search of peace and marijuana, both of which couldn't be taxed. Father William roundly condemned the coexistence of the two. According to him, this was the desecration of a holy place. He also disliked the way inhabitants of Desertvadi combined foreigner-watching with pilgrimage.

Besides all this, his favourite in the whole of Desertvadi diocese, Desmond D'Souza, had recently started living with a Frenchwoman there. Father William was heartbroken—not only was Charlotte on drugs, she was also a non-believer, in spite of having been born Catholic. Desmond was the apple of his eye. He was the only boy in the diocese who had done his MA and actually become a lecturer.

Father never tired of citing his example as Roman Catholic, especially Goan boys, were supposed to be ill-educated. Girls, on the other hand, did very well. I had thought Desmond would marry Neela Gupta, though that would have been a shock to Father William, too.

Ms Neela Gupta was Marwari. She taught us at the government college. She had been to England on a British Council scholarship. She lived with her parents near our house. Desmond D'Souza, whom we called 'sir', was younger than her. They were the youngest

English lecturers at the Desertvadi College. Everybody said it
was a pity that Ma'am Gupta hadn't married—what a nice girl
she was. It was rumoured that she had been in love with a very
handsome man who was a non-vegetarian and belonged to a
different caste. She had sacrificed her love for her parents, who
were vegetarian and very religious.

'Oh what a great girl,' people said.

I visited Ma'am Gupta very often. She always said how
stultifying it was to teach in a college like ours. I found out
what stultifying meant and felt slightly insulted. But probably,
she didn't mean me.

She said one always had to keep students like Pigeon in mind
while preparing one's lectures. Poor Pigeon was awfully stultifying.
In her last class, he had wanted to know why D.H. Lawrence
wrote such dirty stuff and why Ma'am talked so much about this
'poet Freud', who wasn't even mentioned in the syllabus.

Ma'am Gupta had spent ten minutes explaining the relevance
of Freud to the novel *Sons and Lovers* to Pigeon. Pigeon started
worshipping the ground beneath her feet as a result.

Everyone liked Ma'am Gupta. She had large eyes and long hair.
I knew Desmond D'Souza liked her too. Very often, I would see
his scooter parked outside her home. Ma'am Gupta drove an old
Fiat. She said it narrowly missed being a vintage model. I knew
about the vintage car rally that was held every year in Lutyenabad,
so I laughed very loudly when she said that and suggested that
she wait for a while, perhaps it would qualify eventually.

Once, when she was reversing the car to get out of the staff
parking lot, the gear got stuck in reverse. I was removing the
festoons of dried flowers, grass and paper from my moped that,
by the end of the day, always adorned the vehicles belonging
to girls. There were some boy students who specialized in such
decorations. I saw Ma'am struggling with the gears. Then Desmond
D'Souza also drew up beside her. They both tinkered with the
car for a while. As I was leaving, I saw Desmond driving the car

in reverse and Ma'am sitting in the backseat to navigate. I told Vinita that day that I was sure they would marry each other, despite him being Catholic. But then Charlotte carried him off to drugs and Pushkar.

When I reached Andy's home, I was introduced as the girl he was going to marry. I felt very self-conscious when his friend's mother remarked how lovely I was. She said it more to Andy and his family. The four of us got into a taxi to go to Pushkar. The mother kept apologizing for biting into our time. The friend kept smiling knowingly. I began to wish I hadn't come. They stopped on the way to buy some sweets to offer as prasad in the temple.

I asked Andy whether it was necessary for us to accompany them. 'They can easily go on their own. We can have some time together…'

'Oh Geeti, it doesn't look nice. After all, they are my guests. The least I can do is show them around.'

Too many things didn't look nice to Andy, I thought. But the friend and his mother seemed genuinely fond of him. None of my friends' parents cared for me much. Vinita's mother was too suspicious of what Vinita and I discussed in private. She tolerated me only because I was good in studies. Ratan's mother, on the other hand, looked ready to adopt Andy.

Pushkar had a lake that was considered holy. The friend's mother wet her toes in it and prayed for her son and Andy. She was extremely religious and gave alms to every beggar who approached her. Soon, we were surrounded by them. She prayed devoutly in every temple, especially in the Brahma temple, which was supposed to be the only one of its kind in the world. I wondered what Father William would say if he could see us now because while his mother prayed, Ratan stared openly at the foreign women. He also had a great time looking at all the village women who wore colourful lehengas and backless cholis. Shugni Bai too used to have a figure like this when she was younger. I felt insulted by the remarks he made about their erect figures. Andy seemed to be enjoying all his jokes immensely.

When we returned, I was pressed into staying for the family lunch. I was beginning to dislike all the family lunches. Andy's mother was supposed to be a great cook and I felt pressured to compliment her on all the dishes she put before us. I was even supposed to ask her for the recipes. I was supposed to help her lay the table and start eating only after she herself sat down. All this had started as a joke between Andy and I, but now I felt it was on me.

❧ Wedding ❦

The preparation leave had started. It was very hot and there were frequent power cuts. Vinita was getting married twenty days before the exams. The boy and his family had liked her very much. No, they couldn't wait because he had to go back very soon, and no, he couldn't come again—the constraints of a green-card holder.

'It's going to be so hurried,' complained Vinita. 'I won't even be able to go to Jaipur to order my lehenga. My mother will have to do that.'

'What about the exams?' I asked her.

'Oh, that's all right, Vinod is going back five days after the wedding. I'll have clear fifteen days to prepare.'

'Aren't you excited?' I asked her.

'Where is the time to feel all that?'

Usha hugged Vinita and cried. The tenth family that had come to see her had also rejected her. Her father was ill again. He had three daughters to marry off, poor man, everyone said. Even though my mother said I ought to be studying, not getting distracted by weddings, I often went to Vinita's house. My preparations for the exams were almost over. My brother, now touring Lutyenabad, had gone especially to the USIS Library and sent me Xeroxed material on Wallace Stevens and the other writers in the Twentieth-Century American Literature paper.

I wanted to go to Lutyenabad and study at that library. 'It must be good to have such facilities,' I told my father. I wondered what it would be like to study in a place where everybody had access to so many books and notes.

Hundreds of saris were being bought for Vinita, along with hundreds of gold-embroidered lehengas. There were also things like a dinner set, a silver tea service, bed linen, table linen, nighties, and even bras and panties. I asked Vinita how much her father earned. She said all that stuff had been bought over the years and that some saris were as old as she was; her mother had kept them all in a big iron trunk. She asked me not to worry, my mother must have kept much more for me.

I knew she hadn't and I wondered what Andy's mother would say when she saw my trousseau. We were not rich, we were middle-class. Mummy always said the middle class overspends on their daughters' weddings and at least some families should set an example by having simple ceremonies.

Suddenly, I didn't want to think about Andy any more, not like this anyway... trunks, jewellery and saris. But I was attracted to the glamour of a wedding like this. Enviously, I fingered Vinita's gold tissue sari, for which she had a matching tissue purse. I would look nice in it too. I would also look nice in the sheer lace bra and panties. Wasn't Vinita embarrassed to discuss all this with her mother? They were animatedly discussing whether she should wear her pink nightie or the yellow one on the wedding night. Her mother wanted her to wear the pink one—it was quite transparent and also had a lot of lace.

'Pink makes you look fairer,' her mother was saying. 'Your wedding lehenga is such a lovely shade of pink.'

'Geetika is so fair,' she suddenly added. 'She can wear any colour she likes.'

This was the first pleasant thing she had ever said to me. I knew fair meant blonde, really. None of us were fair. Yet it was

nice to be called fair. Andy also loved my complexion. He used to
ask teasingly whether I had *firangi* blood in me. I was very proud
of my complexion, though I always said that being fair was no
big deal. Nevertheless, I never sat out in the sun without covering
my face. I also applied face packs of honey, lime and besan fairly
regularly.

Vinita's family was big. Every evening, they would get together to
sing and dance. Vinita danced quite well too. A video cassette was
made of her dancing. She told me it would be sent to her in-laws.

Her in-laws had sent a lot of stuff for her. There was what
was called a 'vanity case', full of American lipsticks, perfumes
and eye shadows. Vinita's mother had bought expensive saris for
all the women in Vinod's family. My mother would never do
all this. Did Andy's mother know how different we were from
everybody else?

Last time Andy had come, I had tried telling him. 'I want
to talk to you, Andy, for hours and hours. I want to be able to
say what I like to you.'

'But we are talking, aren't we, Geetika?'

'I want to talk only to you, without any interruptions. I've
always wanted to be able to say it is difficult being different...
I've been lonely but—'

'I've never felt that. I think Mummy has just spoilt us by
always being around. That's one advantage of having a mother
who stays home.'

Andy had started talking a lot about his mother, how she
had tried teaching in a school when he was three and resigned
promptly when she came home one day and found him eating
mud, how attached she was to him and his younger sister, how
she had no life outside the home, how worried she was about
his health.

I felt I must respond by telling him what a fantastic person
my mother was. But I didn't want to praise mothers. I wanted

to be out of the confines of homes and families, out and free…
I wanted nobody and nothing between us…just for a while…

Two days before Vinita's wedding, Andy rang up early in the morning.

'I have some good news for you,' he told me. 'This friend of mine has gone out of town with his parents. They have left the key with me. We can meet at his house today.'

I dressed in my best T-shirt and jeans. It felt like I was meeting him for the first time. My heart was thundering. I was so excited I could barely formulate a legitimate reason for rushing out when I was supposed to be studying.

The friend's house was not very far from mine. I reached much before Andy and stood outside staring at the garden.

'Did anybody see you entering?' Andy asked breathlessly, as soon as he entered.

'I don't know. Why are you so late?'

'Just as I was leaving, my mother said Ranju had to be dropped to her friend's house…'

'We get one day to ourselves and you spend half of it dropping your sister here and there.'

I knew I was being unreasonable. Andy was just twenty minutes late. He looked quite crestfallen.

'Where have you parked your moped?' he asked.

'On the top of a tree,' I snapped back.

I was getting quite irritated. I knew Andy was scared that somebody would see us together and there would be talk. But that day, I did not care about anything. I just wanted to hug him tight and cry, and then laugh and joke and laugh some more.

'You know it is for your sake that I am being so careful. My parents already know about us.'

'I don't care about what anybody has to say. I don't care if my parents come to know.'

'Why, you are a brave girl, like Jhansi ki Rani!'

At last we could laugh together. I glanced furtively at my

watch. We had just one-and-a-half hours together. A precious half
hour had gone in squabbling. Andy went out to hide my moped
behind some bushes. He came in after ages.

'What were you up to?'

'There was this friend of mine, Vivek, passing by. He knows
that this particular guy is out of town. It would have seemed too
suspicious if he had seen me entering his house.'

Andy looked so young, so thin, so lost. He was so scared. I
put my arms around him to comfort him.

'You won't leave me, will you, Geetika?'

'Why do you say that, Andy?'

'I don't know. You are so lovely, I'm far beneath you.'

'I don't feel like that. I love you, Andy.'

'You mean that, don't you?'

'What's wrong with you, Andy?'

'I know you don't like my mother. But she is my mother,
Geeti. I can't... I can't change her...'

'I... I like her, Andy, but I don't get enough of you, you
know? She is always around.'

'There will be enough time for that after we get married.'

I didn't want to think of marriage. My mind was too full
of silk, chiffon and gold embroidery. My mind was too full of
my poverty.

Andy was kissing me, which was nice but he was touching
me in places that embarrassed me.

'You are very, very sexy. Do you know that?'

I didn't know I was sexy. Nobody had called me that. Perhaps
Andy was lying. My heart was hammering. His finger was in me,
moving in and out rapidly. He was panting.

'I wish I could make love to you...'

His finger was plunging further and further inwards. It was
hurting me. I told him to stop. Suddenly, I felt a warm gush.
I was bleeding.

Andy said, 'Oh God, did it hurt?'

I felt like crying. I was probably not a virgin anymore. Oh God! We hadn't even gone all the way and I had lost my virginity.

'Why are you crying, Geetika? How does it matter?'

'Now I will *have* to marry you,' I said, trying to smile.

'Oh, tell your husband you did it yourself,' Andy said. 'Although I know better...' He was laughing. It was all right.

'I don't believe in going all the way before marriage. We must have something to look forward to,' he said.

How strange he was, I thought. But perhaps this meant he actually loved me. But was marriage that important? Something to save up for? Like Vinita's mother had saved all those saris for her? And was this all there was to it—blood, that Booba had told me about, years ago?

⊰ *Anger* ⊱

Mummy, look, I got the highest marks in English dictation... Look, Mummy, look, Papa, look at me... Look at me! Is the dress I am wearing all right? Look, do I look nice? Am I beautiful, intelligent, lovely? Why does no one ever look...

'Mummy, where are you going?'

'Out, beta, I have a meeting.'

'Why do you go out every day?'

'I have to work.'

'What should I do? I am bored.'

'There is so much to do. Didn't I get you paint brushes and water colours?'

'I don't want to paint!'

'Those colours have just been lying on your table. You've made just one drawing since then.'

'I don't want to stay here all alone. I will go to Kiran's house.'

'It is too late to go to Kiran's. You are old enough to play on your own. What was the need to get colours if you didn't want to use them? You can't focus on anything, can you?'

'I...don't...want...to be on my own.'

'Read a book, then.'

'I have read them all. Get me a new one.'

'Geeti, stop troubling me... I am getting late.'

'Papa, you are also going...'

'Yes, beta.'

'Don't go...'

'Grown-up children shouldn't behave like this.'

I hated them; they cared only about themselves... What about me? Nobody wanted me. I was like Bunty in Mannu Bhandari's Hindi novel, *Aapka Bunty*. Nobody had wanted Bunty either—neither his mother nor his father. They were divorced. Divorce was a bad thing.

What if Mummy and Papa decided to get a divorce? Like Bunty, I would then have a stepmother and a stepfather. Some stepmothers were so bad. I wouldn't be given anything to eat all day...and Bhaiya...there would be no money for his education. He would get even thinner, his eyes would look sunken... Bunty's stepmother was not bad, but she didn't really want him. Perhaps I wasn't really my parents' daughter at all. No, how silly I was being; I had seen Mummy's photographs when she was expecting me... But I might have got exchanged in the hospital!

When would they come? Not yet anyway, not till very late. It had just been half an hour since they left... Why should I be left alone day after day? Everybody worked but people took care to come home in the evening. I picked up the newspaper and tore it to shreds. God, what had I done! Suppose Papa wants to read it again at night? They would know who had done this. I picked up the pieces and hid them in the store room.

❧ Exams ❧

I could never sleep during exam time, even though I had revised and re-revised the course quite thoroughly. My mother said I had no self-confidence. Perhaps I didn't. It would be catastrophic to do badly. Andy had sent me a best-of-luck card. He had also given me a silver ring with the message 'until I can afford diamonds'. He had asked me to wear it during the exams.

As usual, I had a good cry before every paper. Vinita was not nervous at all; she had not even been very nervous during her *vidai*—amazing girl—though she had squeezed out the required tears.

We had all gone for Vinita's wedding, though my mother kept asking what was the hurry to get her married. Why did parents feel so insecure about their daughters?

Vinod was short but smart, everybody said. He talked to everyone—so 'humble'—even though he had been abroad for so long; he didn't have an accent; how lucky Vinita was! Even my mother liked Vinod. When Vinita's younger sister hid his shoes during the *saptapadi* ceremony, he did not hesitate to give her 200 rupees, as was the custom. He was very patient throughout the long puja, even though Vinita kept yawning.

She wore her pink nightie on her wedding night. She told me Vinod had fallen in love with her at first sight. He had told her she had a fantastic figure. He says 'fantastic' so cutely, she said. All the girls in class asked her teasingly how it was. Vinita blushed and said, 'Hmmmm.'

She told me afterwards that they hadn't really done it; they couldn't—it hurt so much, but Vinod was so considerate. He had said she was tense and it was only to be expected the first time.

I asked her whether it was the first time for him also. She said no, of course not, all those American girls, they find dark men so attractive; Vinod is short also, and they like that.

I asked her whether she minded him having made love before. She said no, of course not, it was all before marriage and men will be men—if girls were game, one couldn't expect them to be saints. I then wondered why Andy had not been able to do it up till now... Perhaps no woman had been game. Andy was short and dark as well, but he had never been to America.

It was the day of the Twentieth-Century American Literature paper. I reached half an hour before time, as was my custom. I liked to study the place—so much depended on where one sat. I liked to sit directly under the fan. Usually, I was able to make the invigilator shift my place.

Tony was at the college gate, waiting, it seemed, for me. We had not spoken to each other since the fainting episode.

'Geetika, tell me about Wallace Stevens, yaar. I kept trying to ring you up yesterday…'

I wanted to tell him to go boil his head but somehow, I couldn't. He was so ugly that he looked pathetic. As usual, his pimples had the sheen of perspiration on them. Vinita was married, poor boy. He noted down everything I was saying on a small piece of paper.

'How will you remember all this?' I asked him. I had just told him that poetry in the modern age was a reaffirmation of faith through the expression of doubt in the breakdown of Christianity, and so it was a microcosm of our doubts and faiths, and so the peeling of an orange in Wallace Stevens had to be seen as being as much of a ritual as partaking of the holy bread and wine…

'Thanks, Geeti, how do you spell microcosm?'

The first question in the paper was on Wallace Stevens's poem 'Sunday Morning'. I stole a look at Tony. He was writing rapidly. He probably had a phenomenal memory. I looked at him again. He had the piece of paper in front of him. He was cheating. I knew Desertvadi Government College was infamous for this, but I had never seen anybody cheat before. I had heard that the dadas in college cheated with knives stuck in their desks to warn the invigilator off. Tony had not even bothered to do that.

The invigilator asked me not to stare here and there and concentrate on my own work. Coward! Couldn't he see that half the students—all the boys—in the room were cheating?

Dadas were known to have beaten up lecturers if they tried to keep them from cheating. Lecturers are a beaten lot, my father used to say; there is nothing left in colleges. My father had entered the teaching profession very enthusiastically but he did not want me to get into academics.

⊰ Mummy ⊱

There was nothing to do except cry or masturbate.

Vinita was in Los Angeles, and there was nobody else to talk to over the phone. I didn't want to talk to Usha. She was at last engaged to a doctor who had just completed his MBBS. He was an orphan. Usha's parents said that was a good thing—no mother-in-law to make her life miserable.

Even Sangeeta, who had had an abortion, was married into a very rich family from Calcutta.

'God, what deception,' everybody said. 'What if they find out?'

Sangeeta had been kept under lock and key for six long years. Some people said she had been sent very far from Desertvadi. How far, who knows?

But did Desertvadi really leave anyone? Did it allow anyone to escape? It was entering my soul through my nostrils. Every day I breathed in Desertvadi. The summers were so long and interminable. Papa was asking me to prepare for the civil services and take the exams next year. I couldn't see that far because of the dust. All day, my nails were digging into my palms; all day, I was thirsty. Yes, there was something to do besides cry and masturbate—there was desert water to drink. I made cups and cups of tea to quench my thirst.

Andy was coming next week. 'Go meet my parents,' he had written. 'Go meet them, Geetika. Tell your parents about us. What about marriage? Let's get married; take your civil services exam after marriage. So many women do.'

Ma'am Neela Gupta said, yes, prepare for the civil services. Undoubtedly one of the best career options these days. But do something alongside. What about an MPhil? There is no MPhil course available in Desertvadi, so go to Jaipur; better still, go to Lutyenabad.

I wanted to ask her why she hadn't married but, instead, I asked her why she hadn't been able to complete her PhD yet. She heaved a sigh and said she had always been unambitious. In fact, she said that her friends had pushed her into applying for this British Council scholarship. It was nice being there. England was so lovely. She said, 'Why don't you go abroad? There are plenty of scholarships.'

I sat and filled forms with my father in the evenings—civil services preliminaries, MPhil courses in Lutyenabad and Jaipur, Probationary Officer exams for banks, Inlaks scholarship for going to England...

My mother asked what was the point in wasting so much energy? Why was I so unsure of myself; wouldn't it be better to decide what I wanted to do? I wanted to tell her about Andy.

Ma'am Gupta was at the door, talking to Mummy. She sometimes came over to discuss Hindi novels. She was very fond of Mannu Bhandari's works. She was handing something to Mummy... It looked like a letter.

Oh God! Mummy was coming directly to find me.

'What is this, Geeti? Who has been writing to you at your college address?'

I had given Andy my college address. The office people must have given the letter to Ma'am Gupta, knowing she lives near my home. Or she must have picked it up in friendly spirit, which was more likely. It wouldn't have occurred to her that the girl who studies so much could also be having an affair. I had been planning to go to college to see the post today. Oh, why didn't I go yesterday?

'Let me see,' I said. 'Must be Vinita... She must have misplaced this address.'

'Why are you lying, Geeti? This letter was not posted from the US.'

I looked at my mother. She had not been keeping well. She looked thin and pale. What was she thinking? How little I knew her. All that I knew was she would be very troubled when I told her. Did she understand the need to kiss, to make love? She had married late, after her younger sister.

Her younger sister, fair and plump, had been the beauty of the family. My mother hadn't wanted to marry at all but my grandfather had insisted. I could never imagine Mummy and Papa making love. They never shut their bedroom door. Mummy looked so stern, always.

'It is from Andy—Anirudh.'

'Why is he writing to you?'

'He likes me, that's why.'

'What do you mean?'

What did I mean? We kiss and frig each other off in the cowshed; when we talk, his mother listens at the door; I hate his mother, she is triumphant about the size of her bra; Andy and I tell each other that we are in love.

'How could you, Geeti? We have always given you all the freedom. Why did you feel the need to go behind our backs? Does anybody you know have this kind of freedom? Did Vinita?'

'No...but...'

'What is the extent of this friendship? Have you talked of marriage?'

'Yes...'

'Then what about a career? Why are you applying everywhere like a madwoman? I thought you were genuinely interested...'

'I am... I will take the civil services exams.'

'Where have you been meeting him?'

'At his house.'

'You will not meet him anywhere else except here. Sit in

the drawing room and behave with dignity. How could a girl like you behave so cheaply? His house! What about his parents?'

'They know.'

'They know what?'

'That we...'

'That we, what?'

'That we plan to get married.'

'You have discussed all this with his parents? You are twenty-one. What did you find in Andy? He is neither good-looking nor does he have a great job. He doesn't even look very intelligent. Geeti, how could you?'

She was crying. Mummy never cried very much. I tried to put my arms around her But she pushed me away. I didn't know what to do. So I cried too. She went back to her work.

I was lonely again. I didn't know what to do. So I wrote a letter to my brother. I cried as I wrote. I told him I loved Andy. Then I tore up the letter.

Mummy asked about Andy's parents in the evening. She had met them at the play performance. They looked typically Punjabi, she said; his mother didn't look very educated. What was the need to commit myself, she asked, why couldn't we just be friends? Girls like me didn't have boyfriends; they met boys on an equal footing. Why had I been so troublesome? she wondered. There was so much in life and I could only think of boys. I had wanted to write to boys when I was merely fifteen... What was wrong with me, had I no self-control?

ৰ *Bhaiya* ৰ

Sahil had hazel eyes. He was so good-looking, like Bhaiya. My heart hammered when I saw him. Sahil didn't live in Desertvadi. He lived in Lutyenabad, which was a very big city, indeed. He had come with my cousin to Desertvadi for a holiday. My cousin didn't like Desertvadi very much but Sahil said he loved it. They stayed with us. Sahil was very shy. He didn't speak to anyone except me. I fell desperately in love with him.

I asked my cousin so many questions about him that my cousin complained that I was like the census man. I asked him who the census man was. He said for a girl of fourteen, my general knowledge was appalling. It must be so because I was leading a protected life in Desertvadi. The census man was the man who came to take the census, what else? I was very ashamed of myself and hoped Sahil wouldn't come to know how stupid I was.

Sahil used to sit on our terrace and strum his guitar. He had brought it with him from Lutyenabad. He told me that one day he would have a rock band of his own. He loved the view of the Aravallis. He said he wished he could stay here, always. I asked him why he didn't; he could take up a job here. He said he was only in college and it would take so long.

He was five years older than me. I told Sheila that one must love a man at least five years older, they were so mature; and Desertvadi was so pretty—we didn't realize how much because we lived here. Sahil told me that he often wished for a home like ours. He said it was so British to live the way we did—just four of us and a dog—and I was by myself so often. He had to escape to the garage to be by himself, his house was so small. His grandmother was all over the place all the time, yelling and screaming at everyone. I asked him what he did by himself. He said he played the guitar and sang. He also wrote poetry. I showed him my poems and he said they were so sad. He asked me why I was sad.

When my cousin and Sahil left for Lutyenabad, I was heartbroken. I cried and cried. My mother said I was a silly girl, and that my cousin would come again. Sahil sent me some of his poems. One of them spoke of a girl with sad, sad eyes and a flower-like face and lips like honey waiting to be made. I asked my mother whether I could write to him. She asked me to show her his letter. She said it was a sentimental letter and I was not to reply. I didn't…

Sahil wrote to say he understood why I couldn't reply and that he would wait for me to grow up. I wrote a long letter to my cousin instead, asking him to convey a hello to Sahil. I was really in love with Sahil.

I told my brother I was in love with Sahil. My brother, Sanju Bhaiya, was most understanding. He said it was perfectly understandable to be in love, but I must grow up a bit to enjoy a fulfilling relationship with boys. I was quite a child, and Sahil was quite mature. Besides, he probably knew many girls and I didn't know any boys and I wanted to study, didn't I? This would distract me from my books. I told him that girls in school, like Justine and Sheila, had boyfriends. He said they were Anglo-Indians and our society was different from theirs. I told him that Justine's boyfriend was not an Anglo. My brother said unfortunately, our society has double standards for boys and girls.

I asked him whether Justine was a bad girl. He said no of course not; he had met her at sports meetings, she was very nice. I told him I hated our society. He said he didn't like it much either. This was the longest conversation I ever had with Bhaiya.

I loved him too. But then so many people loved Bhaiya. The secretary of the Basketball Association of Desertvadi was a Rajput called Dalpat Singhji. My brother was the only non-Rajput in the first five, which was a wonder, everybody said. Dalpat Singhji used to call him his son as he had none of his own.

When my brother left for Mussoorie to train to become an Income Tax Officer, Dalpat Singhji sobbed like a child. My parents looked on disapprovingly. They did not like him, even though, according to my brother, Dalpatji was on his way to success. Whenever his name was mentioned, my father would point out disapprovingly that he was almost uneducated—he had taken seven years to clear his BA instead of the normal three. That doesn't make him uneducated, my brother would counter. He would also call Dalpatji a phenomenon at times.

I often wondered about the strange friendship between my brother and him. What did they talk about? Dalpat Singhji read no books, had no interests. Though he was the secretary of the Association, he never watched a single match. But he said my brother was world-class. My brother said that was a new term he had learnt.

In fact, Dalpatji knew nothing about basketball. He only loved the sports paraphernalia. Whenever sports kits were sent for the players by the government or some private company that wanted to advertise its products, he would lovingly finger the track suits and kit bags. He wouldn't part with them for ages. In fact, only his favourites would get them, if at all.

He once gave me a lovely red tracksuit though I had never played basketball. His three daughters had several tracksuits each, though they didn't play the game either. His wife did not like their daughters wearing clothes that showed off the figure. She herself wore only lehengas, even when she worked in their farms. She would actually put stinking manure in the fields with her own hands, people said. She would never give even a cauliflower to anyone free of charge. Everyone said Dalpatji was scared of his wife, though she never lifted her *ghunghat* in public and never showed her face to any other man.

❧ Sister-in-Law ❧

The letter came in the morning.

Bhaiya had written to say that he was getting married. To a girl called Swati Khare. He had met her in Bombay. She was a physiotherapist.

Bhaiya was posted in Bombay as an Income Tax Officer and he had written to say that he was confident our parents would understand their need to have a quiet, private wedding. Swati's parents were not coming for the wedding either. Theirs was a very conservative Brahmin family and Swati felt the need to define herself outside the family structure.

My mother cried a lot when she received the letter; it was addressed to her. I cried too; Bhaiya hadn't even mentioned me. I told my parents I thought Bhaiya was being very self-centred. My mother said that he was so stupid, he probably didn't understand how much he was hurting them. Then she cried some more. I wondered about Swati. She must be a very unusual woman. They were coming to Desertvadi in three days.

My mother was very tight-lipped when Andy came home that day. I told him about Bhaiya and how Mummy was heartbroken.

'Geeti, haven't I always told you that in India one can never underestimate the importance of the family? Obviously she is heartbroken. Imagine not being invited to her only son's wedding!'

'But Andy, he is doing it for Swati. If the person one loves has these quirks...'

'But doesn't he love your mother? Doesn't he love your parents? After all that they have done for him! How can he forget all that and just be considerate to a woman he met so recently?'

'Wouldn't you do such a thing for me?'

'I am sure you are too sensible to demand this kind of heartless behaviour from me.'

Was I? I was half hoping he would side with Bhaiya. But hadn't Bhaiya let me down? He didn't love me the way I loved him. I loved his brown eyes and his straight nose. I liked the way people turned to stare at him. I liked the way his teachers praised him to my parents. I even liked the way Dalpat Singhji pined for him.

I used to warm his food for him whenever he came home late from his basketball matches. I used to keep that extra bit of ladyfinger for him. Had he forgotten all that? As a child, I had let him break my walkie-talkie doll because he wanted to examine the machinery.

'I am training to be an engineer,' he had told me.

'Your brother has always been slightly selfish, I think.'

I was irritated with Andy. 'At least he has the guts to do what he wants. He doesn't try to please everyone,' I shot back.

'It doesn't require guts to hurt one's parents. And what is the harm in going a little out of the way to please people?'

'You end up hurting people you love...'

'Come on Geeti, that doesn't make sense.'

Mummy was beckoning me from the verandah. Some people had come to see her and she wanted Andy to leave so they could use the drawing room. I asked her whether we could sit in my room.

She said no, absolutely not; we had been sitting and talking for two hours, wasn't that enough? She looked very stern. I wanted to tell her to stop interfering in my life but I couldn't.

Andy had come only for a day.

I went to the station to receive Bhaiya, along with my father and Dalpat Singhji. Dalpat Singhji had become the secretary of the All India Sports Federation. He was now one of the most important people in Desertvadi. He made frequent trips to Lutyenabad and Japan. My mother said it was shameful the way he was squandering public finances. My father said he genuinely loved Bhaiya and we should not comment on things that didn't concern us. Mummy said my father was getting carried away by Dalpat Singhji's success.

Swati Bhabhi was small and lovely—petite! They looked wonderful together. Dalpat Singhji hugged Bhaiya and cried. I wanted to laugh because his tears were falling on his luxuriant moustache. The moustache looked very wet. I hugged Swati Bhabhi; she was so small, I felt tall and awkward beside her.

My mother had prepared Bhaiya's room for them. She had put a new bedcover and curtains. She had bought ten saris for Swati Bhabhi. She had also taken out some jewellery from the locker for her.

Mummy didn't have much jewellery. She had refused to take very much from her parents as she was a Gandhian. I particularly liked the necklace she was giving Bhabhi and asked her whether she was keeping something of the same sort for me as well. She told me that she did not believe in differentiating between the daughter and the daughter in-law. As Bhaiya was older, his wife would get preference. These were the principles she lived by.

Swati Bhabhi told her she didn't believe in accepting expensive gifts but Mummy insisted that she keep the few things she was giving her.

Swati Bhabhi did not talk much, except to say that I was not to call her 'Bhabhi'. Nevertheless, I asked her a lot of questions. I gathered that her family was quite rich but she had got a scholarship after school and had supported herself ever since. She had been living by herself as a paying guest with a Parsi family for three years. In fact, she was rather reluctant to talk about her family.

I told her about Andy and asked her what I should do. She said I was too young to marry; I should work for a while before making that decision. I asked her whether I should try for a job in Bombay. She said she didn't know what kind of a job I would get with an MA from Desertvadi. She did not invite me to stay with them, but Bhaiya did.

My mother said she was not a warm person at all. She gave me a skirt as a present. Swati was earning a lot—she had a good practice in Bombay. Dalpat Singhji said it was an ideal marriage; Bhaiya would have a good position in society because he was a government servant, whereas she would bring in a lot of money because of her profession. My father agreed with him, though he said money was not all that important.

I went to see them off at the station. Bhaiya looked eager to return. He asked me to come for a holiday to Bombay—they were going to buy a car soon, they would take me around...

My heart felt heavy because Bhaiya was leaving. It felt much more final than when he had left for Mussoorie for training. But even Dalpat Singhji was not crying this time.

◁ Jaundice ▷

Andy's mother wanted to know all about Swati and Bhaiya. She said that it was quite understandable that my mother should be ill—she had received such a shock. She asked me whether they were coming down to look after her.

I said no, the thought of calling them had not even crossed our minds. This was a lie. Papa had booked a trunk call to Bombay on Mummy's insistence that they be told. Swati had sounded very concerned. She said that jaundice at this age was very dangerous and that I should look after her very carefully. Bhaiya too sounded very worried.

Andy's mother said it was not my duty to look after my mother; the daughter-in-law should be doing it.

I couldn't imagine Swati squeezing out the juice from oranges or going down on all fours to clean vomit as Mummy was sick so often. They had not said anything about coming; Papa said they probably had other commitments. I saw Mummy quietly wiping her tears when he said that. I decided I would never love Bhaiya again—Mummy looked so pale.

Andy said I was a great girl and a fantastic daughter. He told me he loved me for the intermingling of the East and West in me. I didn't know what he meant; he probably meant it was very Indian of me to look after my mother.

I had come out of the house after ten days. I didn't want to discuss anything with Andy's mother. I wanted to go out and take a ride on his scooter with the wind tugging at my hair. But Andy's mother went on about illness, jaundice and duty. I was suddenly irritated and found myself telling her I didn't want to talk about Bhaiya. She was taken aback. Andy quickly said that I should be going back as Mummy was all alone.

'Geeti, what was the need to be so rude to my mother? She was only being sympathetic.'

'There is no need to criticize my family in order to be sympathetic.'

'Well, your brother has been rather irresponsible. Imagine, his mother is lying ill here and he can't find time to come home. Even if he is busy, he can at least send his wife.'

'His wife is working as well. Do you realize that?'

'So she can't be expected to do even the barest minimum for her husband's family?'

'That's the way we are. That's the way we think.'

'You are not like that, Geeti. Here you are looking after your mother after topping the University. You could have been out exploring future prospects instead. You are not like the rest of your family.'

'Why, what's wrong with my family?

'Well, your people are rather cold. They have known about us for so long now, but they still haven't bothered to meet my parents.'

'It will be rather awkward for them to meet your parents.'

What would they talk about, Andy's parents and mine? I didn't really want them to meet. It would not be just a social visit. Besides, my parents hardly ever entertained, they were always busy. We had no dinners at our home. At times there were social workers who were passing by and so they ate with us. That's all!

Some days back, Sridevi had come for dinner. She was plump and attractive. Her hair cascaded down to her hips. It used to be longer but she had chopped it off because she accidentally peed on it when she went to the fields to attend to her morning call, she had announced at the table. I had never heard anybody talk like that before.

Sridevi had been a well-known theatre actress in Lutyenabad before she decided to renounce the world and throw herself into social work. She worked among the Bhils, like Father William, but she did not convert them. She organized them into unions to fight for the rights that the world had denied them.

She had been arrested twice, but she had contacts in the highest places and had been set free both times. Her father was a well-known lawyer. She told me we did not realize how the other half of the world lived. Bhils, in the villages she worked in, had to walk for miles to fetch drinking water and vegetables were a luxury that no one could afford. She made me feel very guilty about the kind of life I was leading. She asked me to visit her in her village; she had built a house there and had even married a Bhil. My mother said she was rather strange, though she was doing good work.

But people who worked in remote villages always had an edge over people who worked in and around cities, and full-time social workers often felt so much superior to those who had other commitments. Mummy had not renounced the urban world like Sridevi. Sridevi had gone on to win a national award for social work. Did Mummy feel like a failure? At times she did look dissatisfied... What a hard life it had been for her. She never took a holiday.

Whenever Shugni Bai was on leave, Mummy would make straight for the kitchen after coming back from work. I had taken advantage of her all my life. I had only complained about her absence, about what I called her neglect of me. I had never paid attention to her fragility. Now she was ill with jaundice... and I had made it worse for her by getting Andy into the picture. Why couldn't I be the daughter she had wanted me to be? After all, she had a right to expect something from me...

Her bilirubin levels had become alarmingly high. Papa and I were very worried. She had started looking very weak. Bhaiya came down for a day to see her. There was an amazing change in her. It was the first time after a month I saw her smile. I had been looking after her for so long; she had not smiled at me. This was what love was about—it was irrational, unreasonable.

Would Mummy be like Andy's mother too? Hugging and kissing Bhaiya, trying her best to show Swati who came first? Why didn't anyone love me like this? Even Andy was so entirely rational: 'Nothing must change for Mummy. It is not fair if a mother who has devoted her life to raising her children begins to feel she has lost her son just because he's gotten married.'

Had my parents just lost their son? Had I lost my Bhaiya? But when had he been mine to lose? I hardly had any memories of us playing together as children—he was so much older. He only broke my toys occasionally: my walkie-talkie doll, my clay pigeon. He used to be away so much, playing basketball all over the country. I used to tell everyone at school about him. A princess from my school hostel had confessed that she had a crush on him. There was an almirah full of the trophies he had won, in my parents' room. There was also a photograph of his in which his eyes looked very light—almost hazel like Sahil's.

Perhaps Sahil would have loved me madly, if Mummy had only let him.

◦ Plans ◦

Dalpat Singhji didn't call on us very often. Bhaiya and he used to meet at the Association office. So I was surprised to see him in the drawing room. Perhaps he had come to ask after Mummy. Mummy was much better now, though she looked very drawn and stern.

He hardly had any time these days for Desertvadi, Dalpatji lamented. Last week, he told us, he had gone to Japan for a day; he had to sign some papers there. I asked him what all he had seen in Japan during his many visits. He said he never went out of the five-star hotel in which he was put up, except to go to departmental stores where he couldn't buy anything because of the high prices. I asked him how he had managed to get so many things from there. A Sony Walkman, tracksuits for everybody, for his nephews and nieces and even for his wife, VCRs, cameras etc. He said they were all gifts—the Japanese always gave a lot of gifts. I wanted to laugh because I knew what that meant. Bhaiya had told us how Dalpatji managed gifts.

Once, a Japanese official in India had given him a Citizen watch. Very excitedly, Dalpatji had thanked him, saying, 'Daughter give, very pleased.'

Both he and the Japanese gentleman knew very little English. Dalpatji, after conveying his gratitude, had gone on gesticulating wildly, saying, 'Daughters three...three daughters... All liking Japanese watches.'

The gentleman had bowed deeply and sent him two more the next day.

These days, Dalpatji was involved in the all-Asia sports meet that was going to be held in Lutyenabad next month. His one-day visit to Japan had been in that connection. As usual, I made tea for him, serving it as he liked—in a glass. He beamed and asked whether I wanted a holiday in Lutyenabad.

'Oh yes,' I replied. He turned to my parents and asked whether they would consider sending me for the sports meet.

'How can I go?' I asked, 'I don't play any games.'

He said it didn't matter—they would be recruiting a lot of people, especially women, to do things like escort the foreign teams from one place to another, make the announcements at the matches, hold the placards at the march pasts, etc. I could do something like that; his daughters would be doing the same. He would see to the arrangements of our staying, etc. My father nodded and said it would be good exposure for me.

Oh, what fun! I would be in Lutyenabad for almost a month. It would be such fun to meet so many foreigners. I would miss Andy's next trip to Desertvadi, though. But it had been four years since I had last gone to Lutyenabad. That had been with my parents and we had stayed at my aunt's. My cousin had irritated me by wondering endlessly how we could bear to live in a place that didn't even have a decent ice cream parlour.

Sahil's house was very close to my aunt's. I would wait eagerly for him to come out in the evenings. My thoughts ran to that last visit.

It was June and scorching hot outside; still, I was out at five-thirty, waiting for him.

My aunt said, 'Come in, Geeti dear; what are you doing in the heat?'

I told her I was watching the traffic, Desertvadi was so quiet.

Sahil came out at six-thirty. He was quite surprised to see me hanging on the gate. 'Oh, Geeti, what a surprise. You have grown up, kid!'

He had put on a little weight but he was just as handsome. I asked him whether he had written any more poetry. He said where was the time? He was in his final year of college and had to study so much; he didn't even get time to strum his guitar.

'You didn't reply to my letter, Geeti. I waited so long for a reply.'

'I couldn't, Sahil. Mummy, you know...'

'I must get to know you better, Geeti. Write if you can... You have become even prettier.'

My heart had lurched. He was so handsome. There had been a flutter in my lower abdomen when I told him we were going to be there for just two more days. He made a face and said worse luck. He said he often dreamt of Desertvadi.

'You belong there, somehow. You look out of place here,' he said.

Is he referring to my bell-bottomed trousers, I wondered. People in Lutyenabad were wearing what were called 'drainpipes'. I couldn't meet him because, again, my aunt had arranged various sightseeing tours for us for the next two days. We saw the famous Minar and the famous Fort; we even went to the zoo.

I wondered if Sahil had forgotten me. Last I heard from my

cousin, he was looking for a job. My cousin was still doing his MBA, being slightly younger than him. It was very difficult to get things out of him anyway. Besides, I had been too involved with Andy to bother too much about Sahil.

It was decided that I would go to Lutyenabad. Mummy said it would be a kind of higher education for me, though she asked me to behave with dignity and to remember that Dalpatji was very conservative.

The whole country was gearing up for this sports meet. It was called the Sportsaid. Hotels and flyovers were being constructed for it. I didn't quite know what flyovers were, but they reduced traffic congestion, which was a good thing, according to the newspapers.

◁ Journey ▷

Two daughters of Dalpat Singhji, Nandita and Sandhya, were going to Lutyenabad for the Sportsaid. Both were younger than me, Nandita only slightly so. I didn't know them very well, though we had studied in the same school. They failed their examinations very often, which was why Nandita, who was twenty, was only in the first year of college.

Dalpat Singhji often rued the fact that they were not like me. They both were rather plump and dark. He was even more worried about that—it increased the dowry by several thousands, he would say. Rajputs had to give a lot of dowry in cash. But lately, Dalpatji had ceased to be so worried about their dowries. He had been able to keep away VCRs, stereo systems—all Japanese. Cash can always be whipped up later, he would say.

My mother had once suggested that perhaps it would be a good idea if they could be trained for something like nursery teaching before their marriage.

No question of that, Dalpatji had replied; the Rajput community was far too conservative—besides, his daughters would never need to work.

In the train, I had to sit with Nandita and Sandhya. They
giggled a lot between themselves. I noticed that they didn't say
'hukum' to each other or behave like the royal Rajput girls in
the hostel. They talked a lot about basketball players, especially
men. Some of them were their rakhi-brothers. They were going
to be there in Lutyenabad for the Sportsaid. In fact, a lot of
people from Desertvadi were going to Lutyenabad and it was
only because of Dalpat Singhji. I was also going because of him,
perhaps because Bhaiya was away collecting income tax in Bombay.
I was a stand-in. I had brought a P.G. Wodehouse with me. I
tried to immerse myself in it.

'Geetika, do you know Andy?' Nandita asked me suddenly.

'Yes, of course, we acted together in a play. Why do you ask?'

'Oh, Lakhan Singh was telling us that you visit his house
often, from college.'

'Yes, we are good friends.'

I wondered what else they had heard. What must Lakhan,
the dada of the college, the custodian of feminine morality and
honour, have said about me?

'Jija-sa'—he must be calling Nandita 'Jija-sa'—'Looks like
Sanjayji's sister is going to marry Andy. They are meeting a lot
these days.' He must have looked both scandalized and stern.

What do they imagine we do together, Andy and I? How
did we look together in their minds? Ridiculous, kissing and
frigging, both of us thin like beanpoles. I didn't want anybody
to think about me in that way. It was seamy and cheap. I *was*
cheap, perhaps, as Mummy had said.

Nandita and Sandhya were giggling again.

'When will you get married, Geetika?' asked Sandhya.

'I don't know. I must find someone first.'

'My God, are you really going to look?' asked Nandita.

They were quite childish, these two. They had never been
allowed to think of a man in any other way. But was I any better?
In spite of everything, I had gone ahead and lost my virginity,

or hadn't I? I couldn't even be sure of that.

'Will you marry Andy?' Sandhya persisted.

'I don't know, I don't think so. Why? Have you heard anything about us?'

'If there was nothing to hear, how could we have heard anything?' said Nandita, being perverse.

I decided I didn't like them. So narrow-minded, like the rest of Desertvadi. I would have to be with them in Lutyenabad for one whole month. Dalpatji had clearly said that the three of us had to stick together; Lutyenabad was a big city, we were not to stray.

Sandhya was telling Nandita that Lalu was taller than Abhay. Nandita said so what, wasn't Abhay fairer and a much better player?

I knew it would be safer to have them on my side. I tried to humour them by asking whether Sandhya had a soft corner for Lalu. They told me in no uncertain terms that they were not 'like that'; Lalu was a brother, so was Abhay—their father was a very strict disciplinarian and I was not to talk about them in that way.

I also decided I didn't like day journeys by train. The landscape was so dry. It was dusty even inside the train. The mirror in the toilet showed a stained, dark face. How awful I looked! It was as if Desertvadi had got into the train with me. Mercifully, it wasn't hot. The weather was changing. It was November already. The results of my MA had come out in August. I had topped the list of successful candidates. I had got the highest marks not only in the whole of Desertvadi but the whole of Rajasthan. Was I intelligent? I didn't feel very intelligent. At times, Vinita seemed to be much sharper than me. She was much better at remembering dates. I had been so confused between the French Revolution and the publication of the *Lyrical Ballads* in England—one was 1789, the other 1798. But Vini was not interested; she never read a single book out of the course. She must be in California now. How lucky she was!

I could have been abroad too, if my parents had gone ahead

with the proposal from the doctor's family. I didn't have a pert bosom like Vinita, but they could have liked me for my poetry. Two of my poems had even got published in a women's magazine. I knew I wrote well. But the editor of a popular weekly had written back to say that my poems were morbid; I wrote well, couldn't I send something happier, something heart-warming?

Father William had said that he often asked himself the same question, why did I write so much about death? I had told him I was afraid of Mummy dying; she was so pale and weak. She had always been delicate. He said all of us have to die. But I knew it was a good luck charm to write about death—I could keep Mummy alive that way.

◁ Elite ▷

It was night when we reached Lutyenabad. The station seemed huge and alarming—a contrast to the homey Desertvadi station, which always seemed to be bursting at the seams with crying, naked children and women in lehengas. Lutyenabad station was crowded too, but in a different way. People seemed to be busier and more purposeful here. I wanted to have coffee because last time we had come to Lutyenabad, we had had coffee at the stand near the bookstall. Papa had said, 'Excellent coffee.' Dalpatji said this was no time to have coffee; he would take us to a restaurant for dinner. Desertvadi hardly had any decent restaurants, Nandita said.

I didn't know much about restaurants because Papa didn't like eating out. Once, when he had been buying eggs from a poultry farm, he had seen the chef from a restaurant called Elite buying dead birds. Poultries were not supposed to sell dead birds but anything was possible in places like Desertvadi, he said. Also, once during the Urs, which was held in the memory of a Sufi saint at the Dargah, water shortage had hit Desertvadi; there was a rumour that restaurants were using water from open sewers for washing utensils. Desertvadi, especially the old city and the

Khadim Mohalla, was a city of open drains. These drains were originally meant to collect rain water that flowed down the hills but now they collected the city sewage also.

Papa was also against fizzy drinks and chocolates. He said they affected the teeth; Americans have bad teeth because they have junk food all the time. As a child when I used to go to the movies with my parents and feel thirsty during the interval, Papa always refused to buy me a drink. Enviously, I would watch other people buying chilled drinks from the vendor who would go around the hall beating a spoon against a glass bottle.

Papa was a great believer in home cooking but Mummy hardly ever cooked. Our food was cooked by servants. Papa never complained much about that, unlike Kiran's father, who would refuse to eat unless the food had been prepared by Kiran's mother. He would merely point out the shortcomings of the cooking—too much oil, too little salt, undercooked meat. Mummy always just pursed her lips in response. I, of course, never dared to criticize the food.

In college, I would go occasionally to Elite with Vinita. We would go there after watching the morning film show. Only one movie theatre in Desertvadi had the Sunday morning show dedicated to English films. All Macaulay College students would come for the show. At times, getting tickets was impossible because the missionary schools would also get their hostellers for it. One had to reach the hall an hour before time in order to get the tickets. But we would do it because it was fun—one met so many people one knew. We used to dress very carefully for these Sunday outings. Later, at Elite, one would meet the same people.

Two gentlemen met us at the main gate of the station. The car they had come in was a Government of India car. The license plate said so. I decided Dalpat Singhji must be a very important person for the government to send out its vehicle at ten-thirty at night to receive him. The men didn't look impressive at all. I thought they were clerks in his office. We were going to a place called Pandora Road for dinner. Sandhya and Nandita wrinkled up their noses, saying in whispers that these government officers were such 'cheapstakes'. They were referring to the two gentlemen.

Apparently, these two were bureaucrats—they were trying to get a foothold in the Sportsaid through Dalpat Singhji. This is why we were being taken out for dinner. Last time they had taken Dalpatji and his family to a five-star hotel, they had come with an industrialist who had paid the bill, Nandita said. This time they had not come prepared for going out, that was why we were going to Pandora Road, said Sandhya. Pandora Road was not much of an improvement on Elite. Dalpatji said, next time we must take Geetika to a five-star. I had never been to a five-star hotel. I wondered why he was saying 'we' when the bill was being paid by the other people.

Pandora Road had a cluster of small restaurants. I thought Elite was so much better; it had a garden—these restaurants were almost on the road. The restaurant we went into was small and cramped. Lots of men seemed to be laughing loudly and everybody seemed to be chewing on huge chicken bones. I was amazed to note that most people were using their fingers. Whenever we went to Elite, we were most careful about using the knife and fork properly. In fact, I only ordered dishes that could be eaten easily as I was a bit clumsy with cutlery. Meat with bones tended to fly off my plate when I attempted to cut it. Papa said it was because I had no practice. He himself had excellent table manners. When he lived in hostel during his master's, everybody used to dress for supper and eat only with knives and forks.

The two gentlemen were most deferential to Dalpatji. Dalpatji placed the order without bothering about anyone else. He asked me whether I liked chicken, though. They chatted about various things but mostly about the Sportsaid. It seemed Dalpatji had direct access to various ministers. He was on back-slapping terms with the sports minister. The two gentlemen revered the minister as God and Dalpatji as his prophet. I felt very important sitting so close to such a man. Dalpatji spoilt it a bit for me by speaking atrocious English; the two gentlemen spoke only Hindi.

'So Dalpatji,' said one of them, 'I hope our work will be done? We will be eternally grateful to you.'

'Yes, yes. I give word,' said Dalpatji.

'If you continue to be kind to us, we can have some fun in life. Otherwise what are government servants…merely glorified clerks.'

'No, no ji, you run country. Ministerji says he depend on bureaucrats for everything.'

'Sir, let us know if there is anything we can do for you.'

'No, no. I do work for friendship. Yes…great shortage of vehicle, your government is miser. I run the show singlehanded, they give me five cars…Nandita and Sandhya go shopping to Carol Bagh, not know Lutyenabad. You please, sir, arrange for that…small thing for big government officer.'

When Dalpatji went to the loo, they relaxed visibly and began talking to each other in Bengali. I heard one of them say '*anyay katha*'. I knew that meant injustice. Our dance teacher in school used to say that to the maths teacher, whenever the principal demanded that she get a dance programme ready in two or three days. I wondered what injustice Dalpatji was inflicting on them.

⊰ P.M. Stadium ⊱

We went on a sightseeing tour to a huge stadium called the Prime Minister Stadium the next evening. It was so huge, I felt like a midget.

Dalpatji had shown us around as though it were his favourite cauliflower bed. 'Look at that,' he had said, pointing towards the giant scoreboards, 'Electronic, all from Japan.'

I was fascinated by the four giant steel towers that overlooked the huge pit of the stadium.

'Phloodlights,' Dalpatji had explained. I suppressed a giggle; he had meant floodlights.

This was where the opening ceremony of the Sportsaid was going to be held.

'This stadium is the pride of Ministerji,' explained Dalpatji. 'Here, everything will be held—athletics, phootball phinals…'

'We have passes for everything, don't we, Papa?' asked Sandhya.

'Yes, yes, I will show you everything.'

I felt strangely liberated, yet sad, in that huge stadium. This world, where people locked together in combat…where sportspeople, all in peak physical condition, proved the superiority of their skills, was fascinating but so exclusive. Sanju Bhaiya had a lot of skill but too little stamina. So he had not made it to the top. Dalpatji had told Mummy that he must eat a lot of meat. This stadium was for those who had grown up on the right diet, with adequate practice. Crores of rupees had been spent on them. They were winners.

The eight-lane athletics track gleamed a kind of brick red in the fading light. Feet shod in the latest Japanese footwear would soon thunder on it. Forms clad in tracksuits would soon march across it, unfurling the glory of their countries. We returned to what were the official basketball premises. We were putting up in Dalpatji's office. He had told me that I could visit my aunt after the interviews; till then, he would make me enjoy myself. Of course, he didn't mean to suggest anything remotely inappropriate—it was just the risky combination of Hindi and English he used that transformed innocent utterances into innuendoes, making me giggle helplessly.

The office was quite big, comprising two adjoining rooms. The smaller one was curtained off, and Dalpatji's couch was there. Nandita, Sandhya and I spread our bedding on the carpeted floor of the bigger room, which contained a table, a few chairs and a whole lot of files. Both Nandita and Sandhya fell asleep almost immediately. I could hear Dalpatji's snores from the next room.

I always had trouble falling asleep in a strange place.

I decided to read the magazine I had bought earlier that day. It had a special feature on the Sportsaid. It lyrically described the competitive spirit of the games and also listed India's medal hopes. I sleepily read that India had very bleak chances of getting anything at all in basketball. But the magazine noted proudly that the sports scene in India was looking better and better, and soon we would be ready to host the Olympics.

⊰ Lyson ⊱

There were fifteen days left for the Sportsaid to begin. We were going to be put in something called 'lyson work', Dalpatji said. There would be absolutely no work, he added, except hobnobbing with foreign basketball teams.

We were to fetch them for the matches from the Games Village, which was their place of residence, and drop them back. We were to travel in special coaches. We were actually going to be paid for this! We were going to get two silk saris as uniforms, and identity cards, which we had to wear like necklaces at all times.

It sounded like a lot of fun. It was only right that I should earn a bit before making a decision about my studies, I told myself.

I still found Lutyenabad rather alarming. The traffic on the roads unnerved me. Desertvadi was also crowded, but not quite like this. There, one had to veer through the slow-moving throng of pedestrians, bullock carts, cycle rickshaws, tongas, cars and tempos. I always avoided travelling in tempos, as one had to bend double to get into them and remain crouched until one got a seat. Tempos plied between all the busy localities of Desertvadi, and even the nearby villages. They were usually full of women in lehengas and men in colourful turbans, whom the tourists found fascinating. In Lutyenabad, there were only huge buses, fast cars and kamikaze scooter-rickshaws. Whenever I attempted to cross the road, my mouth ran dry and I clung on to Nandita and Sandhya. They were quite at home among the milling millions and laughed at me when I blanched at the prospect of getting into a bus.

Our interviews for this 'lyson' work were scheduled for the following day. I asked Sandhya what 'lyson' meant and she said I ought to know since I was the one who was an MA in English, not she. I was quite nervous. I had faced an interview board only once before. That was after school, for what was called the National Talent Search Exam. I had done the ten-plus-one scheme.

In that interview, I had been quizzed about General Science. We found out later that this was because I was going to take Humanities in college. Students who were going to specialize in Sciences had been quizzed about Arts and Literature. This was to ensure that only those with an all-rounder personality were selected.

I had been able to answer most questions. The only thing I had forgotten was the name of the doctor who had performed the first open-heart surgery. All I had remembered was that his name sounded like a breed of dog, and I had said as much. The two men in the interview board looked nonplussed but the third, a lady, had burst out laughing. She said yes, yes, St Bernards were great dogs but they couldn't perform surgeries.

'Dr Christiaan Barnard!' I had exclaimed, before adding, 'He has arthritis now and cannot operate anymore.'

I got the scholarship.

I hoped they wouldn't ask me too many questions about sports at this interview. I found it very difficult to remember names of sportspersons—Nadia Comăneci, Li Juang or whatever they were. Sandhya and Nandita said nobody would dare ask anything—what was Papa there for?

The interviews were held at a place called Purana Maidan. It was huge and overwhelming, like everything else in Lutyenabad. As the name suggested, it comprised mainly large grounds, dotted with big halls and office premises. Dalpatji told me it was also called the Exhibition Ground; various exhibitions and trade fairs were held there every year.

The interviews were being conducted by the Basketball Federation of India in one of the offices adjoining 'The Hall of Territories'. Dalpatji asked us not to worry because everybody on the board were 'his men'. His men were everywhere. He looked very much like a gangster when he said this. He managed to look quite formidable because of his moustache, which was large, grey and luxuriant. Only I knew he had wept into it for Bhaiya.

There were about fifty people waiting to be interviewed. I was surprised to see so many boys. The girls were wearing saris or salwar kameez. I was in a salwar kameez too, as a concession to present company. Nandita and Sandhya did not wear jeans. I knew Dalpatji was very strict in matters of dress.

The interviews had not begun yet, though half an hour had elapsed since the scheduled time. Dalpatji had dropped us and disappeared into the offices. Nandita and Sandhya were giggling with their rakhi-brother Abhay. Many Desertvadi people seemed to be around. I did not know any of them, though they all seemed to know Sanju Bhaiya. They smiled indulgently when they mentioned him; he was not only a good sportsman but also intelligent enough to clear the civil services—and above all, he was a favourite of Dalpatji's.

Most of them made a great fuss over Nandita and Sandhya. One even managed to get them cold drinks, though all the shops in the Maidan were closed. I got a bottle of cola too, as I was standing with them. I sat down in a corner, feeling rather out of sorts.

How different we must seem to the Lutyenabad people— huddling together, talking about Dalpatji's sphere of influence in hushed, deferential tones. The Lutyenabadis were speaking to each other in a curious mix of English and trendy Hindi, somewhat like the Macaulay College dialect. I noticed that the girls seemed to think nothing of going up to strange boys to ask for information. Two of the girls were even smoking.

'Are you some minister's daughter?'

The boy asking me this was dressed in blue pleated trousers and a checked shirt. He had a cigarette in one hand and a magazine in the other.

'No, of course not. Why do you ask?'

He was dark-complexioned, with gleaming black eyes.

'Here we are, standing and waiting for over an hour, and only some of you get cold drinks.'

'Oh, I have come with Dalpat Singhji, that is why…'

'Who is this Dalpat Singh?'

'He is…er…something in the special committee for the Sportsaid. A family friend. He is also from Desertvadi, you know.'

'You aren't from Lutyenabad, then?'

'No, no, from Desertvadi…in Rajasthan.'

'Yes, I know. Macaulay College is there, isn't it?'

He was smoking rapidly. I offered him half my drink, as he was eyeing it thirstily. 'I can wash the top of the bottle, provided you don't mind *jhuta*,' I offered.

Surprisingly, he accepted it gratefully and finished the drink in one big gulp.

'Which school do you go to there?' he asked.

'Excuse me? I have just completed my MA.'

He smiled and said I must have got many double promotions.

'Have you also applied for this lyson work?' I asked him.

'What did you say?'

'Dalpatji said we were going to get into lyson work.'

'*Liaison* work,' he said. 'We are going to be Liaison Officers, if we are selected.'

⊰ Interview ⊱

Nandita and Sandhya were staring at me. I knew that they disapproved of my talking to this boy. I was, in any case, hoping he would move on. I was so embarrassed at mispronouncing 'liaison'. He must be thinking I was a rustic from some village. Suddenly, a girl swooped down on him.

'Hello, Ratish. When will the interviews begin?'

He said, how was he to know? He was neither an astrologer nor God, and if anybody was to know, it would be me, as I had contacts in the highest places.

She turned to me and said I must be from Desertvadi. I asked her how she knew.

'You look so lost. It's sticking out a mile you're not from the city,' she replied.

She had a mop of hennaed hair and skin pitted with pimples. She said she had met Dalpat Singhji several times in connection with this job and everybody knew that only his favourites would get it.

She took out a lipstick and daubed her lips with it, then she dusted her face with a compact. She didn't seem to mind that Ratish was watching. He was on his fifth cigarette and too busy blowing smoke to care. She turned to him and said, 'Hope you are dropping me home, Ratish. It is going to get very late.'

He said yes, yes, and melted away in the crowd. She watched him leave and then turned to introduce herself. Her name was Annu and she too had just completed an MA, in Political Science. I asked her how she knew Ratish and she replied that she had met him a couple of times in these offices. She talked rapidly about herself. She was from a college called Rosalind House. She had never been out of Lutyenabad and did not know where Desertvadi was. She thought it was in Madhya Pradesh.

Her eyes kept darting here and there. Suddenly, she spied someone she knew and disappeared, shrieking, 'Hi, Vishrut!'

I went back to Nandita and Sandhya.

The interview was quite dull. There was a board of three bored-looking gentlemen. One of them feigned surprise that I had come all the way from Desertvadi for a one-month job. Another whispered to him that I was Dalpatji's candidate. He shrugged and said, why was this farce being enacted then? He probably felt very brave putting forward all these objections. He asked me whether I felt confident about escorting foreign teams. I said yes, nonchalantly. He looked sceptical and remarked that I looked too young for the job. I told him I was twenty-one. My interview was all of five minutes.

Nandita's and Sandhya's interviews took less than three minutes each. I asked them how it had gone. They said it was okay. They also said this was nothing, the real thing was the allotment of teams.

Dalpatji agreed to drop me to my aunt's house after the interview. It was rather late, almost eight-thirty. I didn't want to be closeted with Sandhya and Nandita in the office where we were putting up. We would get our regular accommodation only after the selections. I hoped I would run into Sahil. He must have changed. Become plumper. He had already been putting on weight back then. Did he think of me at all? Even if he did, what was the use?

Andy...I still had not replied to his last letter. There was a time when I used to write to him twice a week. Now... there was nothing to write. I couldn't keep telling him I loved him. Anyway, the word 'love' sounded rather empty. Had I grown up?

Whenever I thought of him, his mother's face blotted out his. She shrieked so much, yelled so much at the servants, talked so much. Her voice kept echoing in my ears for hours afterwards. I had kept going to his home even after Mummy told me not to. At least I didn't have to put up with Mummy's stern, pale visage that way.

Andy was also very uncomfortable in my house. His eyes kept darting to the door. He would always sit on the edge of the sofa, which set my teeth on edge. We couldn't carry on any conversation as he was too busy being nervous about someone overhearing us.

In his home, there was no question of any other conversation other than a discussion on the non-availability of good green vegetables in Desertvadi or the problems of a bachelor living by himself. Andy's mother was always there to make a merry threesome. Since the day I had told her to stop talking about my family, she had spoken very little to me, but she had continued chatting away even more with Andy in my presence.

She kept talking about all the things required to set up a home: refrigerator, washing machine, gas range, food blender. I had an uncomfortable feeling it all was for my benefit. I had tried, tentatively, to sort things out with Andy. He had told me not to be silly—his mother was old-fashioned and probably did expect a great deal at the time of marriage, but he would talk to her when the time came. Everything would be all right.

Anyway, the moment she left the room, Andy wanted to kiss me. He never wanted to talk. I was getting tired of all that smooching. It did not excite me anymore. I wanted to talk to him, say so many things… I wished he would tell his mother to leave us alone, but he never did. He told me she was a heart patient—she had angina pectoris—and one had to be very careful about her feelings all the time.

I hated the way she called him her 'Annu', I hated the way she drew him up to her pillow-like breasts.

My cousin was home; aunt and uncle were away at a dinner party. After the pleasantries, I introduced the topic close to my heart. My cousin looked at me strangely and said, 'Oh, Sahil! Didn't I tell you he is getting married? He has got a job in a bank and is marrying a fellow officer. She is very nice.'

❧ Training ❧

We were supposed to be under training as Liaison Officers—all of us: Nandita, Sandhya, Annu, Ratish and Vishrut, the boy with whom Annu flirted.

'I must flirt with all the boys,' said Annu to me in a business-like fashion. She began with Vishrut.

Vishrut was hairy like a grizzly bear. He had been a basketball player on the national team but his career came to an end when he wrote an article in a newspaper criticizing the functioning of the Basketball Federation.

Nandita and Sandhya told me he thought too much of himself; he was a boy with a reputation and had to be avoided at all costs—especially, Nandita added maliciously, as I was so fond of talking to boys.

There was no need to avoid Vishrut as he was completely monopolized by Annu. She hung on his arm, giggling all the time; she even took him home for tea. She told me many things in a breathless, disconnected manner—that The College and Rosalind House had a special relationship, that she smoked, that in Rosalind, anybody of any consequence smoked, that she was waiting to get married, preferably to a rich guy.

I asked her what she was doing with Vishrut in that case. She said it was all right—she was only flirting with him. I asked whether she minded people sniggering at her. She said probably only the Desertvadi people were sniggering, and they didn't matter; after all, they were *dehatis*, not exposed to Lutyenabad culture at all. She said would flirt with Desertvadi boys too, and then they wouldn't be able to say anything.

She told me I was different from Nandita and Sandhya because I spoke good English and wore jeans. I was not a dehati like them.

Ratish did not seem to be interested in flirting with anybody. He spent his time smoking and gulping down an amazing number of cold drinks. I would often find his eyes fixed on me. They disturbed me a great deal, they gleamed so much. I could never bear to look directly into them. I would always giggle self-consciously whenever I found him looking at me. But he never smiled back.

We were being trained in Purana Maidan. It was a cheerful place. I particularly liked the small eating places, of which there were many. We spent most of our time waiting for lectures. Often, we were shifted from one office to another in search of the man in charge of the training programme. He was called Ojha. Ojha was small and plump and specialized in extolling the virtues of the government. He was very sensitive about his position as the in-charge and felt that the continuous giggling of Annu and Vishrut was an insult to it. He told us that the government was doing everything—he would wave his small arms imperiously—*everything* for us, and we should not be so ungrateful as to cadge free cold drinks whenever we could.

I read whatever literature on the Sportsaid I could lay my hands on. India had spent as much as 1.6 crore rupees on training on sportsmen and women for this event and 800 crore on the construction and renovation of the stadia. One Hindi rag weepily pointed out that in a country where people died of starvation, such expenditure could only be called scandalous. I was reminded of Papa's observation that Hindiwallahs were essentially pessimistic. I was half-ashamed to note that I felt the Hindiwallahs were correct in this instance.

We learnt nothing in the training programme. What it did was give us ample opportunity to get to know one another. I asked Vishrut about The College; he said it was a great place to be.

'It's kind of fun,' he said. 'The chick scene is damn good.'

'Chicks from Rosalind or from The College?' I asked him.

'Chicks are chicks, how does it matter? I thought it would be better here.'

'Why, what is wrong with the scene here?'

'Well, this place has either *behenji*s or BTMs.'

'BTMs…?'

'Behenjis-turned-mod—like Annu.'

'And what are behenjis?'

'Aha, Dalpatji's contingent from Desertvadi, of course.'

'What nonsense!'

'You, of course, are a child. Why aren't you at school?'

I asked Annu what behenjis were. She said they were girls who put oil in their hair, giggled when they saw boys and studied in colleges like Gauri Devi Mahavidyalaya. I asked her what BTMs were, then. She looked at me suspiciously and asked who had told me about them. When she heard it was Vishrut, she sprang up, saying, 'That show-off Meerut boy, I will kill him.'

Vishrut had done his schooling in Meerut and wasn't keen on advertising that fact.

The next day, Annu cut Vishrut dead and started flirting with the sports minister's nephew instead. When she disappeared for the fifth time to have coffee with him, Vishrut pulled me aside and said, 'Geetika, just warn Annu, yaar. This boy was in custody last year. He was almost convicted—escaped only because of his uncle. He was accused of raping a Harijan girl; I'm sure he won't mind a Rosalind girl this time.'

I wondered at this game they were playing. I had never known boys like Vishrut or, for that matter, girls like Annu. I had never been to the films or to the theatre with them. I couldn't bandy jokes with them, I couldn't hang on their arms casually.

Perhaps I was a behenji. I knew my dress was wrong—except when I was in jeans. Annu had told me that no one in Lutyenabad wore the kind of mill prints that I did. She also told me to do something with my face—I looked like a school girl. She was quite impressed, though, with my knowledge of current affairs.

'Oh, you are the studious kind. I find studies a big bore. I did my MA because my mother pushed me into it. I wanted to become an air hostess and see the world,' she informed me.

Annu had also done some modelling. Her mother had refused to let her model for a jewellery store because it required wearing an off-shoulder dress.

Twice, we had to attend lectures with other officers who told us how to deal with foreign teams. Some countries, like North and South Korea, had to be kept far away from each other; security was most important; we were not to let any stranger get into the coach with us; discipline and national pride were important too, and those responsibilities lodged mainly with the women—we were to give the foreigners a glimpse of the exalted moral standards of Indian womanhood and, under no circumstances, were we to enter the rooms of the players.

Vishrut nudged Annu and said, 'Hear, hear.' The two had made up. The training ended with these two lectures.

⊰ Sportsmen ⊱

We had been put up in a hostel near Purana Maidan. There were six of us in a room. The Indian table tennis team, which was practising at Purana Maidan, was also close by. We were using the common mess, which also catered to the sportspeople. We had to pay the mess charges—they were quite high. I was surprised that Nandita and Sandhya didn't mind spending that much on food. They were rather tight-fisted unless they were buying something they could take back home with them. They never spent on cold drinks, for instance.

One day, I saw them having breakfast with Yadu, who was the oldest girl in the room. Yadu worked in the Railways and, as I learnt later, was having an affair with Dalpatji. All three of them were eating from the same plate.

'Why don't you ask the waiter for another plate? Your omelette is almost falling off,' I said to Nandita.

'We like eating together. They are my little sisters,' Yadu replied.

The waiter came with tea for them. The teapot was big, but there was only one cup.

'Thank you, sir,' said Yadu.

I giggled, and the waiter turned to look at me.

'Why can't you learn to behave like a grown-up,' said Yadu sternly to me, 'instead of talking so much and grinning foolishly?'

'But why did you call him "sir"?'

'I think you are quite stupid. Can't you see we are saving money this way? He is charging us for one plate but giving us three. Your stupid giggles may have spoilt everything.'

Nandita and Sandhya looked balefully at me and, having finished their shared breakfast, strutted off with Yadu.

I was becoming more and more wary of Nandita and Sandhya. They ordered everybody around, even Yadu. Abhay, who was also a Liaison Officer, was constantly running errands for them. Nandita giggled a lot when he was around but he always called her 'Jija-sa'. The only person who couldn't be ordered around by them was Sonali, whose father was the Speaker of the Haryana Legislative Assembly. She was a confident girl of about eighteen who wore the trendiest of clothes. Dalpatji was most concerned about Sonali's welfare. She had come after the interviews, but had been made a Liaison Officer anyway.

The Indian table tennis team kept mainly to itself, except for Mridula Kulkarni, who was from Bombay and only a reserve player in the women's team. Mridula had short, curly hair and a ready smile for everyone. She became a good friend of mine. She told me she hated everybody in the sports bureaucracy, and it was a good thing my brother had got out of that world while he was still young. She said the Table Tennis Federation was least concerned about promoting the sport. They wanted power and nothing else. In this country, sportspersons are treated like shit, she told me. 'The only game India is even halfway decent at is cricket, and that is because it is free of this damned bureaucracy,' she added.

I wondered how Bhaiya had been able to tolerate Dalpatji and his ilk.

'We have to lick their boots for everything, even for the rubber to use on our bats. For every foreign trip, we have to sit at their feet and wag our tails. Look at Vishrut—he is out in the cold because his secretary cannot stand him. Everybody knew about his case, but what was done? They can destroy us like this after we have spent the best years of our lives representing this damned country.'

Mridula was very bitter. I asked her why she didn't leave. She said she was too old to do anything else and had been appointed a bank officer under the sports quota. This was the first time I had heard of such a quota.

I thanked the stars that Bhaiya had not gone on to become a world-class sportsman, as predicted by Dalpatji. I also felt guilty about the red tracksuit that Dalpatji had given me. Perhaps it had been at the cost of somebody like Mridula. She still had not been assigned the tracksuit and kitbag that the other players had received.

But Bhaiya never criticized Dalpatji. He always said it was the system that was at fault, not individuals, and that Dalpatji was doing a great deal for the cause of sports by cultivating excellent relations with the government and securing all sorts of unprecedented concessions for players.

I wondered how he managed to overlook the obvious fact that Dalpatji treated sportspersons like playthings. Bhaiya had such a strange relationship with him. Dalpatji had once said Bhaiya was innocent like a cow. I had laughed the whole day upon hearing that.

Nandita told me that Mridula was miffed because she had not made it to the team.

'Why do you keep sitting with her and listening to her stories against the Table Tennis Federation?' she asked.

'Why shouldn't I?'

'The secretary of the Federation is Papa's man.' she replied. 'And you're here because of Papa. You know that, don't you?'

⊰ Team Allotment ⊱

The basketball players were due to arrive in another three days. Before that, the teams had to be allocated. There was a scramble among the liaison officers for Japan and South Korea, I heard. I couldn't understand why nobody wanted China or North Korea, given that they were equally good teams. In fact, China was sure to emerge as champion. Nobody wanted India, of course—that I could understand.

'Which team are you getting?' Vishrut asked me rather mischievously.

'I don't mind any. I don't know a thing about basketball.'

'When Dalpatji asks you which team you want, say South Korea. You won't get Japan, of course—that is for his own daughters,' said Ratish.

'No, no, I am going to kiss Dalpatji and ask for South Korea,' said Annu.

'What is so special about South Korea and Japan? I would rather be with China, if there is a choice,' I put in.

'Communist countries don't give any gifts whatsoever, whereas Japan and South Korea give things like Walkmans, transistors, watches etc.,' explained Ratish patiently. He turned his face to the side to blow out smoke. His nose curved slightly at the bridge, I noticed.

'I want those shoes with air pads,' said Vishrut.

'I want to marry a Japanese industrialist's son,' said Annu.

'Japanese women make much better wives than giddy Rosalind girls,' said Vishrut. 'You would never qualify, Annu.'

Ratish told me afterwards that, on second thoughts, it would be better for me to choose an all-women's team, failing which I was to avoid Muslim countries completely; the men were desperate.

'You look quite incapable of taking care of yourself,' he said with a smile that made his eyes gleam even more. 'I am glad Dalpatji is here to look after you.'

I was suddenly reminded of Lakhan Dada. Ratish was also tall, though not as broad. Andy was such a child compared to these men. But then it occurred to me—was it Ratish's concern for me that made him disregard how prejudiced he sounded against Muslim men?

As usual, he was smoking when he said, 'Tell me about Desertvadi. Is it a nice place to live in?'

Ratish had always lived in Lutyenabad. His father was the Chief Chemist at a pharmaceutical firm, and Ratish had joined the same firm after completing his MBA.

Among the Liaison Officers, Ratish was the only one who had a car. He was also the only one who had a job. I asked him what he was doing here. He said he was vicariously satisfying a youthful desire to take part in competitive sports. I asked him how he had managed to get a leave so soon after joining. He said it was a bit of a family concern, as his father was also there. I asked him why he smoked so much. He said he was waiting for someone to tell him to stop. He didn't smile at all when he said that. He looked directly at me, instead.

The team allotments were out. I got South Korea, Nandita and Sandhya both got Japan as it was a very big team, Vishrut got North Korea and Annu got Thailand, which was an all-women's team. Ratish got Bahrain, which was all-male.

Vishrut exclaimed, 'Oh God, I am stuck with paupers!'; Annu screeched, 'I can't communicate with an all-women team!'; Ratish smoked silently.

There was dissatisfaction in other quarters too. The sports minister's nephew had got Pakistan and was hopping mad; Sonali had got Taiwan and was complaining it was not even on the map; an IAS officer's daughter got India.

Nandita said dogs always bark, but the kings do as they pleased.

The IAS's daughter strutted off to speak to her father, who was also around in one of the offices. She came back saying triumphantly that this was not the official list, it would be made again. Sandhya made a face at her.

I wondered what went on in these offices. Was it all that

they did, these IAS officers and these busy Association Secretaries? Who would get which team? Whose man would work where? Whose daughter would get the Walkman and whose nephew the Japanese watch?

The next day, we got our saris—after having stood for four hours in vain on the previous evening. The official list was also out. I got Thailand, Annu was given South Korea and the minister's nephew got Bangladesh—he was not a nephew, I found out, but only a not-so-close relative. The IAS's daughter got the Philippines.

I wondered whether Annu had really kissed Dalpatji to get South Korea.

◁ Arrival ▷

When I reached our room, Yadu was painting Nandita's toe nails. Her feet were dirty; it was surprising that Yadu could bear to keep them on her lap.

Nandita said, 'You are having a great time in Lutyenabad, aren't you, Geetika?'

'Yes, of course,' I said.

'Well, just be careful of Papa; he doesn't like girls mixing so much with boys.'

'Why has he given Annu South Korea, then? She talks to boys continuously.'

'That is different. You have come with us and you are Papa's responsibility. You came back with that boy Ratish in his car, last evening. It was so late.'

She turned to Yadu. 'Di, apply some more polish on the right toe nail. It's looking faded,' she commanded Yadu, who was putting away her make-up tackle.

Sandhya was making faces in a corner. She said, 'We didn't realize you are such a fast girl. You look so innocent.'

In Desertvadi parlance, a 'fast girl' meant a girl with loose morals. I told Sandhya to shut up. Yadu scolded me saying I must learn to speak properly. They left, banging the door behind them. I was all alone in the room.

Mridula had told me about Yadu and Dalpatji. He had got her a job in the Railways under the sports quota and a posting in a small town where he could visit her in the privacy of a government flat.

She took great care of Dalpatji, even here. She had brought some pickle especially for him from her sister, who lived in Lutyenabad. One day, I saw her pressing his shirts with a small, portable iron. At times, she ironed Nandita's and Sandhya's clothes too.

I wondered about Dalpatji's wife, who worked on his farms. She had not come for the Sportsaid. Did she suspect anything? Did Nandita and Sandhya know about Yadu and their father? Did they condone such a relationship? They seemed to be quite prudish. Yet, they were jealous because Ratish had been talking to me. None of the Lutyenabad boys had tried to talk to them at all. Even their rakhi-brothers were not paying them enough attention. Annu had flirted with Abhay for two days; he now followed her around like a dog, a glazed look in his eyes.

Nandita had taken him to task on the second day for spending 200 rupees on Annu.

'Abhayji,' she said, 'I heard you took Annu out for dinner yesterday.'

'Jija-sa,' he stuttered, 'she said she would show me the new restaurant in Circular Place.'

'You are not satisfied with Papa taking you out? What if he finds out? You had come specifically to watch the matches, hadn't you?'

'But Jija-sa…'

'And your mother? What if she comes to know you are spending 200 rupees on a girl you hardly know?'

Lutyenabad was different. Annu was so free. I would like

to be like her, though I wouldn't flirt with Abhay or with the minister's nephew. Ratish was clearly more interested in me than in Annu. Was it because I was prettier? I was not bad-looking. I stared into the mirror. God, there was a pimple sprouting on my cheek! I did not get pimples very often. Did it have to come now, when I was in Lutyenabad?

Nandita had a pimple cream. I would have to ask her for it. How I wish she were less judgemental and more pleasant to deal with.

I *must* get out of Desertvadi, *must* come to Lutyenabad. I would like to know more about Ratish. What perfect skin he had!

The teams were arriving. They all had officials escorting them, called *chef de mission*. Desertvadi people did not even try pronouncing that—they shortened it to 'mission'. We were supposed to contact the mission at the Village, where they were staying.

Ratish informed me my team had arrived, then disappeared to contact his own. I had to make several phone calls from the Village Information Centre to the players' residence to reach them. I was disappointed to find out that my team spoke almost no English. I wanted to know about Thailand. Two of the girls were very friendly. The older one had two children, and the younger, prettier one worked as a postwoman and was engaged to be married. This was about all I could gather from their frenzied gesticulations.

The chef de mission stayed aloof, even though he spoke passable English. He wanted a whole lot of information about their stay, the matches etc., none of which I could provide. He seemed rather irritated by my lack of knowledge.

That evening, I missed the coach that was to take me from the Village to my hostel. My team had taken so long to come to the phone, and then even longer to come to the Information Centre. They had then proceeded to disappear without informing me.

It was around eight-thirty at night. I did not know anything about Lutyenabad buses. Worse, I had no idea about the roads or which direction I was supposed to head. I still found the big city alarming.

Though the Information Centre was swarming with people, I couldn't recognize any of them. None of the Desertvadi people seemed to be around; they must have left together. I stepped out of the gate, feeling rather unsure of myself. The road looked quite deserted. I would have to take a taxi—there seemed no point in waiting for a bus.

Suddenly, a motorcycle drew up right beside me. There were two men on it. They studied me carefully, as though I were an object. One of them said the goods looked okay. The other said, not too hot. They laughed, and one of them reached out and stroked my breasts. The other blew me a kiss and said, 'Some other time.' They drove off.

I found myself running back to the Village gate. I didn't even realize I was sobbing. I collapsed on a chair in the Information Centre, unable to breathe. The beast—I had seen the beast... They could have... I would have been unable to do anything. I could still feel the burning insult on my nipple.

'What happened, Geetika? Why are you crying?' Ratish was standing there with the inevitable cigarette between his lips. I was again reminded of Lakhan Singh and the library incident. I wanted to jump into his arms and just keep crying. Instead, haltingly, I told him what had happened.

'You stupid girl,' he said. 'Why do you do these foolish things? Don't you know how unsafe Lutyenabad is? Don't you ever read the papers? Where are those stupid Desertvadi people? Why have they left you alone here?'

I cried most of the way in Ratish's car. He patted my hand and cursed the men on the motorcycle. I was rather surprised by the variety of abuses he heaped on them in both Hindi and English. It was curiously reassuring to feel his anger. He gave me his card with three phone numbers, instructing me never to venture out alone and to call one of them if I ever needed help.

I was an animal too, wasn't I? Andy and I—we were all animals. The scenes in the Hindi films that had excited me so much... they were all lies—those shrieks, those artfully torn clothes. There was nothing titillating about rape. This would have been flesh torn from the body. I had seen the beasts licking their chops.

There was the age-old biological drive to come together between the sexes. That was all, wasn't it? One called it marriage, affair, rape, family, honour, shame. All were the same below the waist...blood...and Booba...wrapped up in jeans, saris and the protection Ratish found so necessary... That body—I shall save up for you, like the trousseau Vinita's mother had...lacy, pink nightie, fodder for that animal that panted on the throbbing motorcycle... That body smelling of sweat and alcohol... Dalpatji and Yadu... Payment by sex... And the Sportsaid, where only the spiritual Indian woman had to be exhibited...

I tossed and turned through most of the night.

⊰ Ceremonial ⊱

Ratish asked me whether I would like to see the opening ceremony of the Sportsaid. It was to be held at the Prime Minister Stadium. Dalpatji had already promised to 'manage' my ticket, along with those of the others. I would rather have gone with Ratish than with Nandita, Sandhya, Yadu and Abhay, but I didn't want to alienate Dalpatji.

'Are you also coming?' Sandhya asked, seeing me getting ready with the others.

'Yes, of course.'

'Look at Papa, Nandita. He is taking the whole world along, but he won't give a ticket for Lalu.'

Lalu was also from Desertvadi. For the past week, I had seen him follow Sandhya around.

'What can I do?' said Nandita abstractedly, vigorously rubbing a Japanese lipstick on her lips. 'This has absolutely no colour,' she complained.

'I am going to fight with Papa,' said Sandhya.

I noticed she was almost in tears. I felt slightly sorry for her. 'If you ask him, I am sure he will give a ticket for Lalu... Can't Lalu buy a ticket?' I asked.

'In which world are you living?' said Yadu, 'The opening ceremony tickets were sold out months ago. They are available only in black now—two thousand rupees per ticket—and the seat won't even be in a good place. Buy a ticket indeed!'

'Everybody is going,' said Sandhya. 'Even people who only criticize us. But people like Lalu, who have been loyal to Papa all their lives, are going to be left behind.'

'Don't cry, Sandhya,' said Yadu, putting her arms around her. 'Can't you see how busy he is? He must have overlooked Lalu's case. I will speak to him...'

Nandita was applying mascara. Suddenly, Sandhya screamed at her, 'You're not worried, are you? Your Abhay is going...'

'Tell Geetika to go with her Lutyenabad boyfriends,' Nandita replied. 'I overheard one inviting her for the opening. You can use her ticket for Lalu.'

Mercifully, Dalpatji arrived at that very moment to take us to the Prime Minister Stadium. Yadu at once cleared a chair for him.

'I can see it is a special day for you, sir,' she said, lowering her voice. She always called him 'sir'. Dalpatji, outlandish in a bright red jacket, perked up.

'Yes, yes... With great difficulty I leave minister's side today. I wanted to make sure my daughters are okay. But why are the girls not ready, Yadu?'

'Sandhya is angry with you, sir. And I am angry because she is angry.'

Sandhya jumped at Dalpatji and began complaining about the ingratitude of certain people who only knew how to take...

'I will not take this Lalu-shalu. I have not taken the

responsibility of the whole world,' said Dalpatji.

Sandhya dissolved into tears. Dalpatji got even more irritated and enquired what relation of hers was Lalu that she should go mad in this manner.

'She is a child, sir,' interceded Yadu. 'She feels all your special people should get a chance to see the opening ceremony. Don't yell at the child...'

I watched the tableau unfold before me: daughter, mistress and the ridiculous figure of Dalpatji...the shadow of a formidable wife growing cauliflowers in his fields in the background.

After ten minutes, Sandhya was happily running down to the mess to tell Lalu that he could come along with us.

'So, Geetika, you must tell Sanjay that you saw the opening,' said Dalpatji, beaming at me in the official car that was ferrying us to the stadium.

We got good seats. Not as good as Dalpatji's, of course, who sat with the minister, just behind the Prime Minister. Lalu, to Sandhya's chagrin, sat far away from us.

It was a long event, almost three hours in duration. The crowd cheered when the mascot of the Sportsaid, Gappu—a plump little calf made entirely of flowers—was exhibited. I enjoyed the march past of the players, even though the Indian team looked the sloppiest. The sportsmen and women shuffled lazily on the tracks, their pink turbans and colourful saris looking quite inappropriate for the occasion. Every team, except the Iranian, was led by a hostess carrying a placard bearing the name of the country on it. Nandita told me the Iranians had refused to walk behind a woman as it was against the principles of Islam. 'Muslims are quite odd,' she added.

I was feeling quite bored listening to Nandita and Abhay giggle. Nevertheless, when the cultural function started, it took my breath away. Folk dances from all over the country were performed. There was such perfect synchrony among the hundreds of dancers that it seemed incredible. In Desertvadi, I had at times attended the Independence Day and Republic Day functions held at Patel Maidan. The cultural events were unfailing disasters, with the fifty-odd dancers failing to keep time to the shrill, taped music. This was in a totally different class. The Karagam dancers from Tamil Nadu and the Dandia dancers from Gujarat kept perfect time with exquisite grace to the changing rhythms. It was like a different world. It seemed amazing that these worlds could coexist, the world I knew in Desertvadi and the perfection I was witnessing now.

◄ Ratish ►

Was I taking Ratish for a ride? He had been looking after me rather aggressively since the incident at the Village gate. He saw to it that I was put into the coach every evening; otherwise, he would always be ready to give me a lift. He even said I looked very nice in jeans.

I had told him I had no road sense, which was really a way of asking him to look after me. In a way, I was leading him on. I liked him looking after me. He took over so easily, impervious to the hostile stares of the Desertvadi people; he even outstared Dalpatji.

Andy, on the other hand, flinched so easily—anybody could make him nervous. 'What will the gardener say?' he had objected once when I tried holding his hand in his garden. Otherwise, he couldn't keep his hands off me.

How disloyal I was! Not only was I taking Ratish for a ride, I was also comparing Andy to him. What would Mummy say if she ever found out?

I cornered Annu and, quite out of context, began telling her about Andy. Her only comment was that he didn't seem to have much of a future ahead of him—executive trainees in remote, unknown places were certainly not half as good as MBAs in Lutyenabad, and not even one-eighth as good as those employed in multinationals. So what, in God's name, was a girl like me—

quite good-looking—doing with him?

I knew she would run and tell Ratish at the earliest opportunity. It had not escaped her that he had been paying me special attention. In fact, she had enviously remarked that village innocents had all the luck in the world. I knew she was referring mainly to Ratish's car, which was not only new but also his own—his father had another.

Money was frankly important to Annu, though when I once asked her whether she would marry the minister's nephew, who owned acres of farmland in Punjab, she had replied, 'Not even if he owns half of Lutyenabad'.

Other things, like the ability to speak English, were also important to her. Mummy always said it wasn't important to know English. But it mattered to me too; people from Hindi-medium schools were somehow backward, like Pigeon, who had failed in two papers. However, I didn't make a religion out of it the way Annu did.

Annu also complained that the Sportsaid was proving to be more efficient than a marriage bureau—for everybody except her. Two of her friends had got engaged. Rekha, a woman who used to giggle about her work and had been talking about how making announcements could feel orgasmic, was also in love. She was thirty-five and unmarried, and had fallen in love with a fellow announcer who was thirty-two, married and had two children. His name was Nilayan, but everybody called him Neil.

Neil loved her for her womanliness, Rekha told me. His wife was a journalist and a very ambitious woman. She had no time for the house—unlike Rekha, who could cook, sew and embroider. Rekha told me men didn't like ambitious women. Neil and Rekha had gone to a holiday resort for a couple of days. She came back looking radiant. I asked her whether it had been like announcing and she blushed. Neil and his wife were talking about divorce, she told me.

It was rather boring escorting my team from the Village to the Lutyenabad Sports Complex, where the basketball matches were being held. The Complex was impressive. I liked roaming around in the lawns, especially since the weather had turned quite pleasant.

I also enjoyed talking to the Lutyenabad people, who all seemed to converge there. I gathered a lot of information about various facets of life in the city from them.

Annu complained often about travelling by bus. She said it was demeaning to be pawed by desperate, middle-aged men. Vishrut quickly replied that perhaps she would prefer being pawed by younger men.

The Thai team lost in the very first round. Neither of the girls I talked to seemed to mind very much, though their chef de mission—who, I later found out, was also their coach—gave the team a severe lecture. He seemed far more sincere than them.

Ratish easily forgot his resolve to see as many matches as possible. He spent all his time talking to me, as Bahrain—his team—had also lost in the very first round. They seemed to be very fond of him. They took him out for lunches and dinners. Ratish said they were not interested in the matches at all; they only wanted to see the discotheques and night clubs in Lutyenabad.

I was sickened by the way Indians wangled gifts from the foreigners. Nandita and Sandhya had even brought an empty suitcase for the gifts their team was giving them. They kept very quiet about what they got. Annu, on the other hand, showed everybody the perfumes, shampoos, etc., she had received. She had even got a marriage proposal from an Iraqi journalist who used to hang around with the Liaison Officers in order to arrange interviews with the winning teams. Vishrut said there must have been some confusion because of language—it wasn't marriage the guy was proposing, he was probably just propositioning her.

Vishrut himself had managed to get the shoes he desired from his team and was rather triumphant.

I wondered what the foreigners must be thinking of us. If

one of them ever dared to give even a badge to somebody in public, there would be a crowd begging them for more. The coach drivers, conductors and even the security personnel seemed to be thirsting for things like badges and tie pins. I was reminded of the Pushkar beggars.

I told Ratish it was humiliating.

'Come on, Geeti,' he said. 'It is quite understandable. People are not here just for the love of the game...'

'But to beg like that, Ratish...'

'You are too idealistic. And what is this on your cheek?'

'It's a pimple...'

'Looks like Lutyenabad is not suiting you at all... All this pollution...and you must wear goggles in the afternoons to protect your eyes.'

'Why aren't you with your team today?'

'We had a quarrel.'

'After all those lunches and dinners, I was thinking they would take you to Bahrain with them.'

'They would have if I had done what they wanted me to do.'

'What?'

'They expected me to find them girls at the discotheque. As if I am a pimp or something.'

I thought he had been very principled. Would Vishrut have done the same?

What are your plans for the future, Geeti?' Ratish asked, suddenly.

'I want to take the civil services exam...'

'Whatever for? You don't look like the aggressive lady officer kind.'

'Working women are not always aggressive, Ratish. My mother works.'

'Lectureship is different. It is the best job for women. You can work and look after your home and children...That is important, too...isn't it?'

I did want a home...and Mummy... All those lonely days I spent when she could have been home, had she chosen not to do that extra bit of social work... Now it was my turn to make a choice.

Did I want that kind of life? Stinking utensils in the sink on the days Shugni Bai didn't come, egg-bread-milk for breakfast, lunch and dinner... No... I wanted to keep house, plan my drawing room...the well-ordered life I saw in toothpaste and textile advertisements—the life I imagined Ratish lived...

I don't know, Ratish. I haven't sorted it all out yet.'

'Haven't you spoken about it to your boyfriend? What does he feel about the civil services?'

'I don't know... We haven't talked about it yet.'

'You are marrying him, aren't you?'

To my horror, I found myself crying. I just couldn't stop the tears.

'I don't know, Ratish, I don't know...'

⊰ Combat ⊱

There was a hushed expectancy in the air. North Korea and South Korea were facing each other in the semi-finals. Well-dressed, well-fed South Koreans sat in small groups, good-naturedly urging on their team. Quite a few seemed to have come to see the match. It was a matter of life and death for the North Koreans. They formed a small, tight contingent, all dressed in identical tracksuits. They even had a leader holding their national flag. They cheered when he raised it and looked desperate whenever the other team scored. In my heart, I also cheered for them. It wasn't fair that one half of a country should look like that. It wasn't fair that Lutyenabad and Desertvadi should coexist...

I told Ratish that at heart, I was a Marxist. He said that, at heart, everybody was—him too.

'But then, with an MBA and your job in a private firm… Aren't you rather far from Marxism?' I asked him.

'Do you really know what multinationals are?' Ratish countered.

'I know they are not the champions of the proletariat.'

He seemed genuinely surprised by my knowledge, however sketchy, of his profession.

'Geeti, I don't think it is a sin to make money. Everybody does it. I am going to do it. Tell me sincerely, don't you want money and all that it can give you?'

I did want money. I just had never thought much about it. But I couldn't be like Mummy and Papa, always saying it didn't matter. I certainly did not want to be poor.

'But Ratish, to some people—like my parents—money genuinely doesn't mean anything.'

'Geeti, that generation was different; and, perhaps, your parents were lucky to be able to keep their principles. My father started off like that…' He broke off and looked at me. The full impact of his eyes made me stutter.

'Started off like what…?'

'We are *bania*s, you know. Money is, frankly, all-important to our community. But my father joined the Communist Party. In those days, all university students were Leftist. He decided not to go into our family business and, because my grandfather died early, there was nobody to manage it. My father's cousins gradually swallowed everything; even the shop had to be sold. And then, my sister died…'

I wished fervently I could find something to say. It was an intimate moment. I didn't want it to pass. The match was over. A lot of people were milling around, yet the two of us had formed an island of our own.

'She had always been delicate, and my father was earning very little money from the party… They were living hand to mouth. She died suddenly, after a fever… She often got those, so nobody bothered very much about it. I was four then and my older sister was six; the one who died was just two... My father went into depression after that. He blamed himself for her death, cried incessantly...'

How unreal it sounded—the death of a child due to the idealism of the father! In a Hindi film, the embittered man would have turned to crime.

'Then, of course, things changed. My mother realized that life could not be built on platitudes. She made him take up a job in a private firm. He joined as a mere trainee, hating it all the time. You know, the advantages we have had, good education, etc., are because of money. It is false to underplay its importance.'

Perhaps Ratish was right. Even Dalpatji had said Bhaiya was lucky to be marrying someone who made good money. It would have been different for us as well, had Papa made a lot of money. I could have flown from one place to another like Sonali. I could have had jewellery.

Ratish's mother sounded formidable. But did she have a choice, with a child dying in her arms? For all her social work, Mummy was hardly the domineering kind. She never called Papa by his name. She called him 'ji', just that. Though Papa made tea in the morning, I knew she was rather embarrassed about it. She had never asked Bhaiya to do any work in the house. I was expected to warm his food and lay the table for him.

Mummy always asked Papa for money. She never spent any of her own accord. Yet she always said she believed in the equality of the sexes. People in Desertvadi said Papa was a most understanding husband. I knew that actually meant henpecked.

Ratish's father sounded henpecked too. I asked him who wore the pants in his house. He said there was no question of his mother wearing the pants, she wasn't a hysterical feminist. She was content staying home; in fact, she had sacrificed a lot for his father's career. She had done a course in corporate culture, and some of his father's success was due to the excellent interpersonal relationships his mother had helped him cultivate.

Ratish's world sounded so strange, so different from mine. I could imagine his mother. She must be a very sophisticated person. I was fascinated by middle-aged ladies who painted their nails and wore lipstick. I asked Ratish whether his mother had short hair. He laughed and replied it was shorter than mine.

ᔕ Return ᔔ

Only too soon, it was time to leave. Dalpatji said that since I had seen the opening and my team had lost, I had nothing much to do—I might as well go back. I suspected he wanted me to leave because he was uncomfortable about me spending so much time with Ratish.

The day I was supposed to return, Annu invited all the Liaison Officers home for lunch. She lived in a pokey little flat, but her mother was very affectionate. She had made many things for us and seemed especially fond of Ratish.

Rekha also came. Ratish had told me that Neil would never divorce his wife and that Rekha was wasting her time.

'But she is in love with him.'

'Geeti, he is taking advantage of her. He will have his fun and then leave her high and dry.'

'How do you know?'

'I have seen the world, that's why. Besides, I know Neil's type. They have affairs but can't commit themselves to anybody.'

But I couldn't bear to say any of this to Rekha. She looked so happy and lost in dreams. I just hugged her and wished her all the best.

Vishrut played the fool all afternoon. He pretended to propose to Annu while her mother was in the kitchen. Annu looked very uptight and said she wouldn't marry an impoverished, out-of-favour basketball player for all the money in the world.

I told Annu I would miss her.

'Other people will miss you too, Geeti,' she said.

'What do you mean, Annu?'

'Some people I know. But you are "hooked and booked", aren't you?'

'Yes.'

'Well, be happy then, and invite me to your wedding.'

'I am not getting married yet.'

Nandita and Sandhya looked at me as I bid farewell to all the Lutyenabad people. They stood apart, by themselves. I hoped they would not tell too many tales of me in Desertvadi. I was trying to avoid Ratish. I wouldn't know what to say to him.

Suddenly, he asked me for my address book and then handed it back to me with a small gift-wrapped packet.

Nandita and Sandhya were going to stay back in Lutyenabad for more shopping, even after the Sportsaid. I was returning alone, on a Haryana Roadways bus. The journey would be long, but I didn't mind. I wanted time to mull over things. The weather was not too bad either—it was the beginning of December. I had a light cardigan on.

What had my stay in Lutyenabad taught me? Mummy had said it would be a kind of higher education. I had not learnt anything I did not already know about sports, except that in spite of formidable investments, the country was quite inadequate, even by Asian standards. Bhaiya could hardly have been world-class! But I had learnt that Dalpatji was a reality I could not accept. He did not care whether the Indian team won or lost; he only cared about the requisite number of Scotch bottles that had to be presented to a journalist in order to get good coverage in the papers. No, I couldn't accept that reality.

I couldn't even accept the IAS officers who had fawned on Dalpatji to get a foothold in the Sportsaid... Money... It all came back to money, and the power that went with it.

Money was important, Ratish had said. Money and a way of life in which a woman's job was not so important, but her contribution to her home—very important! It sounded regressive. Yet Annu, who had no intention of taking up a career, was liberated in a way Mummy would never let me be. Mummy's insistence on a job, and nothing but a job, was shackling me... Higher education could also mean breaking free from a constricting value system.

Desertvadi, here I come—after a month, only to go away again. I had begun to miss home. I would miss Ratish too. He had given me a diary with the message, 'To the cutest girl I have ever met, with best wishes.'

Would I never see him again? Perhaps I could write to him. I wanted to know more about him. But then Mummy...

Really, this was ridiculous! I was twenty-one. I had the freedom to try and run the country by joining the IAS, but not the freedom to write to a man. But did I want to have Ratish only as a friend? I was attracted to him—he was so attractive, so protective! I wanted to be protected.

God, did I have to be attracted to every man I met? Perhaps there was something wrong with me.

Annu was so sensible; she knew she was not in love with Vishrut. But me? It was every guy I met.

Perhaps I was what they called 'oversexed'. No girl I knew masturbated like I did; that was supposed to be a thing boys did.

When I was very small, Mummy had caught me squatting and rubbing myself on the floor. She had looked very stern. The next day, she had got me some homeopathic medicine. She had said it was a disease that had to be cured. I knew it wasn't a disease; I could stop if I wanted to.

I became very careful to hide it from her. I started doing it in school. The teachers would ask whether I wanted to go to the loo, that's all. When my friends asked me what I was up to, I told them it was a disease and I was taking medicines for it.

Then one day, Mummy found out I was doing it at school,

somebody must have told her. She was very angry and told me I must stop, or I would have problems later on. I asked her what kind of 'problems'? She said, *problems*, that's all. So I stopped doing it at school and did it only in the bathroom, or when no one else was home.

Now I knew what it was...

The driver was leering at me. Does he know what I am thinking? Does it show on my face that I masturbate?

Ratish thought I looked sweet and innocent.

The bus halted at a stop. An urchin appeared with a cup of tea for me. I told him I hadn't asked for it; he said the driver sahib had asked him to give it to me.

I did want tea...

I called the conductor bhaiya and asked him the time. He told me at once and leered all the more. What would these two do if they could get me alone!

It had always been so difficult talking to Mummy about these things. Kiran's father always used to hug and kiss me a lot. I didn't like that. He would hold my hands and say how soft it was. I had never been able to tell Mummy about that either.

But Ratish—no, I was not going to lose him the way I had lost Sahil. I would tell Andy I wanted time; I wasn't yet ready for marriage. Then, probably, I would come to Lutyenabad for a while, to do my MPhil... Other decisions could wait.

I drifted off to sleep.

When I woke up, it was dark. We had reached Desertvadi. The bus emptied quickly. My luggage was the last to come down. The conductor asked me very sweetly how I was planning to get home, since it would be difficult getting conveyance at this hour.

The driver offered to drive the bus up to my house.

I jumped into a tonga without bothering to reply.

Part Two

MPhil

❖ Jana ❖

I was getting married.

The henna on my hands was not very intricate, not like Desertvadi henna, which women applied with a small stick that tickled the palm so much. This was Lutyenabad, where the woman from the boutique had charged a fortune for a blotchy pattern made with an icing gun.

Papa was horrified by the expenses. 'Marriages are backbreaking,' he said. He bent backwards and his back broke, and there was blood running into the henna; red juice from the green henna leaves intermingling with red blood... The woman from the boutique said, 'You will have to pay extra for this...'

It was hot like hell in the hostel, though it was only eight in the morning. I had started dreaming of marriage again. Shugni Bai used to say it was a bad omen to dream of marriage as it presaged disaster, death. Disaster had come already.

Yesterday, I had received a letter from Papa. I had been dreading it. 'Hope you are preparing for the civil services. Rao's Study Circle is very good; have you heard of it?'

You bet I had—half the hostel was preparing hard for the civil services... All these scholars from across the country!

But Papa, I don't want to... Ratish doesn't want me to... Somehow, the two had merged somewhere. I had told him that I was not going to take the civil services exam. What did I want? Did I really know? Ratish said lectureship was better for women as it gave ample time for the house as well...home and children... Did I want children? Lakshmi, the only friend I have made in the hostel, says I have wide, child-bearing hips.

I don't want to take the civil services and that is final... *Papa*... I will have to write to Papa, tell him my childhood dreams are dead. I have grown up. Here I am in the Jana Postgraduate University in Lutyenabad, having a grown-up affair about which everybody knows—even you do, Papa.

Yesterday, I had dinner with Ratish at a five-star hotel; the bill came up to one-fifth of your salary. I can't boast about it as it is against certain principles that should have been mine. What should I write that won't break both our hearts? I must cry again as I used to in Desertvadi and tell no one about it... I must try and think... I must try and think without crying...

I could hear Lakshmi shrieking in the next room, 'What's love got to do with it, do with it!' She must be getting ready to go to the library.

Lakshmi took lessons in Carnatic music. Her Paattu Vaathiyar—music teacher—lived quite close to the university campus, but she only sang Michael Jackson, Cindy Lauper or Madonna after her lessons.

Lakshmi was an Iyer. She often said Iyers were the most intelligent race in India, closely followed by Bengalis. She was doing a PhD in Economics and her supervisor was a Bengali. She was an unashamed communalist when she wasn't being an egalitarian Marxist. Her supervisor was intense-looking and bearded. I saw his photographs often in the *Times of India* and *India Today*, especially during Budget time, when he would tear apart the reactionary policies of the government.

Lakshmi was anti-establishment too, but then, so was everybody else at Jana, which had the distinction of sending the highest number of candidates to the civil services every year.

I had fallen in love with the campus. It was sylvan, lush and green. It didn't look like the Lutyenabad I had known during the Sportsaid. Ratish said it was the centre of pseudos of the country. Lakshmi was not a pseudo... Some mornings, she had chandan markings on her forehead. When I asked her whether she had performed puja, she would sing something inappropriate like 'Beat it, beat it'. I knew she was embarrassed about religion.

She was passionate about her subject, which included working out a theoretical model for price rise. She had told me it was an out-and-out Marxist project. She worked late into the nights, scribbling equations and singing to herself.

I knew I must catch her before she disappeared inside the library.

'Hi, Lakshmi.'

'Just beat it, beat it!' she sang and danced.

'What time did you get up?'

'Six, lady! I have done my washing for the week. Rushing to the library. *Life* magazine features the Jackson family this time… I must get hold of it.'

'Aren't you meeting your supervisor today?'

'No, no, no. Today, his wife will read the paper he wrote for her at the School of International Studies. While everybody will be spellbound by her brains and eloquence, he will sit in the back row and wonder why he married her.'

'Jealous cat. She is better looking than you are.'

'Certainly not. I look like Michael Jackson's twin sister.'

She ran off, still *beat-it*-ing it. I liked meeting her in the mornings; she always raised my spirits. She had the reputation of being an eccentric genius in the hostel.

⚜ Structures ⚜

I had decided not to go for classes. I wanted to think… I had to take a day off to think, now and then…when structuralism became too much.

Structuralism was a disease that my supervisor had caught in Sorbonne. Now she was infecting all of us—three of us—who wanted to work on novels for our MPhil dissertation. Structuralism could be anything in France: Greta Garbo's face or striptease or even graffiti on the walls.

'Choose any novel,' we had been told, 'and take it apart.' We were putting literature in its place, along with Garbo's fortunate face…

I wished I could write to Papa and tell him about all the exciting things I was reading. Instead, I had to break the news of my insurgency to him. There are other things in life, Papa, other things I want to do. I want to drink of life—I have been thirsty for so long. No more waiting. I can't bear to take an exam any more.

And I am in love, Papa; you know that, don't you? I live for the evenings and Ratish. I have grown up, Papa. Grown up enough to take a decision. I am planning my life, at last. My life has to be drastically different from Mummy's and yours. It has to be structured in a way yours wasn't. We were so different from everybody else we knew in Desertvadi. I think I am beginning to enjoy the anonymity of belonging to the mainstream. Ratish has so many friends. I like them, I like the parties we go to. I will even like his parents when I get to know them.

I must make a phone call to Ratish and discuss this letter with him. I quickly put on my salwar kameez and ran out. It was unbearably hot, even for my desert-hardened head. I wrapped the dupatta around my head like a turban.

In Jana University, one somehow got the licence to dress as one pleased. Lakshmi would often wear salwars with T-shirts, and tracksuit jackets with kurtas. Men inevitably wore kurta pyjamas and kolhapuri chappals. Ratish always stood out because of his immaculately ironed shirts and trousers when he came to visit me.

The receptionist cooed over the line, then there was a splutter and some music, and finally Ratish's voice.

'Hello, sweetheart. Why aren't you in class at this time?'

'Didn't feel like it… Ratish, I got a letter from Papa yesterday. He has written again about the civil services.'

'Oho, why are they so hung up on the civil services? You are not sitting at home twiddling your thumbs, are you?'

'They don't see this as an adequate substitute.'

'Try and explain the situation to them, Geeti. Government jobs are all nine-to-five, or more. How will we have a family life, then?'

'I don't know. They just don't seem to understand...'

'Geeti, you will have to be calm, darling. Don't forget they are your parents.'

Family was very important to Ratish. It had been important to Andy as well. But Ratish was never critical of my parents the way Andy had been. But wasn't Ratish undermining the importance of my career? Wasn't my childhood plan of joining the civil services important?

Yet, it was more Papa's and Mummy's dream than mine. What did I want? Would Ratish have been supportive if I made it absolutely clear that I would not settle for anything but a career in the civil services?

Why was I being difficult? It was important to be happy and I was happy—for the first time in my life. Ratish had taken over my life so effortlessly. All the unpleasant aspects of life, like paying the admission fees in the university office, standing in a queue to get my hostel accommodation—Ratish had managed all that.

The sun was making my head reel. I wanted go and lie down. I had to read 'Science Versus Literature' by Roland Barthes. This was amazing... I was taking copious notes, and yet I didn't have the faintest idea what my dissertation was to be on.

That was the least of the problems, my supervisor had said...

⁂ Boyfriend ⁂

Are you dead, Andy? I have left you far behind. So, are you dead to me?

What happens when relationships end? Do the ghosts also die? It was so painless for me to say, 'I don't think it is working out'... It was so difficult for you... You cried so much. I didn't know you could cry. But you didn't say even once that your mother...

Do you know that it is she who will always be your wife? She is there, deep within you, cradling your soul...

There is communication because there is no communication, thundered the supervisor in a sudden spurt of lucidity.

Three dark heads bent obediently over the notebook to glean these pearls of wisdom.

'When I say cat, you may think of a black cat, a white cat, a fat cat, a thin cat...'

I wondered where to put this in. I was going to write a dissertation on *A House for Mr Biswas* by V.S. Naipaul, I had decided last night. At what point should I bring in the feline? This brand new structuralist approach... For the past twenty minutes, this impressive lady from Sorbonne had only spoken about the difficulty in identifying cats. I had even drawn one in my notebook. Structuralism had spread far and wide, she had told us; it had reached Cornell, where a professor had simplified it at once for the simple non-European brain. Only Americans are capable of such simplifications, she had added laughingly.

Cornell, America... Vinita.

Vinita had changed so much. She now had a baby girl. She did all the household chores herself, she had told me. She had become plump. Her breasts had lost their upright quality; she had even started applying a lot of make-up—bright lipstick, mascara and eyeshadow.

She wouldn't know about American universities though—that wasn't the America she had gone to. She had gone to drudgery and loneliness... No servants to chat with all day long.

In Ratish's house, there were servants... Lakshmi said Ratish was far too predictable. She said I was predictable too. That I would get married in a hotel, watched by a whole lot of people I didn't know; that I would have two easy deliveries and be pleasantly miserable all my life. She even predicted I would get fat.

When I told her I wasn't predictable and would make her sit up one day, she began singing 'Girls Just Want to Have Fun'.

Every discourse has a mediatory role as an instrument of change.

Who would mediate between my estranged parents and me?

Which discourse—the discourse of commitment or the discourse of tradition? Lakshmi or Ratish?

Ratish had come to Desertvadi to say that he loved me. Mummy had said it was absolutely dreadful the way I could never make up my mind about boys. She had cried. Andy had cried too; Papa was the only one who hadn't. And then, suddenly, there had been a letter from the university saying I had cleared the written exams for the MPhil programme, would I appear for an interview?

I was where I wanted to be for the first time in my life, though the umbilical cord of parental expectations was yet to be cut... Ratish said he valued family and respected my parents, and that I should be gentle with them... Cruel to be kind, kind to the potential children in my womb. What if there weren't any? What if I couldn't have any? So much of our planning would go haywire, Ratish. I would have been cruel for nothing.

There would be nothing to do except cry or make a phone call to your office... No patter of little feet. What would I do with you then?

Tonight, we are going for a party, I will ask you then.

Words are either arbitrary or associational.

Is that a word, 'associational', or was it coined in Sorbonne this very summer? Lakshmi says it would be better to check the professor's antecedents; perhaps she is not from Sorbonne at all.

Lakshmi looks down on our department anyway.

Economics people have this strange nose-in-the-air attitude towards languages. Our department was housed in the School of Languages, so everybody thought it was a Linguistics department... But we were doing literature, three of us. One was from Utkal University, Orissa; another from Ramakrishna Mission, Pondicherry; and I, from Rajasthan University.

I was disappointed that there was nobody from Lutyenabad in our course. All Lutyenabad students went to the Capital University because all the jobs were there. I had heard that there was a danger of never landing a job in Lutyenabad after doing an MPhil from Jana University.

So Andy, your curse may yet materialize—if I don't have children and I don't get a job. You had said as much, hadn't you?

'You will never be happy, Geetika, never... Don't think you can find happiness by wrecking mine.'

But what could I do, Andy?

'Geeti, my mother wants us to marry,' you had said.

'But Andy, my parents do not want me to marry yet.'

'Look, the situation is getting very difficult for me. My parents are rather worried about the fact that your parents have not made any overtures to them.'

'Why don't you explain to them—'

'I have done enough explaining. Your brother got married without even calling his parents for the wedding...'

'What does Bhaiya have to do with this?'

'Geeti, I can understand my parents... They didn't question my decision to marry you. Surely, they are entitled to some sort of say in my affairs.'

'I am not saying they are not...but what am I to do?'

You could never answer that one, could you, Andy? It just went on and on—your duty towards your parents, the obduracy of mine. I was tempted, sorely tempted, to just tell my parents that I was marrying you that very day but Ratish's card saved me.

It came by the evening post the day you left Desertvadi after extracting a promise from me that I would speak to my parents. It was a lovely card; it said: 'I can't forget you, little one'.

It became easier to write that letter to you, dear Andy... It became easier to tell you, when you came running after receiving that letter, that it won't work... But it wasn't easy dealing with the lava of your frustrated anger as it burnt down my unsuspecting ears whenever I picked up the phone for months after that.

'You bitch, you found somebody else at the Sportsaid, didn't you? Don't think you can ever be happy with him...'

Discourse becomes necessary because of the ambiguity inherent in the nature of language.

But I understood even what you didn't say... I knew that I had wronged you, Andy. I did not cry as much as you did; I would have to make up for it. I had always appeased the gods by crying... This time, I slipped up...

✦ Virgin-Whore ✦

It was a house in Greater Kailash that we went to—a Shaivite name, the great Kailash, I told Ratish. But Ratish was not listening; he was groping for his lighter. Just as well. He did not appreciate my sense of humour. He appreciated my figure, which was slight and non-embarrassing. Ratish hated to be embarrassed.

His friend was called Hari Prasad. His parents were away, so his girlfriend Munmun was acting hostess. She had been married but had recently left her husband. I asked Ratish the reason for the separation.

'They had a problem, Geeti. He didn't satisfy her sexually.'

'How do you know?'

'Hari told me...'

'Are they going to get married?'

'She hopes so, but they won't. Hari's parents will never agree.'

'But he appears to be so much in love.'

'He falls in love with every girl he meets.'

How often Ratish said that—'fall in love with every girl'... But he had been right about Nilayan and Rekha. After the Sportsaid, Nilayan had gone back to his wife.

'But is this all right... Shouldn't Munmun be told?'

'Look, it doesn't matter. Hari is not the only man she is seeing. For girls like her, it doesn't matter. He satisfies her, that's enough.'

Munmun didn't pay much attention to me. She flitted around, talking easily. How attractive she was, round-faced and bright-eyed! Now and then, she would put her arms around Hari. All the men in the room seemed to be looking at her. She did have a lot to look at…

My sari was too dull for the occasion—this is what came of listening to Lakshmi's impassioned advice. This type of beige-and-brown combination suited women who have definite views about the political scene. I would have to wear reds and yellows…or chiffons and de Chines that Lakshmi found so vulgar…

'That's a very attractive sari. Sambhalpuri, isn't it?' Munmun said.

'Yes.'

'When are you getting married, Geeta?'

'Geetika… I don't know yet…er… What about you, Munmun?'

'Let's see, I am in no hurry. I have been married before. Why aren't you drinking anything?'

I had finished my cola. I was desperately hungry. I knew dinner wouldn't be served for another two hours—it was only ten. People ate so late at these parties.

The room was big and indifferently furnished. Ratish used to say that banias didn't believe in spending money on consumer goods. They made investments in gold and real estate, only. But Hari must be spending a small fortune on drinks today. There were so many people. Men were grouped together, holding their glasses. Very few of the women were drinking. I too couldn't bring myself to have any of the strong stuff. Somehow, Mummy was always there at the back of my mind. What would she say if she saw me here tonight? She would be shocked that I was at a party with all these heavy drinkers. I should be in the hostel room. Mummy had a shrewd idea of what I would be up to in Lutyenabad, which was why she had opposed my plans so much.

'What will you do in Lutyenabad that you can't do here, Geetika?' she had said.

'I want to do my MPhil, Mummy. You know there is no course available here in Desertvadi.'

'But you always wanted to appear for the civil services; for that, you don't need an MPhil.'

'What if I don't get through...'

'The UPSC allows three chances...'

Three long years in Desertvadi with the constant danger of the phone ringing... 'You bitch... You found somebody else at the Sportsaid, didn't you... If you think you will ever be happy... You will suffer all your life as I am suffering now... You are incapable of finding any peace, ever... You were playing with me all this time, weren't you?'

No, Andy, no. I am no player. Everything is dead serious for me. It is so difficult for me to know whether I am being true or false. There is always this part of me that keeps watching the other half sardonically. When I was kissing you, I always knew how ridiculous we looked together. Now, along with loving Ratish, I am also watching his friends down their umpteenth drinks. They are so well-dressed, these men, their T-shirts sometimes stretching over the beginnings of pot bellies, all designer stuff. They are lawyers and doctors and chartered accountants. They drive around in Marutis. They drink hard in the evenings.

I am attracted to their maleness—the smell of aftershave lotion and the ease with which they spend thousands—it reminds me of television commercials. I also know that they are inspired by the very same commercials—there goes Vimal suitings, smoking the spirit of freedom, wife wears jewellery from Zhaveris, where trust is a tradition or vice versa...probably has a Videocon washing machine, the TV would be neighbour's envy, owner's pride. No, they probably had imported televisions: Sony, National; floors would have to be Indian... Marblex floors for the kitchen and bathroom... I would like all that too: cold coffee in the evenings for the children, no Bournvita to help them grow, and for me, tea...

Dinner was really late.

I needed to go to the loo.

'So your friend Ratish has found a doll.'

'Darling, why do you hate him so much?' This was Hari's voice. After a couple of drinks, his voice tended to sound less cosmopolitan—the ds and the rs got emphasized.

'I know he is trying his best to break us up.'

'Come on, Munmun'—there was silence. 'I love you.'

'What is this Gita girl doing?'

'MPhil from Jana.'

'Beauty as well as brains—and the distinction, probably, of never having even looked at a man…'

'On the contrary! Geeti was having a torrid love affair when Ratish discovered her.'

'You are joking… What about virginity?'

'I don't know. I was surprised too. He must have been really in love.'

'Or madam must have been exceptionally clever. Doesn't look it, though.'

The voices moved away. That was jealousy! The lovely Munmun was actually jealous of me… I looked in the mirror; I wasn't bad-looking… But she was jealous of an unbroken hymen…

⚜ Watermelon ⚜

Lakshmi was sitting in her room, pondering over a huge watermelon.

'I was waiting for you, Geeti. I picked this up from Sarojini Nagar Market.'

'How did you manage to carry it on the bus? It weighs at least five kilos.'

'You know that boy Dipankar from the History Centre? He carried it for me because I was also carrying all that,' she gestured to a pile of packets.

Lakshmi ran wild the day she got her scholarship grant. She bought wool that was selling at a summer discount, a whole lot of it; she was planning to learn knitting and make sweaters for her sister in England. She had also bought cheap T-shirts, cotton pants and a blow-up of Michael Jackson.

I couldn't picture Dipankar carrying a watermelon. I had seen him a couple of times, talking to Lakshmi. He was altogether too suave. Instead of the usual kurtas and kolhapuris, he wore jeans and bright checked shirts. He even spoke differently from other Jana scholars, which meant without a Bengali or an Oriya or even a Bihari accent. Lakshmi had told me he was from Capital University and had migrated to Jana because of ideological differences with his supervisor.

'He is bright—Bengali, after all,' she had told me, paying him the highest compliment.

'Is Dipankar also taking the civil services exam?'

'No, no, Geeti, the whole world is not power crazy. He is really interested in academics. Do you think I should have offered to share it with him?' asked Lakshmi, pointing to the watermelon.

'You could hardly have done it at the bus stop.'

'Let's go and give him some now.'

I had never been to the boys' hostels, though girls were allowed inside. Previously, even the boys had been allowed into the girls' quarters, but recently a rule had been passed against it. There had been several demonstrations against this 'regressive' step, but the authorities had not relented.

Lakshmi jumped up and cut out a huge piece of the watermelon. We trotted off to the hostel, which was some distance from ours. It was evening and already quite dark. Lakshmi was muttering 'Billie Jean is not my girl' to herself. I was hoping she wouldn't dance on the way—that still embarrassed me.

Lakshmi was known for her uninhibited ways throughout Jana University. Very few knew how inhibited she really was. She never changed her clothes in front of anyone; even I was shunted out. Though she was interested in sports, she had never learnt swimming because she didn't want to get into a swimming costume, she had told me. She was even getting sari blouses stitched long enough to cover her midriff as she had just landed a teaching assignment at one of the Capital University colleges and would have to wear saris to work.

Lakshmi had a tiny waist and a big bosom that she tried her best to camouflage. I knew she had never known a man intimately. Yet, she wouldn't hesitate to dance and sing on the roads.

The boys' hostel was built on the same lines as the girls': five storeys and rows of single rooms. Most of the rooms were locked. The boys probably got back much later from the library than we did. Dipankar's room was on the third floor. Lakshmi sprinted up the stairs much faster than I did. I noticed that, in spite of her unorthodox attire, she managed to look quite curvaceous. She was built like Munmun, in fact, but how different they were! Munmun wore itsy-bitsy blouses and chiffon saris, and though she had liked my thick cotton one, I was pretty sure she never wore such saris herself.

Dipankar's room had a pall of tobacco in the air. There were newspapers, books and journals strewn all over. A brightly woven counterpane covered the bed.

Dipankar was an attractive man. He had a baby face with crinkled, laughing eyes. He seemed delighted to see Lakshmi. I was surprised by his voice—it was low-pitched, tobacco-thick and altogether too sophisticated to emerge from a mouth that was smiling so much.

'Hello, Lakshmi. I was wondering whether I would get to taste the watermelon.'

'Meet my friend Geetika. She is in the School of Linguistics and English.'

'Hello, Geetika. I didn't know you were doing English…'

I was thankful Dipankar didn't ask the usual question about whether literature was taught at all in what was primarily a linguistics department.

We chatted a while about this and that. I was distracted by

the way he kept smiling at Lakshmi.

'Did you see the Baul performance last evening?' asked Dipankar, looking at both of us.

'No, I couldn't go. Geetika had gone for it.'

'It was rather good,' I said colourlessly. No, I didn't want Dipankar's attention the way I had wanted masculine attention in Desertvadi.

'You know, Lakshmi, at a point I wondered about the intimacy that these dancers shared. It wasn't only religion, it was also sexual, you know...a definite homosexual element...' he was saying.

'Well, they are ascetics...' Lakshmi began.

'The erotic eremite bit...That's not true of Bauls, though,' said Dipankar with a smile. 'I was wondering whether it is inherent in the nature of worship...'

Suddenly embarrassed, I started looking at the newspaper on his desk; I could see his name in print—Dipankar Banerjee.

'What is this that you have written?' I asked him.

'Oh, just some reviews. These papers don't pay too badly and one also gets the book.'

'What have you reviewed?' asked Lakshmi.

'Salman Rushdie's recent publication, *Shame*.'

'I really like his work,' I said.

'Well, he is rather distanced from his subject matter...'

'I liked his *Midnight's Children*,' said Lakshmi.

'In *Midnight's Children*, which definitely had a lot of potential, he did engage with his subject matter in a way... But in *Shame*, which is a kind of *roman à clef*, the suavity bothered me... And one wonders about his motivation—he is sitting there and writing about India and Pakistan... Obviously giving the *gora log* what they want to read.'

I was wishing I hadn't opened my mouth.

'I would say that for most Indian writing in English,' said Lakshmi. 'This quest for foreign readership is rather apparent. I find Tamil literature so much more fulfilling.'

I didn't even know Lakshmi read Tamil.

'I read a bit of Bengali,' said Dipankar. 'I would tend to agree with you. Regional literatures don't suffer that much from this kind of what they are calling "epistemological shift" these days.'

'Geetika writes in English...' said the wicked Lakshmi.

'Oh, do you!' said Dipankar tolerantly, smiling at me. 'Poetry?'

'Yes, er...and some prose, just a little bit!'

I could feel my cheeks burn. I wanted to run from there. Dipankar was again smiling at Lakshmi. I didn't belong here. I wished Ratish would come and take me away to his chiffon crowd.

It was rather late when we emerged from Dipankar's hostel.

'So, Lakshmi... I didn't know he was such an admirer of yours.'

'Are you jealous, Mrs Geetika Ratish?'

'I didn't like him very much...and I didn't know you read Tamil.'

'What are you getting so uppity about... Because you couldn't defend your Salman Rushdie?'

I didn't know what had bothered me. Perhaps it was the ease with which Dipankar had used the term 'epistemological shift'.

'He is cute,' said Lakshmi, 'but he is not an Iyer.'

⚕ Hopscotch ⚕

'Let's run back to the hostel. Can you skip on one foot?' asked Lakshmi.

I had played hopscotch as a child.

Hopscotch, *don't drink so much... How many pegs did you down today, Ratish? None of your bloody business... But I am your... Not my keeper... Get off my neck, get off... I hate you when you are drunk, I hate Hari when he is drunk, why do you drink with him... Shut up...get off.*

I shall play some game...today...hopscotch... I was out of breath.

'Lakshmi, you know Hari's girlfriend is seeing two other men simultaneously?'

'So what, Geeti?'

'Ratish doesn't want him to marry her.'

'It isn't any of his business, anyway. Why do these men keep discussing their private lives?'

'Only after they are drunk. Munmun is very attractive.'

'Then probably she will manage to hook him. Why are you so bothered? Let's run!'

'I am bothered about his drinking, Lakshmi. All of them drink so much.'

'You sound like a paranoid wife.'

'What do you know about wives? You have never even had a boyfriend.'

'Why... I am in love with Michael Jackson. I will marry him...'

'Not poor Dipankar?'

'Silly girl, why should I marry Dipankar?'

We ran some more.

I flopped down on Lakshmi's bed.

'Tell me, this Hari Prasad, he is a bania too, isn't he? Do his parents know about Munmun?' Lakshmi asked.

'No, and probably he has no intentions of telling them. He won't marry her...'

I could hear Ratish's voice in my ears: 'His parents will never agree...that type of girl...'

Ratish was rather conservative in such matters. But he had been right about Rekha. After the Sportsaid, Neil had left with a promise that was never kept. Rekha still lived in a morbid little flat with her sick mother. She taught in the mornings, cooked in the evenings and arranged flowers in vases in the drawing room. She could still paint and embroider but Neil had gone back to his unkempt house and never written to say why.

I was lucky. Ratish wanted to marry me, he really did. He had come all the way to Desertvadi to say that to me, in spite of Andy. He had said it didn't matter, it didn't matter to him even if I had gone to bed with Andy... Very few men were that forgiving. But I also knew he had been glad to find out that it hadn't happened.

'Tell me, Geetika, just tell me, I don't mind, but...'

Usha was having a bad time with her husband because of her failure to bleed the first night, though he was a doctor and probably knew the hymen could rupture due to a hundred and one other reasons. Yet Usha was subjected to his insane jealousy... Poor, pimply Usha, who had never even looked at a boy... No boy had looked at her either.

Her husband made her sit with bowed head as he rained blows on her. He had turned her out of his house twice. Her parents had made her go back both times... It was so easy to batter a woman—all that soft, vulnerable flesh.

Ratish loved the texture of my skin. He loved to feel the back of my neck. His fingers were so slim, yet so strong but his limbs were muscular. Lakshmi had muscular forearms too; she played tennis. Ripples of power. I too should have trained for sports as a child...

'Lakshmi, does virginity mean a lot to you?'

'Girls just want to have fun', screeched Lakshmi.

I knew she was not going to answer. A couple of days back, she had been approached by a secret women's group in our hostel. They called themselves 'The Anti-Man'. These women practised and preached free sex. The only rule was: no falling in love, no commitment to any man.

Lakshmi had spat out her refusal. She had cried in her room after that... She wasn't that type of girl...

That type of girl...like Sangeeta and Booba.

But Lakshmi also criticized what she called our middle-class morality. Then why did she cry so much... And was she only pretending to look distant and scholarly when Dipankar discussed homosexuality?

✣ Zany ✣

I told Ratish about The Anti-Man. He said he hadn't credited Lakshmi with that much sense.

'Is that so sensible? I mean, shouldn't one at least question conventional morality... I mean they have a point, don't they?'

'What is the point in free sex, Geeti?'

'Well, there is a kind of bondage that love and marriage traditionally impose on women.'

'You believe in marriage, don't you?'

'Yes...'

'And that doesn't stop you from being intelligent and independent, does it?'

'Do you think I am all that?'

'Of course. You have settled quite well in Jana...'

I kissed him. That was nice to hear. Ratish thought I was all right. So what if I couldn't open my mouth when people like Dipankar were around?

'So don't tell me that women who sleep around have a point!'

I felt Ratish's lips on mine and the smell of tobacco. I loved him, I really did—especially when he hadn't had a drink. It was nice to be loved in this manner, when the responsibility of my body wasn't mine. I had made it over to him—he would take care of it, and he was taking care of it... It was marriage, though we hadn't taken the saptapadi.

'Ratish, what if I get pregnant?'

'So what? But also, how can you?'

'You know it isn't a hundred per cent safe.'

'Look, sweetheart, it is better to get pregnant than to take chemical risks with your body. I am not going to let you get on the pill.'

'My mother will have a fit if...'

'I will see to it that you are not an unwed mother.'

Strangely enough, I was not really bothered. With Ratish, nothing seemed to matter. If this was the definition of love, I was in love. How handsome he was! His dark skin... I loved running my fingers up and down his cheek, his arm, his thigh... He was so smooth, with hardly any hair... Like a girl, I told him.

He rounded his lips and raised his eyebrows, and I felt the familiar constriction in my throat. I wanted to flee, hide... but more than that, I wanted him to hold me, kiss me, love me. It didn't even matter that he seemed unreasonably conservative about marriage and family life.

'What about your parents—what would they feel about a daughter-in-law who delivers five months after marriage, Ratish?'

'As long as it is my baby, why should they mind when it was conceived?'

'You have never told me what they thought of me.'

'How does it matter, Geeti?'

'That means they didn't like me.'

'There is nothing to dislike about you. You know, like all fond parents, they were hoping I would marry this girl they had chosen for me.'

'You never told me all this!'

'It isn't very important. Our family friends in Calcutta, they have a hardware business. My parents wanted me to marry their daughter.'

'What is she like?'

'All right. Why do you want to know about her?'

I felt very close to tears. His parents had been very quiet when Ratish had taken me to see them. His mother had asked me a few desultory questions about Desertvadi. But it had been difficult to reply, because her eyes seemed to travel above my head to something beyond.

She was very different from Mummy. She was tall and thin.

I had noticed her bejewelled fingers—she wore diamonds on all of them. Her nails were painted a very light shade of pink. Her short hair curled perfectly, framing her rather long face. Though she was at home, her sari was impeccably ironed. She even had a light touch of lipstick.

His father was grey-haired, fair-complexioned and also very tall. He had been wearing a very white kurta pyjama. I had had trouble sipping the tea, which had been served in bone china cups.

'Why are you crying, honey?'

'Ratish, I find your parents quite alarming… I mean, I don't think they will ever approve of me.'

'Why shouldn't they? You know parents always create problems in our sort of marriages, but things even out in the end. They have to.'

'Our backgrounds are so different. You know, the way of life…'

'How does it matter, Geeti? Stop being silly.'

How could I tell Ratish that I suddenly saw myself as they had seen me—a slim slip of a girl from a small town known only for the elite Macaulay College, who had emerged from nowhere and was forcing her way into a world that was far above her? I knew that nothing about me could compare to the hardware daughter. How they must have hated me.

I nuzzled against Ratish's shoulder—it felt solid and muscular. What would Ratish's mother say if she found me with a bulging stomach?

'Mama, meet your *bahu*.'

She would probably raise one plucked eyebrow, then throw up her manicured hands.

I wanted to giggle.

'You are what is called zany,' said Ratish.

I threw my arms around him and kissed him. Nothing mattered…nothing at all…

❧ Striptease ❧

There was a lot to read on *A House for Mr Biswas*. I had been working hard to prepare a coherent reading of the text. I was to meet my supervisor individually for the first time today. It was important to make a good impression on her Sorbonne-returned mind.

I had also tried to find out more about her. She was not very old; there was an interesting history of divorce from a stifling marriage attached to her. Her husband had been a college teacher in Meerut, like her. Ten years after marriage, she had received some sort of a scholarship to go to the US. She had been at various universities there and had then somehow landed in Sorbonne, where she stayed for precisely one year. Then Jana University had invited her to join the faculty.

At the Sorbonne, she had been introduced to the fatal inevitability of structuralism. She had come back like a crusader to spread the doctrine among the non-believers. Her first lecture had been about the sheer backwardness of the Indian academia. So had been her second and third and fourth. She roundly attacked the pretensions of the fossilized Capital University, which had never heard of the famous Saussure and Jakobson and Lévi-Strauss and Barthes. She was very worried about our Indianized pronunciation of certain French names and had spent half of her fifth lecture writing them down on the blackboard in phonetic script.

Her lectures became noticeably less fiery when she got down to the nitty-gritty of explaining structuralism to us. She gave us a long bibliography of French writers, ruing the fact that none of us had even a smattering of French. She also hinted that the American professor Livingstone Brown from Cornell had already written a handbook for the benefit of undiscriminating minds like ours and there was nothing more that she could add other it. Brown had become the New Testament for our batch of protestors.

I was meeting her one-on-one for the first time... She looked dignified and slightly bored, as she always did.

'Come in, Geetika.'

'Ma'am, I have been thinking about the dissertation...'

'And you have thought of a text—that is excellent. Now tell me, what have you been reading from the bibliography I gave you?'

'Roland Barthes...'

'Excellent. What about the others? You have to read a lot in order to gain even this much.'

The phone on her desk rang.

'Oh no, could you make it Saturday?... No, no, I can't make it on Tuesday... No, not Wednesday either... It will have to be Saturday...'

She put the phone back down and said, 'So, as I was saying, you have to read much more. The students in Sorbonne are so alive to critical theory. They read so much, think so much. Much more commitment is needed for academics than what I see prevalent here.'

'I am planning to work on *A House for Mr Biswas*,' I put in valiantly.

'That is all right. I don't plan to interfere with your selection. I believe in an open system. I wouldn't like to impose a text on you.'

'Regarding Barthes, there are a couple of points, I would like to discuss with you...'

'Yes, it is not easy to understand Barthes. Read Susan Sontag's introduction. Have you read it?'

'No.'

'Read that and we shall meet next week.'

She began dialling. I lingered. She looked at me questioningly. The meeting was at an end, and I had had no opportunity to discuss the text with her. There would be time later, and at least she had told me what to read. Perhaps this was how postgraduate teaching was supposed to be. I must ask Lakshmi how much time one could expect from one's supervisor. It would give her further opportunity to be nasty about the English department.

I found Lakshmi in the library.

'Back already! Didn't you meet your supervisor?'

'Yes, it was a very short meeting. She was busy…'

'When are you meeting her next?'

'Next week. Till then, I have to keep reading Barthes.'

'Why didn't you tell her you couldn't see the point in what you were reading?'

I had been discussing Barthes with Lakshmi. We had read his essay on striptease together. That had made Lakshmi say that perhaps I should work on the actual striptease, which was a regular feature of certain sleazy hotels in Lutyenabad; why bother my head with Naipaul and his likes?

'I think the point will strike me by and by.'

'Geeti, don't be overawed by her Sorbonne reputation. Why don't you talk to some other people in your department?'

It wasn't often that Lakshmi took my problems seriously. My heart warmed to her.

'Lakshmi, I am having doubts about the methodology. You know, she keeps saying her method is very different, very scientific, but she never really spells out the difference. I thought that reading Barthes, for instance, would change my perspective, change my way of looking at say, V.S. Naipaul, but I can't say it has… Besides, she makes me feel very foolish. Do you think I am dumb?'

'Look, Geeti, I don't know much about your subject—I am not sure whether there is much to know about English Literature. I mean, at times, it seems enough to be well read. But you are not dumb, far from it… And you read a lot. You will do.'

In a rare gesture of affection, Lakshmi put her arm around me. We walked to the campus dhaba, where she ordered banana shake and vada sambhar. We sat under a tree and sipped the cloyingly sweet drink.

✦ A House for Mr Biswas ✦

It became increasingly difficult to whip up any enthusiasm about meeting my supervisor. Every meeting was like the first. In fact, if anything, I began seeing her less, and for even less time, than before. People had begun to say that she had only visited the Sorbonne and had done nothing there except present a paper. People were saying a lot of uncomplimentary things about her ever since she had landed an assignment with the Sahitya Akademi to edit an anthology on 'Indian Criticism'. She had suddenly started wearing spectacles—people said she had become intellectual with a vengeance.

I had tried my best to convey my reading of the text to her. '*A House for Mr Biswas* is a story of alienation; I find it difficult to read it as a comic novel.'

'Hmm.'

'Naipaul seems to be a very interesting personality...so distrustful of the world...'

'That is interesting. But you have to understand the methodology of analysing the text. Mere impressions about the text and the author are not enough; you have to read the text—every sentence, every phrase... You know how every sentence leads to the next one. Your dissertation has to show that methodology in a scientific manner...'

I waited with bated breath for more to come...the science of literature...

'What you have to do is divide the dissertation into sections and sub-sections. Take the text apart, like you would do with a complex machine. Isolate every theme...'

'Ma'am, I don't know how to do that.'

She opened the book with a sigh. 'See, here is the text. Now read it and reread it... You cannot escape labour. You people have become so accustomed to imposing interpretations on the text that you forget its concrete reality. It is the text that is most

important, not Naipaul... Look at the first sentence, then look
at the second...'

'But ma'am, what do I do after that?'

'At least do that. Your dissertation is on *A House* and you
must read it like it has never been read before.'

'I have read it thrice already, ma'am. What else do I read?'

'There is so much to read... The whole French tradition. You
could begin with Sartre and Camus, existentialism...'

'But ma'am, Naipaul is an East Indian...'

I wanted to ask her what I was supposed to do with the
existentialists when analysing the novel. What was I supposed
to do with Barthes? Such naïve questions, I knew, they would
only attract her contempt. I remembered what Lakshmi had
said: 'Don't be scared of appearing foolish'.

'Ma'am, I don't understand how my reading of all these affects
my analysis of Naipaul.'

'It is a whole new way of looking at literature,' she said, raising
her eyebrows. 'And I am telling you how to go about it. In the
first section of your dissertation, you make eleven sub-sections,
giving headings to each. Under those, you analyse the themes...'

'But ma'am, why is it necessary to do this?'

'Do you only have objections?' she asked. 'It is necessary
because it is the scientific way of analysing a text. The other two
girls working with me have already started... I am giving you
the framework, am I not?'

I wanted to discuss the whole question of the house. I found
it poignant that Biswas, in the novel, died without ever fully
owning the house... A house was a very important thing indeed,
didn't I know! If I had a house, I could have lived in it with
Ratish... I wouldn't have had to...

This wasn't the scientific way of looking at literature, far
from it... Yet every time I read the book, my heart ached for
Biswas, as if he were me; Biswas *was* me. That way of looking at
literature was sufficiently French, wasn't it? Hadn't Flaubert said

something similar about his novel *Madame Bovary*?

'Ma'am, I wanted to discuss this amazing feeling of identification I have with the text.'

She raised her eyebrows again, 'Geetika, it will be better if you write down all this and give it to me... And yes, I will borrow your text for the week.'

I came back to the hostel. At last I was making some headway. I would write a paper on the novel. Perhaps then, it would be possible to get her full attention.

✤ Family ✤

Ratish had been asking me to spend time at his place. 'You must get to know the family,' he would say, smiling.

I was a bit wary—after all, they had not been very welcoming the first time. It had been easy to stave off his invitations until now, but gradually they were becoming more aggressive.

'Geeti, don't you want to get to know my family at all?' I noticed he wasn't smiling now.

'I do, but Ratish...they don't really welcome the idea of my...'

'Who told you that?'

'You did...'

'I told you they wanted me to marry into a family they know rather well...'

'That makes me uncomfortable, Ratish... They will always compare me with—'

'Geeti, aren't you being rather silly? After all, you are going to be a bahu of the house very soon. They know you are in Lutyenabad...Don't you think your refusal to come to my home can be misconstrued?'

Perhaps Ratish was right. They lived in a bungalow in South Lutyenabad. It was a big house, with gardens in the front and the back. The gardens looked manicured—neat lawns and neat flower beds—a bit like the family itself, which was terribly well-groomed. Ratish had told me they employed two *maalis*. Our garden in Desertvadi used to be in a mess because of chronic water shortage and a maali who was always absconding.

'I will come. I like your house,' I told him.

'Well, it isn't exactly ours. It belongs to the company. We have a house in Old Lutyenabad. You won't like it; it has around thirty rooms—all cubby holes—no attached bathrooms, no proper lighting...'

'Will your parents shift there once your father retires?' I asked him.

'No, of course not. Old Lutyenabad is another world. My parents have been out of it for too long to go back to it now. You know, in that house my aunts still cover their heads in front of my grandmother? My father is trying to work out a way to sell his portion so that he can buy property in South Lutyenabad.'

He kissed me. 'Housing is a problem in this city. But don't worry, you are marrying an MBA, sweetheart... The hardware people had offered a flat to yours sincerely,' he added mischievously.

'Marry her—why do you bother with me?'

'Who will look after you then? Lutyenabad will gobble you up.'

❧ Dahlias ❧

I decided to spend the coming weekend at Ratish's place. How would they take to me? They probably hated me already. But his mother hadn't said anything objectionable—she had only been very silent. It had been so long since the Sportsaid. So much had changed. I was so different from the confused person I had been then.

I knew I didn't *have* to take the civil services... It was difficult for women...children couldn't be brought up by ayahs...home and a choice...

Would I be seeing to the curtains and the bedcovers and whether they matched, in a few years? In Ratish's house, the guest room was done up in shades of blue. The drawing room had been cream and green. The first time I had gone there, I had asked Ratish whether cream was difficult to maintain—didn't it get dirty very soon? He had replied that he didn't have the faintest idea and that I should talk to his mother, who would probably welcome some display of interest in the household. I was reminded of Andy...

Household...home...children... Hadn't I told Sanjay Bhaiya that I had decided on a way of life—just as Swati had decided not to have any children?

Mummy had been so surprised; couldn't Swati manage her career as well as her children? Hadn't she managed herself? Bhaiya said times had changed and couldn't Mummy try and understand? He had expected her to—she who had been so unconventional all her life.

I told Bhaiya that it *was* possible, possible to do both—I would choose lectureship as a profession as that would give me time for the home as well. He said yes, yes, I could even knit in between classes like Mummy's colleagues, only I didn't know how. I had told him I thought his choice was not in keeping with the Indian way of life. I thought of Mummy's pale, tearful face. Both of us were hurting her—Bhaiya because he didn't want a family, and I because I wanted one.

Ratish took me to the drawing room, yelling out to someone called Asharfi, who, surprisingly, turned out to be a man. His mother was also there, arranging flowers in a vase.

'Mama, here she is. At last madam has consented to spend a couple of days in our home.'

'That is all right, Ratish,' she said.

Asharfi took my bag inside. Ratish followed him.

'Your parents may think it rather awkward that you are here... I guess they are modern enough not to mind,' his mother said, sticking a rose next to a dahlia. She made 'modern' sound like an abuse.

'My parents don't know I am here; in fact, I came here only because Ratish insisted so much.'

'He is rather insistent… But boys…men hardly have a sense of propriety. I guess I am just behind the times… But it is all right. I don't mind,' she said, still busy with the flowers. 'You are welcome,' she continued, as Ratish re-entered.

He took me to the guest room.

'Ratish, I think I must ring up my parents and tell them I am here.'

'Whatever for? They will just get worried…'

'I feel a bit guilty. I mean, they don't even know where I am.'

'You are in safe arms,' he said, putting me there.

'Geeti, why are you staying there?' said Mummy's worried voice.

I told her that Ratish felt I must get to know his family. There was silence at the other end. Ratish took the phone from me and told her that everyone in his family was anxiously waiting to meet me. I felt slightly foolish as I took the phone from him again.

'We will come to Lutyenabad and meet Ratish's parents at the earliest,' said Mummy.

'There is no real hurry,' I said.

'Why Geeti? Is everything all right?'

'Yes, of course, Mummy.'

'So, are you having second thoughts about me?' asked Ratish, putting his arms around me again.

'Oh, yes, I am planning to join The Anti-Man…'

'That is only if I let you get out of here…'

Cold, fleshy dahlias were touching me all over.

'What's wrong, Geeti?' asked Ratish.

'I don't think I should be here.'

'You are a difficult case. What's biting you now?'

'I don't think your mother quite—'

'Listen, I heard her welcoming you. All this is nothing but a hangover from your Andy days. All mothers are not wildly possessive and if you insist on seeing the Oedipal everywhere, God help you.'

'Ratish, I...'

'Listen, darling, my parents love me. In time, they will love you too. You must adopt a positive attitude towards them. My only complaint is that you are too negative as a person.'

Perhaps Ratish was right. I did tend to exaggerate things. I cried so much too. It was possible to live differently, not to lay one's heart open to all the slings and arrows. I must try and see things from the other perspective too...

I kissed Ratish.

'This is going to be difficult, a test of willpower,' he said, gently putting me back. 'There are eyes and ears everywhere in this house.'

He went away after showing me the room. I began to put my things in the drawers. The other perspective, what was it? What do I do with the simplification: 'My parents love me; in time, they will love you too'?

Perhaps they will, perhaps that is what loving was all about... Had Bhaiya told Swati to love our parents too? Why was I thinking of Bhaiya? He was no ideal. He had hurt my parents; he had hurt me too...

☙ Crepe de Chine ❧

Was I supposed to go out of my room and have the morning tea with the family? Would someone tell me what to do? It was eight in the morning and I had just woken up. I decided to bathe and dress before going out.

The breakfast table was being cleared when I ultimately went in. Ratish's mother was sitting at the table, absently polishing the lid of the butter dish.

'Asharfi,' she said, 'look at the state of the butter dish. Am I paying you to chat with the maid?'

'It would be better if you dress up,' she said, glancing up at me. 'Though we are not expecting any guests, the Old Lutyenabad people are in and out of this house all the time.'

I was wearing my salwar kameez, the one I usually wore in the hostel.

'I haven't brought too many clothes with me,' I replied lamely. I felt rather out of sorts, tackling the egg and toast with her scrutinizing the cutlery. It wouldn't do to ask where Ratish was. I began asking her about her daughter instead. She was in the US, having got married last year to a doctor there.

'What is Reshma doing?'

'She is setting up her home.'

'It must be rather lonely being home and doing all the housework. This friend of mine from Desertvadi—'

'She is, in fact, finding it rather exciting. You see, she knew what kind of life to expect there. We have all been to the US. Problems only arise for girls who marry for the glamour of going there.'

'Is she planning to work, eventually?'

'She might... You see, we have not given up our traditional roots. Reshma was not brought up to believe that she is destined to get into some kind of a high-flying job; she will work if and when possible...'

She probably knew that my parents wanted me to take the civil services. But what did she mean by traditional roots? Her short hair, polished nails and sleeveless blouse were hardly traditional.

'My parents are very keen that I should have a career,' I ventured. 'I guess it is because Mummy herself works...'

'When there is a need, women have to work outside. It keeps one busy. I should think Reshma has also gone into a family that is like ours... They have similar views, they were looking for a well-bred, simple girl... Family background is so important.'

She got up with a sigh and began calling the hapless Asharfi to clear the table and get on with other things—there was lots to be done.

I went back to my room, half expecting Ratish to be around. After a few minutes, a maid called Naina came into the room with a sari in her hands.

'Memsahib is asking you to put this on,' she said with a giggle. 'This is her sari,' she added unnecessarily. 'She's also sent Reshma Didi's blouse and petticoat.'

I asked her whether she was married to Asharfi. She blushed and said of course not, her husband worked at a hotel.

'Don't you have saris of your own?' she asked me.

I said I didn't have too many. She informed me that memsahib had two almirahs full of saris and so did Reshma Didi. She then enquired about jewellery—did I possess any?

'Why are you asking me all this?' I asked her.

She giggled and said, 'Asharfi was saying that this time memsahib will not be able to get her way...'

'What does memsahib want?'

'Ratish Bhaiya said we were to call you Bhabhiji, but memsahib said that was not necessary.'

After getting rid of Naina, I sat fingering the sari; it was lime green de Chine. It was soft and smelt faintly of perfume—her perfume... I would smell like her if I wore it. I had never worn a de Chine before...

Ratish came in much later.

'What are you doing sitting here? Mama said you came out only for breakfast and then went right in...'

'I didn't know what to say to her.'

'You are being rather ridiculous, you know. You are doing an MPhil and you can't find anything to say... Why haven't you changed into the sari? Will you continue wearing these ridiculous clothes?'

'You never found my clothes ridiculous before this.'

'Well, there are certain kinds of clothes that are acceptable in the campus, and certain others a bahu wears... I mean, if people come, you are going to be introduced as my fiancée.'

'I don't think so. There are express orders against that.'

'What do you mean?'

'Naina said...'

'What are you doing chatting with the servants? Anyway, what did she say?'

'She said your mother has asked the servants not to call me Bhabhiji.'

'I will speak to Mama—and also to Naina...' He strode off.

I was trembling, my throat felt parched... Oh God, what had possessed me to say all that? I could have bitten my tongue off. I ran behind him. Where was he? He wasn't in the drawing room; I ran into a corridor to the left.

I stopped short. I could hear Ratish's loud tone from the next room. I also heard a small sob.

'Beta, I only asked them not to call her Bhabhi because it may get embarrassing for her. Do what you like—we are traditional people. If you like, start living with her... Here is your father, talk to him!'

'Ratish, it is rather strange that you start fighting with your mother the moment this girl enters the house. How do you expect us to react to her? You spring her upon us from nowhere and say you want to marry her. What about her family? I mean, what sort of people are they to send her here like this?'

'Papa, she has come here to do an MPhil. You talk as though she has come here to live with me.'

'Well, Ratish, it is strange that you should be spending so many nights out of the house recently...'

'I am marrying her, there is nothing wrong with that...

'You have always been a fool...'

'That is his affair,' said his mother, intervening. 'He is grown up enough to make his own decisions. If he wants to marry her, it is all right by me—but at least let me interact with her in my own way. As your mother, I should have at least that much right.'

There were other stifled sobs.

'Mama, you know I am not saying anything against that—'

'Then behave accordingly with her,' said his father 'Don't be blinded by a girl you met just a couple of months ago…'

I ran back to my room and sat on my bed. The other perspective, I knew it now. That I had dropped into his lap like a ripe fruit. What remained unsaid was my father's monthly salary. Sobs, dry and loud, racked my body…

☙ Mothers ❧

'Geetika, my son means a lot to me. I don't want to do anything that hurts him,' Ratish's mother said.

She was flicking off talcum powder from the dressing table. She was always doing something…polishing, straightening, dusting. She had walked into the guest room and I had at once begun to feel displaced.

I realized she was referring to what had happened in the morning. Yet her attention was more on the spilt powder than on me.

'Oh yes… Ma—Mama.'

'Naina is a troublemaker…these people always are. As a rule, we don't talk much to them… It is better to maintain distance to preserve one's own dignity.'

I was littering her well-ordered world. I had reached the breakfast table late, I had worn clothes that clashed violently with the tapestry, I had talked to the servants. I felt unkempt, inadequate… Yet this was a gesture on her part that I had to respond to. I followed her out of the room. She straightened the bedcover before leaving the room.

'Are you busy?' I asked her.

'Yes, there's a lot to be done around the house.'

I followed her into her own room. She began putting out

her husband's clothes. How many times would he change! He had already dressed once for golf, another time for lunch. These were probably clothes to relax in…kurta pyjama, white, crisp.

She was threading the drawstrings into the pyjamas with a safety pin, then she prised open the buttonholes in the kurta, which was stiff with starch.

'Can I help you?' I asked her.

'What will you do? I have to do these things myself. Ratish's father is so impatient with buttons…'

She hadn't asked me anything about my life. I could have descended from Mars. She didn't even look at me. I didn't matter, I was a nobody. I wanted to tell her about myself, I wanted her to look at me.

'I like cooking,' I told her, 'I find it challenging.'

'Oh, really…' she said.

'Mummy never had much time to cook… So in a way, my interest is because of her disinterest,' I bumbled on, desperate to tell her about the other way of life, my life.

'Oh, well…We have to entertain a lot. All my husband's colleagues, now even Ratish's colleagues. Life in a society like ours is quite different, you know.'

I knew it was different. But her 'different' was a value judgement. Not being interested in cooking was an idiosyncrasy she wasn't interested in. I realized she was choosing her words very carefully. She didn't want me to get the impression that she had accepted me in any way.

'It must be quite tiring to entertain so much,' I said angrily.

'No, it isn't,' she replied. 'One meets a lot of interesting people, people with similar interests, similar backgrounds. That's how we met Reshma's in-laws…' She sighed and went out to look for her husband, who had to be put into clothes to relax in.

She was creating so many things…the background, the standard—the background I didn't quite match with, the standard I couldn't maintain. She was creating her husband with the rigorous dress routine; she had in some ways created Ratish. Was she trying to create me as well, with a lime green, expensive sari, soft and perfumed?

I was the girl from a disadvantaged background who, upon her son's insistence, had to be grudgingly groomed and made suitable. Did she expect me to refuse to wear what she offered? Did she care? Did she hate me? She hardly knew me.

✦ Stars ✦

I felt limp and listless in Ratish's arms. My head ached; I wished he would go away. Why did his parents have to go out tonight? His lips felt oppressively demanding. This is how a prostitute would feel, squashed and unwilling. I wallowed in my humiliation.

The house was silent, yet noisy with acrimony. I felt waves of resentment engulfing me. Ratish's mother seemed to disapprove of everything about me—my clothes, my studying at Jana, my waking up at eight. His father did make a valiant attempt to be pleasant to me at dinner. He asked me about Desertvadi and remarked that it must be a nice, quiet, unworldly place to live in. He was even interested in the fact that I did some creative writing. But I couldn't forget what I had overheard... 'What kind of people...'

I couldn't let my body be possessed, it was too much mine at that moment; my head hurt so much...what kind of people... scheming people...people after the Gupta bank balance...

Ratish's touch felt like an imposition, so many impositions... My body cried out to be freed...

'What's wrong, Geeti?'

'Nothing... I have a headache...'

'Your eyes are swollen, too. At least tell me what is wrong.'

'You don't own me, you know!'

'What a strange thing to say! What is wrong with you?'

'It's this house... I want to go back, Ratish...'

'What's wrong with the house?'

'Ratish, I overheard your father...'

'Look, Geeti. They are from another generation, have another point of view. What would your parents have said in a similar situation? Their anger is more against me. I know it was an unpleasant thing to hear. But he was saying it to me, not to you. In fact, I told him he had no business saying anything against your parents, and he agreed he shouldn't have. He doesn't know them...doesn't know what fine, unworldly people they really are. Actually, he can't bear to see Mama cry... And Mama has even apologized. Doesn't that mean anything to you?'

'I can understand their situation... Look, I fought with my parents to come to Lutyenabad. I have further alienated them by saying I won't take the civil services... It is not as if I see everything right there and everything wrong here. It's just that I want some distance, some space...'

'Things will change once we are married—they are already changing. What do you expect from me? Am I not standing up for you? Look, you have to have faith in the person you love...'

'Ratish, where will we be staying once we get married?'

'I am glad you asked me. There are solid economic reasons for staying with my parents... On my salary, I can only afford a small flat somewhere far from the city. Why should we face those hardships if we can get all this? And you don't want the reputation of being a homewrecker, do you?'

'Do you realize how difficult it will be for me to adjust? I want to work, even though I am not taking the services, and—'

'Who said you can't work if you stay here? In fact, if you have even a little bit of sense, you will realize that a family structure is advantageous for working women. You don't have to bother about the house; children are taken care of...'

Swati had decided not to have children... But there were other working women who did have children. What was this axiom that children couldn't be brought up by ayahs? Children

were brought up by ayahs—I had been brought up that way...
But the lonely afternoons, the tears... I didn't want to replicate
them for my children, did I?

Ratish did have a lot of common sense, but it didn't make
me feel better. How I wished he would have less common sense.
How I wished he would say, 'I will pluck the stars for you if you
want me to, darling.'

The stars, I knew, were not for plucking. Ratish was putting
on his shirt. I shouldn't let him go, not like this. But all that I
wanted to do was cry...for so much of what I would never have...

⚜ Love ⚜

'You should have confronted them when they were saying all
those nasty things about your family... Or you should have just
walked out,' said Lakshmi, bristling like a hedgehog.

'I couldn't, Lakshmi; what should I do now?'

'Tell Ratish you will marry him only if he moves out of
that house.'

'I could do that, I suppose...'

Could I? Lay conditions like I had never done before? I had
acquiesced to so many things Ratish had said. It had been so
easy to agree. Had I burnt my boats already? Somehow, I felt so
married to him. It seemed ridiculous to say, 'I will marry you
only if...'

Perhaps I deserved what I was getting. I should have listened
to my parents and stayed put in Desertvadi. Desertvadi... No,
there was no way I could have stayed there.

'What are you afraid of?' Lakshmi asked me.

'Lakshmi, I am just no good. It is better to be like you.'

'And be in love with Michael Jackson?' interjected Lakshmi
wryly.

'And be the proverbial ice maiden and have the whole men's
hostel lusting after you...'

'How can I be an ice maiden? I am dark like a farmhand.'
That made me laugh.

'My mother used to say nobody will ever marry me, so she can have me always. She was joking, of course,' she continued.

She jumped up and danced away. *Billie Jean is not my girl...*

I too should have been getting back to academic concerns. Soon, it would be December, and time to submit an abstract of the dissertation that I was to write next semester.

Marriage...probably after that.

Desertvadi had to be revisited. Swati and Sanjay Bhaiya would also be there for the New Year...

I knew I was just postponing a crisis. Trying to make Ratish understand would lead to one. I knew he would feel terribly guilty about shifting away from his family. He was not like Bhaiya. But then, I was not like Swati. I could hear his mother's sobs.

They too loved him—I knew how parents can love...

Ratish had told me they meant a lot to him; he had not been critical of Bhaiya but had just said that such action was unnecessary when parents could be made to cooperate. After all, this was India, not the West, and even the Westerners appreciated the close family ties Indians had.

I was torn between Bhaiya and Ratish. I had known very well how Ratish felt about these things since we began. Would it be fair to push him into a totally different direction at this point? I knew Ratish loved me. Would this not be taking advantage of his love for me?

Why couldn't love be enough? I had thought this was where problems ended. Perhaps, I didn't really love Ratish, like I hadn't really loved Andy... Perhaps I was incapable of loving.

I was aching for Ratish's touch. It would be so easy to fall into his arms and bury my head in his shoulder...

There was a knock on the door.

'Visitor, Geetika,' somebody yelled.

I shot out. Ratish was there, slightly dishevelled.

'It's rather late…Geeti. But I had to come…was missing you like hell.'

It seemed my world was restored instantaneously.

⚜ Sexy ⚜

Lakshmi knocked as I was working on my paper.

'What are you writing?' she asked, peeping over my shoulder.

She liked to read whatever I wrote. She never commented much on the poems or short stories I occasionally handed her, but she would often cut out notices of creative writing competitions and give them to me, telling me what all I could do with the prize money. Her dreams ranged from motoring all across Europe to buying Calvin Klein jeans.

'I can't dream like you do, Lakshmi,' I had told her once.

'Who told you to get stuck with in-law problems at puberty?' she had shot back.

At times, she was remarkably perspicacious. I would get the feeling that she was empathizing with me to a much larger extent than I realized. But she stubbornly refused to comment on Ratish, except to say that his clothes were so well-ironed it appeared as though he put even his socks on hangers.

She sat down quietly on my bed. That was unusual for her. I knew something was wrong. She asked me whether I had anything to eat in the room. I gave her the namkeen I had brought from Desertvadi. She munched on it for a while.

'Geeti, that Dipankar…'

'What happened, Lakshmi?'

'You know, they have started skating in the campus. I had gone for it; Dipankar was there too. You know, he kept looking at me…'

'Aha aha!'

'Don't be silly. You know, my T-shirt was quite wet with

perspiration, that blue one. It is quite skimpy but I was wearing it because I had a sweater over it...'

'You sure generate heat, love. It's so cold. What made you take off your sweater?'

'I had been jogging.'

'Obviously he was staring.'

'Geeti, I hated it... It was kind of sexual.'

'Obviously! He can't quite see you as Ma Durga, can he?'

'I hated it. He never stares like that otherwise.'

She mooned around the room, picking up things. I wanted to comfort her but I didn't know how. I knew that even one wrong move would send her scurrying back to 'Beat It'. Or 'Girls Just Want to Have Fun', which was her latest craze.

'Are you scared, Lakshmi?'

'Of Dipankar? Don't be silly...'

'I didn't mean him, specifically.'

'I don't... I don't want all that... It's kind of obscene. Anyway, he better not harbour any hopes.'

I wondered whether to tell her about Ratish and me. She never questioned my obvious lies about spending so many nights at my aunt's house. She looked like a child. I felt irrevocably aged and sad, but sadder for her.

'What did Sorbonne say?' she asked me.

'"Write a paper and show me"—that's what I was doing. And now that she has borrowed my book, she will at last read the text, I hope.'

'She is a scandal; no wonder the Prime Minister finds so much in common with her.'

Sorbonne had become a member of the new breakfast club of the Prime Minister, who regularly met intellectuals over breakfast.

'I don't know, Lakshmi, I feel she is just disinterested in us, in me. She might not be such a fraud otherwise,' I whispered.

'She has no business being disinterested. She is occupying a flat in prime land of the city because she is supposed to guide

research students. She is not being paid to get bored with them...
I can't understand you, Geetika. Ratish's parents tell you are a
cheap climber and you nod your head and say you understand;
this woman takes you for a ride and you try and defend her
motives...'

'Lakshmi, the problem is I *do* understand. The world looks
so different if you change your angle even by a degree and...'

'Don't try your instant psychology on me, put it in one
of your stories. At times, I think you are a coward. You are a
coward, I think.'

'And what would you do in my situation?'

'Dump him, dump her. Apply for a scholarship abroad, get
out...'

'What is all this about going abroad?'

'I had gone for a lecture to Capital University... There was
this professor from Rochester. He spoke about game theory...
You know, game theory is just overtaking the economics world
in the US? It's fascinating, I am getting very interested in it...'

She launched into an explanation of the game theory. It
was not compatible with Indian conditions or with the kind of
research she was doing, she told me. She was going to talk to
her supervisor about it nevertheless. This was the first time she
had spoken about her supervisor without telling me how striking
he looked when he pulled at his pipe.

'But Lakshmi, you are enjoying working with him.'

'I am. But I feel that he is tying me down. He is much too
bright, you know. Perhaps too intelligent to guide anyone... He
seems to have already concluded what I am going to find out
after three years of work... I can't be tied to his ideology. I have
to know about the rest of the world.'

I wanted to hold on to her. My heart felt chilled. She was
a free bird, fluttering her wings for the skies. I wanted to fly
with her too, but I felt leaden. There were shackles on my feet.
I wanted to hold on to her.

She was right. I was a coward, I just wanted people, Mummy, Bhaiya, Andy and Ratish. I had wanted all of them, wanted their souls, their hearts…and they had all gone away; a part of Ratish had also gone away. Lakshmi was going too. I was at a kerb, waiting, waving goodbyes, waiting and wiping my tearful eyes, sobbing into a green handkerchief because I was Booba and a certain fat landlady would always keep my Sam away.

❧ Wife ❧

When I went to Desertvadi for the winter break, my parents broached the topic of marriage rather tentatively.

'So, Geeti, what are your plans?' Papa said, rustling the newspaper. 'Now that you have decided not to take the civil services, should we plan your marriage?'

'I have to write my dissertation this semester…'

'Are you going to apply for a lectureship somewhere?' Papa asked.

I knew what it cost him to ask this. My parents had given up on a part of me; the Geeti who had stood first in all the examinations was forgotten. This was a Geeti who had had boyfriends ever since she was fifteen. I was angry, my place had been usurped by Swati, who didn't want jewellery, who had no time to dress up. I wouldn't dress up either when I visited Ratish's home, but in Desertvadi, I took pleasure in showing off my Sambhalpuri saris. I had bought three with my scholarship money.

'Possibly, Papa. In fact I have applied already…'

'That is good… What about Ratish's family?'

Papa wanted to know whether Ratish's parents approved of me. But he didn't know how to frame his question—he had never thought he would have to ask me all this. Mummy's daughter should have grown up strong and ambitious, rebellious of traditional restraints. Instead, here was a Geeti who had spent the whole of the previous day scouting around the narrow lanes of old Desertvadi for silver jewellery, a Geeti who was giving up a childhood ambition to become a high-powered officer in order to marry a man who felt that a woman who worked full-time could not do justice to her family.

Mummy had been blunter about her disillusionment.

'Geeti, are you sure you are doing the right thing?'

'Mummy, I am not planning to be a housewife... I just don't want to take up a career that demands so much of my time.'

'You never said all this before. Suddenly, you feel you ought to be home to cook for your husband.'

'Mummy, I am interested in what I am doing. I like the idea of a lectureship. Both of you have been lecturers...'

'Our times were different. We have seen the deterioration of educational institutions. Besides, we did much more than teaching...'

'I want to write also.'

'That is an excuse... Your real reason is Ratish. And you should be careful of complying so readily. He appears to come from a much more traditional background...'

I thought of his mother in her de Chine sari, arranging flowers in a vase. I looked at Mummy. As usual, her sari was crumpled and her hair dishevelled. Lakshmi was the daughter she should have had.

She would resent my telling her to comb her hair, but the state of her sari irritated me far too much.

'Mummy, at least tie your sari properly.'

'Are you going to be ashamed of us now?'

'If you tie your sari like this, then certainly.'

She walked away from me. Mummy was facing a lot of problems at work. The government was not releasing funds for her social work centres. I ought to be proud of having a mother who was doing significant work. I ought to understand the strain she was under...

Mummy and Swati had developed a strange kind of bond.

Swati had more of Mummy than I did, certainly. I was lost in their negations—no jewellery, no make-up, no tradition. Both were tense like live wires, both smiled rarely, both were very critical of each other. When Mummy sent her a sari for *karva chauth*, she returned it, saying she didn't believe in fasting for the longevity of the husband. This was one fast Mummy had observed all her married life. I remembered climbing to the highest point on the terrace as a child to sight the moon, so that she could eat. Mummy had kept the sari away, it was a lovely shade of pink. She looked very old when she showed it to me.

'It was such an expensive sari. She could have kept it just to please me...'

'Why do you keep giving her these things? Last time—'

'She is something to me, isn't she?'

'But Mummy, it is not necessary...'

'As parents, we are not asking anything of Sanjay. Look at other parents... Would anyone have forgiven them for the kind of wedding they had? We just want to keep a good relationship...'

'Mummy, Bhaiya has never been particular about these things...being sensitive to feelings...'

'Then at least she can be a bit more sensitive. In our old age, who shall we seek if not our children?'

'Mummy, you have me...'

'You will go to your own home. You will have your own commitments.'

'I have commitments here too.'

'Then sit for the civil services. Geeti, I want you to have a career, a challenging career.'

'And be like Swati...no children?'

'You will never be like her. You are warm and caring. You will always be able to nurture... But don't waste your talents, Geeti. There is much more to you than just a pretty face...'

I repeated my usual replies, lectureship, writing...

'Geeti, will you be able to do all that? In a family like that, where working women are considered aggressive?'

'Mummy, you don't like Ratish, do you?'

'He is an affectionate person, a loving person, but he is very conservative, Geeti.'

Somehow, Mummy, Papa, Swati and Sanju Bhaiya made me hate myself. Swati was so much of what I ought to have been: the modern Indian woman with a career. I could not talk very easily to her. In spite of that, I couldn't resist broaching the subject that had become a taboo in the family.

'Swati, why have you decided against having children?'

'Geeti, my career is the most important thing in my life today. I am building a practice. I am not going to do anything that takes me away from there.'

'It is an unusual decision...'

'Not really; the world is moving at a fast pace, which we don't always realize if we shut our minds to progress... Women are doing much more than they ever did before.'

'But then, Swati, would you say that the family as an institution is dying out? I don't hear of decisions like yours—'

'Don't you hear more and more of late marriages, one-child families?'

'Sure I do.'

'And Sanju is a part of my decision too... He feels that a child at this point in our careers is only likely to hamper our growths. You two are so different... Sanjay is the only man I met who was actually ready to discuss this whole thing; otherwise, for most Indian men, it is a foregone conclusion: marriage, children and the sickening domesticity... And of course, it is the wife who has to bear the whole burden of it...'

⋇ Feminism ⋇

Ratish's sister was in Lutyenabad for a visit. He was suggesting an engagement ceremony at this point. I hadn't met his parents for quite some time but when Reshma came, I had to pay them a visit. I didn't know why I started thinking of Swati as I sat sipping tea with Reshma.

Reshma was very different. She wore tiny sparkling diamonds in her ears and on her fingers, and had wavy hair that cascaded down to her shoulders. Her life was full of the positives of what Lakshmi called the 'soulless middle class'.

'It is nice to be home and to be waited upon like this. I didn't realize how much I was missing it there,' she said, stretching out like a cat on the couch.

'Are you planning to come back?'

'I don't know, depends on my husband. We will start discussing it once the baby arrives. Neither of us would like our children to grow up there.'

Reshma was expecting her first baby already.

'Yes, it is much better here. The support system is better here, anyway.'

'What do you mean, support system?'

'I mean family and ayahs, etc. There, one would be very much on one's own. Though that would probably encourage the husband to be more supportive.'

'I don't understand this hue and cry about eliciting housework from the husband. I wouldn't expect Rajan to change the baby's diapers after he gets back from work.'

'But what happens if you are working too?'

'I give it up and bring up my children. This is what my mother did—she devoted her whole life to her home. I really don't see how children can be brought up well otherwise.'

'But Reshma Di, more and more women are working outside the home, they are doing such valuable work...'

'And dumping their children on others...'

'I would think children are a joint responsibility.'

'I have never heard of a man giving up his job to look after his family... Not even in the US.'

I thought of Swati.

'But surely there are men who make compromises with their careers... Come on, Reshma Di, there are men who do a fair amount of babysitting, there are men who cook. I mean, if they don't, they should be doing it—'

'Well, Geeti, don't expect Ratish to do it... I didn't know you were such a radical feminist. I hope you have told him of your expectations...'

Reshma had been much nicer to me than the rest of her family. She had even brought me a perfume as a present. I wished we hadn't argued. Ratish's mother was coming in with some saris on her arms.

'Here, Reshma. This is what I have been buying for you the whole of last year.'

Reshma began looking at them one by one.

'Oh, Mama, they are so beautiful; I don't get any time to dress up there. Here, I must do all the dressing up. Do you like them, Geetika?'

'Oh, Geetika is not fond of good clothes. In Jana University, they only dress in rags, that is the "in" thing...'

I was wearing one of my nice saris. It was leaf green with a maroon anchal. I was also wearing the silver earrings I had bought in Desertvadi.

'Hardly, Mama. The sari she is wearing looks very lovely.'

As she left the room, Reshma said to me, 'Don't mind Mama, she will come around. You will find out her bark is much worse than her bite. But Geeti, temper this feminism of yours a bit. I am older than you, so I feel I can say this. You look so soft and feminine otherwise. And really, all these stupid issues... Surely, life is much more...'

It was much more for Reshma. But me, I would have to be apologetic about my background and start with a minus in their world.

✦ Game Theory ✦

'I don't want to marry,' I told Lakshmi.

'Don't. Come to Rochester with me.'

'Are you going for sure?'

'I have applied, I have a fair chance... Only thing is, I still have to talk to my supervisor.'

'Haven't you already spoken to him?'

'Only about my interest in game theory. I still have to tell him I am planning to go. He has been putting in so much time and work into my thesis. I don't know how he will take the news.'

This happened to others—a calm and studied stock-taking, a reasonable decision. In my life, there was only the hysteria of conflicting emotions. Ratish, his parents and mine, crowding in with their expectations and disillusionments...

'I am sick of everything, Lakshmi, I want to run.'

'Geeti, you know what you need at this time? You need a job. I enjoyed myself working at Capital University. It is a lot of fun teaching undergraduate students...'

'I have already sent in an application.'

'You have to do more; you have to go and meet the teachers-in-charge at various colleges.'

There was a knock at the door. Somebody yelled, 'Visitor, Geetika.'

'Here comes the man you will not marry,' remarked Lakshmi.

I told Ratish I would pursue my plan of looking for a lectureship in one of the colleges.

'That is all right,' he said. 'It will be good if you can get something close to home; commuting is a problem in the city.'

'I think I must submit my dissertation before we think of marriage.'

'Why? What's the problem now?'

'It would be rather distracting otherwise.'

'Who will distract you?'

'I don't know, Ratish, I feel I must wait...'

We were driving towards Hari's house.

'Will Munmun be there?' I asked him, more to escape the subject of marriage than to elicit any information.

'No, I don't think so... I have at last been able to convince that fool...'

'Why did you have to get into all this? It isn't any of your business.'

'I feel strongly about friends. Hari is one of my closest. I couldn't let him marry that trollop. His parents would have died of shock...'

'Ratish, is this ethical? I mean, how can you break up people like this? They could have been happy together...'

'Geeti, don't talk through your hat. All that I did was tell Hari where she was when he expected her to be in the office. She had booked a room at the Taj with one of her boyfriends. This was the "business" she was conducting.'

'How did you come to know?'

'I happened to be waiting for a client in the lobby; she didn't see me.'

'But Hari knew she was seeing this other man...'

'Seeing him in the bedroom? It is one thing to know, another to actually see... Geeti, are you just fond of contradicting me or do you actually condone such behaviour?'

'I find it difficult to pass judgements so easily. She can be an excellent person, how does one know? I don't think you should have done this.'

'You just said you don't pass judgements. Hari will thank me for this. Geeti, I think Jana has been pretty bad for you. What made you say wild things to Reshma? Are you aware of the kind of impression you give people?'

'I didn't say anything I don't feel.'

'Talking to Reshma isn't exactly like taking part in a symposium for the liberation of women.'

'You are right, it isn't. And talking to you is like talking to an inquisitor from the middle ages.'

'Geeti, I say openly what ninety per cent of men believe covertly.'

'When did you take the census? And even if hundred per cent believe in certain things, that doesn't make them right.'

'Yes, only you and a couple of more idiotic women must set standards of morality and ideal behaviour.'

I was trembling. I wanted to get down from the car then and there. This was the first such fight we had had. Ratish's face was contorted with rage. I had never seen him look like this before. I had never thought it was possible for us to hate each other to this extent.

Ratish got very drunk that evening. So did Hari. Hari was being summoned to Kanpur by his parents, who had seen a girl for him there.

'Whoever she is, at least I won't find her sleeping with the driver when I come back from office,' Hari said drunkenly.

'Don't be too sure,' I said, as Ratish's bloodshot eyes glared at me. 'Ninety per cent of women may be doing secretly what ten per cent do openly…'

⚜ Trapped ⚜

I felt strangely happy as I sat down at my desk that morning. I had at last taken a stand with Ratish. Finally, he would know that the girl he had picked up from nowhere did have some definite opinions of her own.

Poor Munmun! Why did I say poor? Was marriage that important? She had been humiliated… I had been humiliated too. Why did I feel incapable of taking a stand for myself?

I won't marry you unless…unless…unless that hymen is intact, unless you get out of your mother's lap, unless you stay home to look after our children, unless you promise not to sleep with the driver, unless you move out of your parents' home; unless you promise not to insist on children, unless...

Marriage was conditions and preconditions...What was my precondition? I dislike your mother's home and her propensity to make weapons out of flowers. I feel defeated by red, red roses and healthy dahlias... I want a home free of these encumbrances... What is your price for me, mine for you? You will tell yourself that I cost you your family and all your life, you will wonder whether I was worth that much... I am not sure whether I am. I don't know my worth, not like Swati does. I am presuming, of course, that you would be ready to pay that price. Would you be ready to pay that price?

I looked at the text in front of me. I had reached the point where I could recite the five-hundred-odd pages of the novel backwards. The paper I had so enthusiastically presented to the supervisor had come back without any comments.

'Ma'am, what do you think of the paper?' I had asked her tentatively.

'It is a good paper,' she had sniffed. 'You can use parts of it in your dissertation.'

'Do you agree with my criticism of what I call the traditional way of looking at the novel?'

'Well...your criticism ought to be different from the others, they are not following the structuralist method... You see, your point of view ought to come about only after you have broken down the text, conceived the structures that make it what it is. I suggest you begin on your dissertation without wasting any more time...'

I had left her room with the strong desire to throw the text at somebody and isolate the structures by tearing out all the pages. On an impulse, I decided to talk to another professor in our department.

'Can I talk to you, Professor Ranganathan?'

'Sure, Geetika. Come and sit.'

Professor Ranganathan had been at Jana for a long while. He commanded a lot of respect among the students.

'I am a bit lost with my dissertation,' I said, wondering how to go on.

'We all feel like that before beginning research. It shouldn't frighten you. If I remember right, you were the first to decide what you wanted to work on. That is half the battle won. Tell me, what is troubling you?'

'I can't make head or tail of what my supervisor says,' I burst out. 'She just says "read the text" or "read Sartre, Camus, Barthes", etc., but she doesn't say what I am to do with all of them...'

'She must have told you how to go about organizing your material?'

'She has... I mean she has told me about the chapterization, but what am I writing about? I don't know what I am writing about!'

'I have been hearing about this supposedly new way of looking at literature. I have read a bit of Barthes too. I am not sure what insights you're expected to arrive at, as research students...' He trailed off, 'You see, Geetika, I am sure you are aware of a certain academic etiquette, I won't call it anything stronger than this, which forbids me from giving you concrete suggestions.'

'I am aware of this, Professor Ranganathan. I have come to you only after trying my best to communicate my problems to my supervisor. I am beginning to feel that she is not interested in my subject at all.'

'Tell me what exactly she has asked you to do up till now,' he said, patiently.

I told him.

'Geetika, let me outline the formal situation now, which is not exactly wonderful. There is absolutely nothing you can do about it. You are formally registered with her; you will have to write your dissertation exactly as she tells you to. She can hold up your degree for years if she likes, and that can be disastrous for your career. What she has told you makes very little sense to me. Unfortunately, people like her exist and flourish under our university system. This is all I will say.'

'You mean I have to just...'

'If you are clever, you can exploit her lack of interest to your advantage. I agree that if she insists on your showing how one sentence leads to another, there is precious little room for any research. Just try and complete the whole thing quickly. And yes, I would like to see the papers you have written.'

I could do nothing, nothing at all. I had to sit regularly at my desk, religiously reading the text and writing about it, until the dissertation was done. Nothing I could do; I had invested too much in my MPhil to back out now without a degree.

Had I invested too much in Ratish as well? Did I want to back out now? I was still in love, so much in love... I wanted him here, holding me close to him. I wanted him near me. But there was nothing I could do about his parents, nothing I could do at all... Except believe in structuralism, his love, her structuralism...

❖ Antigone ❖

The Guruvayoor College building was not as imposing as that of the Desertvadi Government College. It was just an ordinary yellow-washed, double-storeyed structure with nothing to indicate that it was a college except for groups of smartly dressed students sitting on the steps and standing in the foyer. They wore jeans and T-shirts, kurtas and salwar kameez of the latest designs—they looked alarmingly confident. I had hoped that the college would have a more conservative alumni than other Lutyenabad colleges, since it was run by the temple trust based in Kerala. There was, however, nothing to suggest anything religious about it.

I walked to the English Department room with trepidation. I was to meet the teacher-in-charge there. I had come to know that there was a vacancy in the college, and that the teacher-in-charge was empowered to make an ad hoc appointment. I was carrying a folder with all my certificates and testimonials.

'Can I speak to the teacher-in-charge?' I asked.

The gentleman reading the paper lowered it and smiled at me.

'Yes, yes! Nandita will be here presently, come and sit,' he said in a friendly tone. 'You must have come for the ad hoc?' he asked.

'Yes...'

'This is a nice place to work,' he said. 'You will like it.'

I felt reassured by his confidence that the job was mine for the asking.

'Nandita, come here, duty calls,' he yelled out to a whirl of green and pink sari swishing across the corridor.

'Coming, Amaresh,' replied a high-pitched voice.

Nandita Dhillon was very carefully groomed. She even had a coat of silver shadow on her eyelids.

'Which courses are you doing in your MPhil this semester?' she asked me.

'I have completed my coursework. I am working on my dissertation which is on...'

'Where are you doing your MPhil from?'

'Jana University.'

'Oh, you are not from the Capital University. How was your name in the ad hoc panel then?'

'I had applied...'

'Well, I would like to ask you a few questions. Let us go to the other room...'

Amaresh had buried himself in the paper again, he lifted his head from it and said, 'Don't bother, I will get out.'

'Have you read *Antigone*?'

'Yes, I have.'

'Can you tell me something about Sophocles, to begin with?'

I realized my mistake. The *Antigone* I was referring to is a modern play, based on the Sophoclean original and set in the twentieth century. I knew nothing about the Greek playwright.

I told her that. She cut me short, remarking that the modern version would make very little sense on its own. I told her I hadn't studied it in the classroom, but had only read it for pleasure. She said that she was aware that other universities had a very limited syllabus, unlike the Capital University, and that is why, in the last semester of this academic year, she was looking for a person from the Capital University who would be able to handle the teaching at such short notice.

'I will be able to handle *Antigone*,' I told her, 'if you give me a chance…'

'You see, it's a question of not taking chances with the future of the students… Frankly, Geetika, I would prefer a student from Capital University.'

I looked at her silver-coated eyelids. She was so well-groomed, so self-assured. She would probably read the paper and have tea once I left—or worse still, she would jokingly tell Amaresh that I hadn't even read *Antigone*.

I wanted to speak to Ratish; I felt ill with disappointment. Lakshmi was away at her uncle's for the week. As soon as I got back to the campus, I decided to ring him up. I dialled his number and, as usual, his secretary cooed over the line.

'Hello, Ratish…'

I told him what had happened.

'Isn't it unfair?'

'It is, Geeti, but these things happen.'

'What will I do if I don't get a job?'

'You will get one… But why are you so desperate? I have a meeting in ten minutes, I have to rush.'

Obviously, he doesn't have unlimited time for me, I told myself, preparing to walk back to my room. He could have expressed some more sympathy, though. This was a major thing in my life, but all these major events seemed so unimportant to Ratish.

Dipankar was having coffee at the dhaba outside our hostel.

Lutyenabad became quite chilly in January; many students sat out in the sun all day. I didn't want to get chilled in my lonely room.

'Hello, Dipankar,' I called out.

'Oh, hello, Geetika,' he said. 'How are you?'

Dipankar was wearing a navy blue blazer with his jeans. Somehow, he reminded me of the students I had seen lolling in Guruvayoor. He lit a cigarette and offered me one.

'I don't smoke,' I told him, flattered that he should ask, even though quite a few girls smoked in Jana. 'Been writing any more reviews?'

'Only of the academic kind,' he said, wrinkling his nose.

It was surprisingly easy to talk to him. He told me about his research with a self-deprecatory laugh. He also spoke about his supervisor in Capital University, who had published one of his coursework papers under his own name.

'The man did not even see it fit to correct a few spelling mistakes I had made,' he said, rolling his eyes.

Dipankar had a certain warmth in his behaviour that I found very comforting. He seemed to be genuinely interested in the problems I was facing with my supervisor. He even asked me about my creative work—without sounding condescending the way he had when I met him for the first time.

'You haven't told me about your other work. How are the stories and poems coming along?'

'All right,' I said. I didn't want to talk about that. I was always at a loose end when people asked me what I wrote. I could never explain my themes to anybody...

'Why don't you send them out somewhere?'

That was another question I dreaded. I did want to publish my work, but it seemed so much simpler to keep it away in a file. Father William, who wrote to me occasionally, said it was important to keep writing—publishing could wait.

'I will...sometime.'

He laughed and said that perhaps I wanted to be like Emily

Dickinson and be discovered after my death. I told him he could do the discovering and go down in history too.

I was in a much better mood by the time I walked back to my room.

⚜ Madonna ⚜

Dipankar was rather nice. It was so easy to be friends with him.

Why did Lakshmi... But he wanted far more from her than friendship. What would he want as a boyfriend? The usual kisses behind the bushes? I had grown up...the thought of kisses no longer filled me with that bubbling excitement. Lakshmi was different with her virginal, curvaceous body. Would Dipankar also have a charter of demands that she would have to fulfil? 'Love my parents, have children, stay at home...'

No, of course not; there were other kinds of relationships in the world. There were equal relationships. Why had I failed to form any? Why couldn't I have a relationship in which...

What *was* the ideal relationship? Once I had dreamt of a boyfriend with whom I could laugh. I had already stopped laughing with Ratish. Was that an end? No, I was not prepared to end this relationship—it had sunk too deep. It would have to run its course. This feeling was too negative to be love. What was it? It was a marriage, the backbreaking marriage I had dreamt about.

I sat at my desk and began to write about the death of Biswas's father and the preparation of his mother for lifelong widowhood. Red henna and black charcoal dust, red and black, colour of life and death in the parting of the widow's hair... The loveless novel of V.S. Naipaul.

Why did I find myself empathizing so much with Biswas? The poverty of his dreams struck a chord in my heart. No, the dream was not poor—a house which is a microcosm of the universe—I too wanted a house where there would be a life I could call mine.

'Hi,' said Lakshmi. I had kept the door open to let some

light in. There was power failure in the hostel and my room was pretty dark in winters, even during the day.

'Lakshmi, I was just thinking of you.'

'You do think of me a lot... I can see that.'

'I was thinking of you and Dipankar.'

She clammed up. Ever since she had decided to go to the US, she had stopped singing with abandon.

'But,' she hummed uncertainly, 'it is a material world...'

'Undoubtedly, but you are Iyer and not material at all.'

'That is a sick one,' she observed.

'I was thinking dirty thoughts about you and Dipankar.'

She flushed, 'Geeti...really?'

'I was thinking of both of you behind the bushes...' I persisted.

'Behind the bushes' was a standard joke at Jana. There were a lot of shrubs and other vegetation on campus in which lovers sought privacy.

'You are frustrated, dear.'

'Are you saying that my diagnosis of Dipankar's love sickness is wrong?'

'No, that is right.'

'What do you mean?'

'Well, dear Dipankar did sidle up to me yesterday saying how unusual I was...'

'Well, well, well?'

'And didn't I think it would be a good idea if we were to meet more often, more regularly?'

'What did you say?'

'I said I had absolutely no time and my work kept me busy twenty-four hours a day.'

I clucked my disappointment. 'Didn't you tell him you would consider his case if he changed his name from Banerjee to Iyer?'

'You have to be born an Iyer, sweetheart... But really, that isn't the only reason...'

I kept quiet.

'Geeti, you don't actually believe I am casteist, do you? Come on, he is too suave, you know, too polished. All that interest he displays in people, it is kind of false. I feel it is kind of false, that is. He probably laughs at them behind their backs. And all those reviews he writes, I mean...so judgemental.'

'It is not a sin to write reviews, Lakshmi.'

'No, it isn't, I guess. He is too much of a Lutyenabad academic, that's it. I would prefer someone with a heavy Tamil accent, like, "What are you writing, Geethika?" or even a heavy Bengali accent like, "What are you writing, Geetikaw?"'

'I am sure it is the bushes that scared you, ultimately.'

'Maybe. You have too much sex on your mind, too much in your writing...'

'You have too much in the unconscious.'

'What's love got to do with it...do with it,' danced Lakshmi with the empty box of namkeen in her hands. 'What's love got to do... You have finished all the namkeen, you sex maniac!'

✦ Epistemological Shift ✦

Yet another interview. This time, it was a proper interview in Lajpat Rai College and not a rendezvous with a teacher-in-charge. A proper interview board was there behind the closed doors: a university expert, a governing body representative, the principal and the teacher-in-charge. I sat outside, sandwiched between two other applicants who were discussing their MPhil papers over my head.

'What about Sen's course?' asked one.

'Sen is going to crucify me. You know he is in there—he is the university expert.'

'Oh no!' wailed the first one.

They looked at me pointedly, hoping I would vacate the place. I sat pretending to be deaf and mute—I wanted to hear more about this Sen who was the university expert and had the power to change my life.

'What grade did you get for your Rushdie paper?'

I pricked up my ears. This was good news—Sen taught Rushdie.

'I got B+. Neena got an A– for her paper, but she had written on *Jewel in the Crown*.'

This was getting better and better. I could talk at length about both Rushdie and Scott. I was beginning to get excited about this interview.

At last, my name was called out. I remembered what Prof. Ranganathan had told me: Agree with whatever the interviewers say and try to tell them whatever you know about the subject.

The board looked alarmingly large. There seemed to be a dozen people at a huge table. I counted them again. There were seven.

There was a mousey-looking lady with jet black, obviously dyed hair, who shot the first question. 'You are...'

'Yes, ma'am.'

She read out my qualifications in an unimpressed tone. One of the gentlemen screwed up his face and began scratching his cheek.

'So, you are doing your MPhil from Jana,' said Scratch Face.

Guilty! 'Yes, sir,' I said.

Dyed Hair fixed me with a gimlet eye. 'In Jana, I presume you work mainly on language, linguistics?'

As opposed to pure literature! In Capital University, there was a separate department for linguistics, which had nothing to do with the English department.

'Yes , ma'am,' I said, remembering Ranganathan. 'I am working on V.S. Naipaul's *A House for Mr Biswas* for my dissertation.'

'I believe that in Jana, you have to submit a short dissertation,' she said condescendingly.

'Tell us about your dissertation,' said Scratch Face.

I remembered Ranganathan again. Go slow on theory, he had said, try and brush structuralism under the carpet.

I told them about the paper I had written for Ranganathan.

They asked me about Naipaul after that and seemed reasonably satisfied with my answers.

'Who is your supervisor?' asked Dyed Hair.

I told her.

'She is a linguistics person, isn't she?'

'Yes, ma'am… I mean, I don't know. I am not using a linguistic approach.'

'What do you mean by a linguistic approach?'

'I mean, a theoretical framework… I am aware that some of my friends are using the structural method to analyse the text.'

'How is it different from what you are doing?'

That was easy. I compared my paper with my dissertation, running down the latter. I realized that the interview was almost at an end and I hadn't been able to bring in either Rushdie or Scott.

'It is just by chance that I decided to work on Naipaul,' I said chattily. 'My real interest was in Rushdie.'

Scratch Face looked up, interested at last.

'Which work of Rushdie's are you interested in?'

'*Midnight's Children*, which is a great book and does not suffer from the kind of epistemological shift that *Shame* seems to display.'

'What do you mean, epistemological shift?' asked Dyed Hair sternly.

I launched on an explanation, comparing the two books and cleverly bringing in *Jewel in the Crown*.

'Thank you,' said Scratch Face, smiling at me and then at Dyed Hair. He had probably seen through my ruse. He didn't look angry, though.

That evening, Ratish, Lakshmi and I dined out. We went dancing after that. Ratish and I teased Lakshmi mercilessly about her dancing, as she danced by herself or with the pillars in the dancing hall.

⚜ Universals ⚜

They were formidable, all of them. They spoke so well, spoke so much; they were not particularly well-dressed, certainly not expensively so, yet I was intimidated as I had never been before. Ratish's mother was intimidating too, but this was different. She was all wrong, I suspected, all wrong... But these women were anything but wrong.

My initial impression of the English Department of Lajpat Rai College was that of a conclave—a witches' conclave. The department was predominantly female. Of the thirteen staff members, only three were men, and two of them were not present the day I joined. I had been appointed to fill the two-year leave vacancy of the third.

On my first day there, I found all the lady lecturers sitting in a circle, and the one with dyed hair, who had been at my interview, was reading out incantations. I was invited to join the listeners. The department room was small and intimate. Chairs with rather dilapidated cushions were arranged around a big rectangular table. In a corner, adjacent to the window, stood an almirah, ambitiously labelled 'Department Library'. In another corner was a small table on which stood an electric kettle and a few cups and saucers. The kettle was emitting urgent hissings.

'We will take a tea break,' said Dyed Hair. 'This will also give us an opportunity to welcome the new entrant to the department.'

She introduced me crisply and efficiently, and handed me a piece of paper listing my timetable. I was to teach two novels to the BA Honours group. Thankfully, I was familiar with both.

The lady on my right said, 'The topic for the seminar is "Teaching English Literature in India". Arundhati's paper is titled "Some Aspects of Third World Poetics and the Dynamics of Pedagogy".'

I mentally deciphered the title, hoping I would not be expected to contribute to the discussion in any way. After we had finished tea and I had answered a few questions relating mainly to my MPhil dissertation, the paper-reading resumed. I found it difficult to concentrate on what was being said. I was alarmed by the words. The word 'pedagogy' came up again and again. At least I know how to pronounce it properly now, I thought. At least... What if they find out what I was thinking? Would they throw me out of the room, out of the college? An English MPhil who can't pronounce 'pedagogy'. There were other unfamiliar words and expressions. What in the name of God was 'principles of inclusion'? Include what?

My attention began to wander. They were a curious bunch. The lady on my right looked formidable. What was her name...ah, Malhotra, Ranjana Malhotra. Was I to call her Ranjana too, like everybody else did? She had cropped grey hair. Her features were set in a very stern expression, with immobile eyes and eyebrows, but her mouth looked vulnerable with slightly drooping lips. She probably never smiled in class. The students probably were too scared to even breathe in her classes...

Next to her sat a very attractive lady. She wore a green sari with a navy blue *pallav*. Her hair, beautiful, silky and lustrous, was tied in a knot at the nape of her long neck. She had a patrician nose, long and elegant, in which she wore a single diamond. She had been introduced as Nandini Jain Iyer. She was also wearing little green gems in her ears. Nobody else wore much jewellery.

Yvonne D'Souza, the lady in a printed nylon sari who had large teeth but a very kindly smile, was wearing gold earrings and gold bangles. She reminded me of Mummy, somehow. This jewellery was probably as much a part of her anatomy as Mummy's gold ear studs... Years of indifferent use had given the gold a lacklustre look.

The youngest of the lot, Sona Kapoor, looked small and sharp. She wore glasses that magnified her eyes. Her white sari was rather crumpled. Her only adornment was a big sindoor bindi. She had been appointed just two years before me.

Dyed Hair—her name was Arundhati Sen—was getting rather worked up about 'the so-called universal value of literature'. I noticed she had a rather deliberate way of speaking. She rounded her lips a lot; Lakshmi would have called her a 'Bengali *roshogullah*'. Everybody was nodding wisely. I found my neck moving in imitation. This was probably the end of the paper.

She had barely stopped reading when Sona Kapoor started talking. She spoke for almost five minutes. She was uncomfortable about various points in the paper, she said, including the simplified term 'Third World'. She went on to point out that that was another kind of universalization. I caught on that 'universal' was something that was simply not on.

Arundhati answered for the next fifteen minutes, insisting that this wasn't what the paper was saying in the first place, and how could she be charged with this kind of simplification? That in fact, the first quarter of her paper just defined the term and, probably, Sona had not been listening at all.

Sona went on to say, in her high, shrill voice, that the first half of the paper contradicted the latter half, because if there was no Third World, then where would the ethos come from? And if one began particularizing every experience, one would come down to every individual and then there would be no theory at all...only chaos and confusion.

I realized that things were hotting up. Arundhati replied, her voice rising too, that it was Sona who was contradicting herself and was probably arguing for the sake of argument. Ranjana Malhotra cleared her throat and, miraculously, everybody fell silent.

Her voice was measured and calm, a respite from the pitched battle that had just been raging. She began by drawing attention to the vastness of the topic that had been attempted in the paper and applauded Arundhati for drawing attention to a facet not widely discussed till now. She spoke about alternatives and wondered whether any existed. Lastly, she turned to me.

'So...Geetika... Can I call you that? Do you agree with

the impossibility of communicating a Third World ethos to the students within the confines of the present system? You are from a different university. Jana, to my knowledge, seems to have a more open system—not as hidebound as we are here. Could you tell us something about your experiences as a student there?'

Where was I to begin? The incompetence of my guide or her despairing of 'students here'? As I fumbled to verbalize my thoughts, Nandini Jain Iyer came to my rescue.

'Sorry to interrupt, but Arundhati, I feel your paper doesn't deal enough with the vexed question of Third World ethos... After all, that would have to be defined in order to go into this whole debate about the constraints of the system.'

'Oh, Nandini, this is what we have been discussing for the past twenty-five minutes...' said Arundhati, rather irritably.

'Then we need to discuss it more; otherwise we will keep going round in circles as we have been for the past twenty-five years, or for as long as we have been teaching...'

Arundhati hotly began contesting the tyranny of definitions. I hoped they would not single me out again. Someone looked at the watch and screeched, 'Oh, my bus leaves in five minutes.' There was a shuffle and everybody began to leave.

'Which way are you going?' Nandini asked me. 'Can I give you a lift?'

There was a liveried chauffeur in Nandini's car. She must be very rich, I thought. We sat comfortably in the backseat.

'Thanks for coming to my rescue,' I told her.

'I thought you needed it. Our department seems to think everybody arrives ready for intellectualizing...' she said drily.

'I certainly do not... In fact, I feel rather inadequate. All of you seem to know so much more.'

'In six months, you will begin to speak the language, never mind the understanding. I am not sure I understand very much...' she said.

Emeralds

'That was rather uncalled for on my part,' Ranjana Malhotra told me the next day. 'I am sorry for singling you out in the seminar. I think I was rather impatient with the bickering...but it was not the best way to deflect the tension.'

'I find it difficult to communicate personal experience in abstract terms; that is why I could not speak at all.'

'Articulation is important in this profession. You will realize its importance as you go along. This is one thing these American universities instil in their students—an ability to communicate effectively.'

I started. Could she read my mind? I had been thinking a lot about foreign education.

'How important is it, Dr Malhotra? Would you say that everyone of any merit whatsoever ought to try and get a degree from America?'

'Call me Ranjana, everybody does. Personally, I am against this brain-drain to the West. We have to work here, get our degree from this country—otherwise, how will there be any development of research facilities here? And there is some measure of our slave mentality operating when we look towards the West for the development of thought. But it is definitely easier working there, and definitely better as far as chances of promotion go when you return armed with a PhD from Berkeley or Cornell. I don't have a foreign degree but then I have been in this college all my life. I haven't progressed to the university to become a professor.'

Most others, I found out, had PhDs from abroad. The Lajpat Rai English Department was unusually accomplished. For one, it was an island of femaleness in a predominantly male college. The two male lecturers were old and colourless, and preferred to keep to the general staff room. Secondly, it was a model of efficiency and academic integrity in a university where the teachers' commitment to their jobs was constantly debated in the public sphere.

In fact, on hearing that I had got a teaching job, Hari Prasad had jokingly asked me whether I was enjoying the two-year paid holiday that I had landed. He had gone on to narrate the story of a lecturer he met every day on his way to work at ten in the morning. This gentleman would be returning from work at that hour. I got to hear of many such stories from various people over time—even from Ratish.

Thirdly, it was an amazingly active department. There were department seminars every week. In fact, I had stumbled into one on my first day at the college.

Arundhati not only had a PhD from Cornell but had also published two books. She was well known in academic circles. Her deliberate way of speaking could become sharp and focused quite easily, as it had been at my interview. I felt she disapproved of the way I had conducted myself there.

Yvonne was quiet and placid. When she spoke, which was rarely, people listened. She had a great fund of common sense, which never degenerated into simplifications.

Sona Kapoor spoke incessantly. She must have been around my age, but she took on everybody.

Nandini was different—different from the department— though I couldn't put my finger on the reason for a long time. She was the only one who would at times rush home, saying that it was her son's birthday or that thirty people were expected for dinner or that Raghu, her husband, was coming home from a three-week trip. The others seemed to have no life beyond the college.

I learnt quickly that it was bad form to talk about personal things but Nandini did—slowly and deliberately, leaning back on the cushion. She told me she had two children, both sons, by her first husband who had serious problems... I longed to ask her the nature of the problems, but I was scared to appear too inquisitive.

'My children are refreshingly normal,' she said.

Nandini lived in a sprawling mansion in south Lutyenabad. The house belonged to her mother, who also lived there. Her father had been one of the leading industrialists of the country, and her mother was his second wife. After his death, the sons of the first wife gradually took over the whole business and Nandini, her sister and her mother were left with an allowance and the big house.

'It is pitifully low if you consider the value of all that was taken away. But the courts decided it was enough for a widow and her two daughters...'

I knew Nandini took annual holidays to Europe. But I saw her point.

'In this country, the sexist bias is institutionalized...'

'But it is the lower classes that bear the brunt of it,' said Sona Kapoor, butting in.

'I think it is real enough in all classes,' I ventured, thinking of Ratish's mother and Reshma and the maxim that women ought not to work.

'The verbalization is certainly more in the upper classes. You have all diamond-chiffon varieties complaining about inequality,' said Sona sharply.

I noticed that Nandini was wearing diamond studs in hers ears. She was the only one who changed her jewellery so often. Ranjana Malhotra sometimes wore a number of glass bangles that would break when she thumped her hands on the table...

'Oh, Sona darling, the kind of women you are talking about wouldn't be seen dead in chiffons anymore,' Nandini said sweetly, too sweetly.

'Fashion trends among the elite are the last thing I would follow closely,' said Sona, even more sharply.

'One has to be aware of what one is criticizing—you know, to get away from the clichéd representations of reality,' Nandini replied, even more calmly.

I was enjoying Sona's discomfiture. She had told me that

morning I was wearing too much perfume. She had come sniffing like a dog to me and said, 'Oh, oh, oh…This is not exactly a cocktail party, you know.'

She had then told me that what I was wearing was definitely an 'evening' perfume, not a 'day' perfume at all. Sona reminded me of a school bully. She was nasty to most people, but deferential to those who could defeat her at her own game. She followed Ranjana Malhotra like a faithful dog, for instance. I felt I would never be able to handle her type of aggression. She was so much of what I was not.

'I do know what I am criticizing,' persisted Sona. 'There is nothing much to know anyway.'

'Oh, dear! You are like my son. Yesterday he said he hated China grass. I asked why and he replied, "Because it grows in China",' said Nandini, undoing her bun, then plaiting her hair and putting it up again.

I wanted to laugh seeing Sona's face. She stalked away after that. I too rushed off to class.

The students of Lajpat Rai College were a mixed lot, I found. The ones enrolled in the Honours courses were sincere and hardworking, and after a few days of tongue-tied shyness, I found myself enjoying these classes. The Pass course classes were different. They seemed to be full of tall, strapping young men. I would often find eyes resting on me speculatively, hungrily, as I struggled with Shakespeare and Wordsworth. I would wrap the pallav of my sari tightly around me before entering the class.

Nandini was sitting with a glum face that afternoon.

'Can I take a lift back with you?' I asked her. Nandini lived very close to Jana. I was still living there, though I had been served a notice to vacate the room. It was presumed I was earning enough to support myself without the benefits due to a student. Ratish said that it was just as well—it would probably help me make up my mind about marriage. My parents were now in perfect agreement with him.

'Yes, of course, Geetika. I was waiting for you, in fact,' Nandini replied.

'Sona was rather sharp with you today...' I said in the car.

'I wasn't any better, was I? Yet, her criticism can probably be justified whereas my situation... I am terribly suspect, ideologically suspect.' She was not smiling at all, 'What makes you so accepting of me, Geetika?'

'I don't know. Am I accepting of you? Perhaps because I have no ideology...'

'In six months, you will. In six months, you will notice the contradictions in my situation as an industrialist's daughter and an English teacher. In six months, you will become at best tolerant of the overbearing patriarchal presence in my home and my flirtations with feminism.'

'And all the time, I will be trying to hide my envy of those lovely earrings.'

'You like them?'

'They are lovely. I have never seen anything like them.'

'They are heirlooms...very old. They are part of a set that belonged to my great-grandmother.'

'I love jewellery, Nandini... How I wish I had some!'

'Tell me more about yourself, Geetika. You never say much about yourself.'

I felt very warm towards Nandini. Lakshmi had left for Rochester. I was left with no friends at all, unless I counted Ratish. But it was difficult to communicate my enthusiasm for Lajpat Rai College to him. I told Nandini I was contemplating marriage. She replied that I ought to sound happier about it. I told her there were problems. She said there always are.

✤ The Anti-Man ✤

Upper-middle class, bourgeoisie, consumerism were bad words, and Ratish was definitely upper-middle class. Washing machines and food processors were not to be talked about in the department room, not even the imported goods that Ratish's mother found so fascinating. In the department room, the inroads capitalism was making in our society were to be censured. Ratish had given me an American sweater, which I never wore to college. Mummy wasn't fascinated by imported goods either. She had never gone out of the way to buy them, never asked people to bring things for her when they travelled abroad.

I used to love the soft, furry imported woollens that some hostellers wore to school. I also liked the pretty dresses they wore. Mummy said that as we were Indians, we must take pride in wearing and using Indian things. She told me a story about Indira Gandhi, who threw her lovely imported doll into the fire during the Swadeshi movement. Patriotism, national chauvinism... In the Lajpat Rai English Department, however, nobody talked of India and Indians in the way my parents did. Uncritical acceptance of all that is Indian is also suspect, somebody had said at a seminar. To valorize all that is Indian was simply not on... Did Mummy do that?

Unfamiliar words—'uncritical', 'national experience', 'metaphysics of presence', 'deconstruction'. Slowly, I was beginning to 'decode' their messages. Most concepts I had grown up with were problematic; my present situation was without any commitment. I wallowed in guilt. Ratish attacked me squarely for the pretensions of the intellectual class: 'Your overfunded universities...you chew that much of the national budget and what is your contribution to national life? A lot of talk, a lot of bilge. Ask your friends why they are so keen on seminars held abroad—every scholar in this country has their eyes fixed firmly on the west.'

'Not really, in Lajpat Rai...' I would begin, but even as I said it, I realized the necessity of commitment.

I wasn't committed to anything. I, too, wanted to be an elite scholar. But how could I ever be one? After all, I had just joined the department. I read avidly but was too inhibited to venture an opinion. They were all so much better read. They would find me ideologically suspect...they would! Where was I to hide my fascination for the world of advertisements—Ratish's world—the world of washing machines and food processors, the world where middle-aged women permed their hair and painted their nails? Nandini...what about her? I didn't know enough about her world. It must be different from Ratish's. What word could one use for it—'feudal'?

I was trying to straddle two very different worlds—Ratish's world, where money was important, very important... Other things were important too, like how one dressed, but ultimately it was money that tipped the balance; and the world of the witches, where there were other hierarchies, although I still couldn't read the signs fully. I knew it was different from my parents' world, the world of small-town colleges. There, the mood had been simpler. Here it was something else—more tense, more unforgiving, more judgemental. It was most obvious during seminars and the verbal slugfests...

Dipankar belonged to this world. He was unforgiving too. He too pronounced judgements in that carefully unaccented voice—which was cold and hard—a very intelligent voice, a voice that made no allowances. But I had begun to think of Dipankar as a special friend. It was so easy to sink into the luxury of friendship with an attractive man in my new life with a job. When Lakshmi had been preparing to leave for Rochester, Dipankar had tried his best to get in touch with her through me. I didn't really mind. I still thought Lakshmi was being unreasonable.

'Hello, Geetika...' His eyes would actually light up. 'Let's see a film together or something. Ingmar Bergman Festival is on in Shakuntalam,' he would say, sounding sincere, friendly, easy.

'You have got a job at Lajpat Rai? Fantastic, yaar! We must celebrate,' he had said, sounding pleased—pleased for me.

'You must give me the phone number of your working women's hostel. When are you shifting there?' He had asked, as if really interested in meeting me.

I found no reason to disbelieve him.

'Let's go on Thursday for the film,' I would say. I looked around for a piece of paper to write my number on; I smiled back at him. It was so easy... I did try to take Lakshmi along for the film but failed.

'Geetika, I am going to be very angry with you if you persist in this...' she had said angrily.

Dipankar could be my special friend. He was a friend worth having...a friend with a developed mind. I started having coffee with him more often. He came out of his room at six every evening. I told him about the department at Lajpat Rai. He seemed very interested. It was very easy to talk to him.

'You know, Dipankar. I probably got the job because of you...'

'How?'

'I quoted your review of Rushdie's *Shame* at the interview and the interview board was floored.'

'Then you must make over half your pay cheque to me.'

'Sure...'

'I know money doesn't mean anything to you; your boyfriend has enough.'

I had introduced Dipankar to Ratish the previous day.

'Have you joined The Anti-Man, after all?' Ratish had asked afterwards.

'What do you mean?'

'Well, I interrupt serious intellectual debates these days...'

'Ratish... Dipankar is—'

'Now that Lakshmi is away, he is probably thinking of settling for you.'

How could Ratish? As if I would cheat on him! As if Dipankar would pollute his thin and academic body with somebody like me!

He was friendly but definitely uppity.

❧ The Critic ❧

'Are you writing anything these days?' Dipankar asked me one day.

I suddenly wanted him to read the story I was writing. I wanted him to discuss it seriously, using terms like 'epistemological shift'. Legitimacy, I wanted legitimacy. Perhaps my story would depict the commitment I so desperately wanted. Perhaps then I wouldn't feel inadequate in the department seminars.

The story was about a rich, married woman who was having an affair with an impoverished lecturer in order to conceive a child that her husband couldn't give her. The husband's sterility was symbolic of the intellectual and spiritual famine in their lives. However, she dumps the lecturer once her objective is realized. The story was in the first person, from the point of view of the woman. Impulsively, I asked Dipankar to read it.

'Will you see it, Dipankar? I have never shown my stories to anybody... You write so many reviews...'

'All right,' he said, looking slightly surprised. Or was it my imagination?

I suddenly felt inhibited. Hadn't Lakshmi said there was too much sex in my writing? Anyway, once written, the stories had to be read and Dipankar seemed intellectual enough to handle all this.

'Have you published much?'

'No, not much. Very little, in fact.'

Dipankar disappeared with my story for a long time after that. I was shifting to a working women's hostel soon, so I was too busy getting no-dues certificates from the university hostel to seek him out. I settled quickly into the new hostel. Lajpat Rai College was much nearer. My commuting time went down by almost half an hour. Evenings were lonely, unless Ratish came by. He was sulking because he thought there had been no need for me to shift. We could have got married instead, he said. My parents were coming to Lutyenabad soon. I told him we could defer the setting of the date at least till then.

I decided to ring up Dipankar. I knew he spent his weekends at home with his parents. The first time I rang, a very Bengali voice said that he would be home in another half an hour. I left a message with my phone number. I decided to ring again after two hours.

'Oh, hello, Geetika… I meant to ring up, but somehow did not get the time…'

'I wanted feedback on my story, Dipankar.'

There was silence. A slight clearing of the throat. 'I don't know why you gave me this story…'

I felt as though I had been slapped, 'For your comments, what else?'

'Well, it is about a certain kind of experience, a frankness about a certain kind of experience… You know middle class, upper class… It is so predictable. I wish you wouldn't give me such things to read. I mean, Geetika…why should you give it to me?'

'What do you mean by predictable?'

'I mean…commonplace…and then, sexual experience described in great detail. What is the point of such a story? Why should it be written?'

'Why is anything written?'

'Well, I guess people write when they have something to say—something about love, friendship, etc. This seems to be a disguised autobiography.'

Suddenly, everything fell into place. The lecturer in the story had been Bengali. Dipankar thought that of me…the age-old ruse…read my pain and make love to me. Dipankar had met Ratish. He thought it was an autobiographical story meant to ensnare his innocent academic self. The rich woman and the impoverished lover!

'Just because it is in first person?' I asked shakily.

'There is no objective distance from the subject matter either…'

'I think we need to discuss it...'

'Oh, I am rather busy these days. I will post the manuscript back to you.'

'But really, these comments of yours...'

'I will ring you up when I have more time. You know I am really rather caught up...'

I banged the receiver down and fled to my room.

I was trembling. The objective distance...was that all that he could say? What about his objective distance as a critic? What about his morality as a critic? He couldn't even fulfil the minimum courtesy of communicating his criticism properly. He could have called, instead of waiting for me to ring up. He could have written. He was too busy even to see me and yet he took the liberty of thinking that I was waiting to rape his intellectual innocence.

I sat in the room, watching the light fade. I couldn't face an evening by myself. I couldn't sit anymore in my lonely room. Suddenly, I knew where to go... Nandini.

✢ Middle Class ✣

Nandini's house was big. I had never been inside one of this size before. Each room was huge—big enough to fit a modern day two-bedroom flat. The ceilings were high, so high that the fans had to be suspended by ridiculously long rods, like those in the Desertvadi College auditorium.

The room I was ushered into had pale green walls and a fantastic Venetian chandelier, also green. On one of the walls, there was a huge, garishly coloured painting of Goddess Lakshmi. It was the usual calendar representation of the goddess, standing on a lotus and raining coins from empty palms. The furniture was rather indifferent—a lot of sofas and some brightly coloured cushions.

'Oh, hi,' said Nandini, coming in. She was wearing a printed salwar kameez.

I felt rather foolish. What had possessed me to come hurtling down in a scooter rickshaw to her house at this time in the evening?

'I was rather depressed, so...'

'Geeti, I am so glad you have come. I was planning to invite you over one of these days. Why are you depressed? It often helps to just talk about it.'

It came in a rush—confused, tearful, hysterical. Dipankar, my writing, me... Nandini was very silent...

'Oh, this is awful,' she said at last. 'It is an awful experience to be insulted in this manner.'

I still hadn't seen it quite like that. 'It is an insult, isn't it?'

'His manner definitely is... The fact that he is refusing to meet you...'

'Nandini, it boils down to me, doesn't it? What I am... That is why he could say all that...'

'Stop blaming yourself for his behaviour. Anyway, what do you mean by that?'

'I mean... It is because I am from Desertvadi, I am not an intellectual, not like him, not like Sona Kapoor, and I am marrying this yuppy MBA.'

'So, you are scared of seeming ideologically suspect... Oh, Geeti, the very fact that you are feeling like this about these people proves it is another kind of snobbery.'

'I am confused...'

'I am confused too. My first husband was like this, critical and judgmental... He is teaching in the US now. When I got married, I was ready to be reformed. I was ready to be metamorphosed into a committed person. He was a sadist, you know. His lovemaking was punitive. I thought it was penance for my being what I am—spoilt and rich. I spent five years with him in Calcutta and I could never understand what he wanted from me... I got out of the marriage bruised and broken...'

She rolled up the sleeve of her kameez and showed me a puckered scar on her upper arm. 'This happened because I bought a food processor...to mash up the baby's feed. I was trading his intellect for consumer goods, he said. He threw a glass at me and then we made love as I bled... I thought I would die. Funnily enough, I felt so guilty...that it seemed all right to die. But then, on the other hand, he kept applying for scholarships to go to the US and I was never allowed to question that. It was terrible of me to want a food processor, but it was all right for him to want better research facilities. When we divorced, he said that only a materialistic person like me would draw a similarity between consumer goods and intellectual challenge. But Geeti, I feel there is a connection, there *should* be.'

Nandini looked very young with her hair down. I wondered why she was telling me all this. Perhaps because I too was feeling fatally attracted to the academic community. But then what option did I have? I did not have a huge house to live in... I did not even have a razor-sharp intellect like Sona Kapoor.

'How did you meet Iyer, Nandini?'

'I met him at an Art Exhibition four years ago. We liked the same painting and started to discuss it. He is a journalist. We lead very separate lives, but it works. He even maintains a separate flat. My sons call it "Raghu's hell hole", it is so untidy. He is fiercely possessive of it, though. There was one more husband in between the professor and the journalist... You can see I have led an eventful life. He was a businessman who thought I would be good drawing-room decoration. My mother arranged that match. That marriage never began at all.'

How different we were! Could I ever imagine three marriages, two divorces? What would Mummy say about this kind of life? Rich and idle... Yet Nandini did not seem idle at all. Surprisingly, I had no trouble understanding this life that was so very different from mine.

'Nandini, my writing is so middle-class...'

'It would have to be. Why should you want to deny your origins?'

'But then should I write at all? I mean…they will never like my writing—Arundhati and the rest…'

'Yes, you should… You should, even if that is the only thing you do.'

'Why do you say that?'

'Geeti, there is such an intermingling of the personal and the intellectual in you…honest…you are honest…'

Nandini had never read a word I had written.

'I know what you are thinking,' she said. 'But this is just an intuitive thing I said. I would love to read your work. But see, from the purely practical point of view, your writing is what you are about, isn't it?'

Yes, it was. This was what I was. I was about writing; that is why Dipankar's callous behaviour seemed like such a betrayal.

Part Three

....

Research

❧ Birth ❧

Push, push, push harder...

It was hot in the theatre... I felt hot and parched...perspiration and the spectre of the grey-haired obstetrician...stern and unforgiving...she who should have been Mother... Mother was far away... Mother was too pale and silent...

It was morning, too early to deliver. I had cried for her all night.

She bent to cut me up...episiotomy...

I was not crying anymore...because I was pushing...pushing it out... She was here, telling me not to make a fuss, sternly and elegantly...her Sambhalpuri sari in place and the gown to protect it from my blood, which was all over the stirrupped table...as I pushed and pushed for mother-life...

A distant voice over the phone, a terribly familiar voice... 'He is not home... Why are you pursuing him again?... He has been through hell.'

'You are educated...why do you yell like this... Everybody goes through it...women have to adjust...what is so particularly feminist about it...

Don't yell, I will give you an injection that will lessen the pain... I can't leave the whole world for you... Stop screaming, aren't you ashamed of yourself... Push, push, push...

'No, don't say *push*...open up, like a flower, like Mother Earth,' the grey-haired childbirth adviser had said.

She was there, groaning in empathy with me. 'Live the pain, a special pain...'

'That's right,' said the obstetrician. 'One more push and it will be out...'

It...*she*...the adviser used to say 'she', but I knew it was a son I was having... A boy.

Congratulations...

Your first baby...

Lucky madam...

Why are you laughing...shut up...don't laugh...shut up...

Take heart, child...

She is hysterical...

I will give her something, it was a long labour, where is her husband... Where is he...where is he...where is he...

Where *are* you, Ratish? You are not husband, not *my* husband...

⊰ Arrival ⊱

Flowers—so many of them—white red and yellow... So many bunches.

Flowers are expensive...must be the witches...

'Somebody to see you, madam.'

A soft touch, a kiss. 'Geeti, how are you? The baby is so sweet.'

Can't answer you, but I need your lap... I need your arms... I need you...

After hours... 'Why did you... Geeti? Why?'

Won't answer...what is the need... You know it all...you know it all...you know it all...

'You could have called me for the birth. I have children of my own. There was no need to be alone.'

No need...no need at all... There was need... A ghost had to be exorcised...a ghost had to be invoked... A pale visage had to dissolve—bedsheet white...cold...in warm blood. Mine.

'Don't talk if you don't want to, close your eyes. I will stay with you tonight. Sleep, Geeti, everything will be all right.'

Mummy, you have come... Pat me to sleep. I hear your glass bangles clinking... You stopped wearing glass bangles when I was in school, but I remember... But this is you, this is you... This has to be you...

⊰ Shame ⊱

It was two in the morning. I had tossed and turned since ten, when the lights were put out...

'Sleep...you need it. We will give you the baby tomorrow; tonight you need rest.'

How do they know? How do they know what I need?

This was the second sleepless night. My son was all of two days old—I was a two-day-old mother. I had fed the baby today; he had opened his tiny pink mouth and had sucked with amazing strength.

He was a strong little boy, a tough little baby—mine...only mine...

What had I done? What if they lynch me in the nursing home, all these family people?

Kill her... She has no husband, stone her to death... corrupt, corruption...polluted.

My bleeding body, it had created... The baby is beautiful, everybody had said.

'Does he look like his father?' the nursing staff had asked.

They would love to know, wouldn't they... There was a father, of course there had to be; babies couldn't be spawned just like that...in a test tube. No, they wanted to know whether there was a husband.

The witches came regularly. I had visitors all day. The nursing staff didn't know how to react. I was the only one who didn't have a mother or a mother-in-law at my bedside, yet the witches were undoubtedly respectable. They were my only passport to respectability.

I had hysterically tried to explain to them.

Explain what? Could I even explain to myself why I was here...why I was here all alone? Why wasn't Ratish here with a thermos of hot coffee? That was what the neighbouring woman had been sipping when the door swung open. Hot, hot coffee warming my throat.

The air conditioner was buzzing busily—it was too cold... I must switch it off, I was trembling. Oh God, it was so cold... Should I ring the bell and call the nurse? I didn't really want to, didn't want her to look tired and put upon... This was hell, hellish cold... My teeth were chattering...

I wrapped the blanket tightly around me, the air conditioner skipped; it would be warmer, soon it would be warmer. It would be morning and I would get coffee in a thermos flask. I would drink the hot, hot coffee.

Hot coffee, tea, seminars or me. The child in Literature... The baby as concept, reading as level of penetration, writing as foetus, publication as baby.

Sex everywhere...sex... Moral turpitude.

'Do you realize you can be fired for moral turpitude?'

'It is not immoral to have babies, sir.'

The Principal was old and grey, wary of the articulate women of the English Department, weary of students striking, tired of matching his wits against the governing body.

I was weary too, of the six-month-old pregnancy, of backache, of grieving for the dead.

'We have certain examples to set for the students, Miss Mehendiratta. I believe you were waylaid by some students...'

Here she comes, they had yelled. Whose baby is that? Does she know herself? The whore...whore... I will oblige her next time, one had yelled; me too, yelled another.

'Yes, I was. They called me a prostitute.'

He flinched. 'Miss Mehendiratta, I am not in a position to understand the situation... But I will write to the governing body. It is my duty... I don't know what action they will take...'

I had come back to the department with a stone on my heart. Arundhati and Sona were sitting there. Arundhati walked away as soon as I entered. I knew she disapproved of me. Sona came to me.

'What happened, Geeti? You look awful...'

'I might be fired for moral turpitude, Sona...'

'Oh, God... Geeti...'

Unwed pregnancy had struck a chord somewhere in Sona Kapoor's heart. She had stopped lashing out at me, though she still disapproved openly of my 'liaison' with Nandini.

'Geeti, I feel I must tell you,' she said, 'Arundhati has convened a meeting of the department today to discuss your case. I think she has had a talk with the Principal also.'

'Sona, I need the job.'

'I will let you know what happens at the meeting. By the way, how is the women's hostel taking it?'

'I changed my hostel when I found out, and registered as Mrs Mehendiratta in the new one. That's all right. Nobody knows there...'

The obstetrician was by my bed. 'You have to register the name of the baby for the birth certificate. Where is the father? Where is your husband, Mrs Mehendiratta?'

'I don't know,' I answered truthfully.

'Who will take you away from here?'

'I will go...'

'You are creating problems for us, Mrs Mehendiratta. I didn't realize... I didn't know... Anyway, it's *your* problem. You may leave tomorrow morning. My paediatrician will see the baby today. And...please settle the dues before you leave,' she added hurriedly.

There was perspiration on her upper lip; the tiny hairs looked dark, like a moustache. She looked tired.

'You look tired,' I said.

'Yes,' she said sternly. 'You women don't make it easier for me. There was a woman six months gone with child, demanding an abortion. Why didn't you...?'

'I don't know...'

'Do you think a society like ours will accept you? Your baby? You have been very unfair to the child. Thank God it's not a girl. Do you have a job?'

'Yes, I teach…'

'And can you support a child on your salary? Where do you live?'

'Women's hostel…'

'Where is the father? Has he run away?'

'No, where will he run… But I don't know where he is… He has gone to America for a while…'

'Why do you women do these things? Why don't you wait for marriage? Why do you spoil your life and other lives with it?'

She swished out; she was a spinster and was spending a lifetime clearing up other people's marital and extramarital messes. She was so correct in her appearance—grey hair in place, sari pinned in place—while the chaotic consequences of love and sex raged all around her.

Women screaming in labour, women asking for abortions… Women like me, who embarrassed the whole establishment by not producing husbands, in-laws or even their own families.

⊰ Dada ⊱

'Geeti, who are we to judge you? We may or may not see the point in what you have done, but we are here to help you,' said Ranjana Malhotra.

'They are not going to take a stand,' Sona had said, settling on the cushion in my room. 'Arundhati and a couple of others feel your motives are suspect. And Arundhati said that merely having a baby out of wedlock is hardly a feminist statement. The men were there and, for the first time, agreed wholeheartedly with her. Nandini was hysterical and all, and called Arundhati a frustrated bitch. It was awful…'

'And Ranjana Malhotra?'

'She and Yvonne felt that the department had no business discussing your private life; Arundhati said you were responsible for dragging it out in the open. In a way, Geeti, it is good that they are not taking a stand.'

'Why, Sona?'

'I have not seen it succeed, ever. The Principal anyway hates their guts and, really, the kind of stand that they are capable of taking is often not understood by anybody.'

'Sona, what do I do?'

'Who did you vote for in the Teachers' Association? I hope you were sensible enough to vote for Ranjan, because he is the one who can save your life now.'

Sona had been campaigning aggressively for Ranjan.

'Look, the University Teachers' Democratic Party is very powerful in the Association. You know Ranjan and I have been seeing each other. I think I can persuade him to talk to the Principal.'

'Will he?'

I knew Ranjan could get things done. His trade union background had made him emerge as the champion of teachers' rights. If anybody could twist the arm of the Principal, it was he. I felt hopeful.

'Another angle is your business connections. Talk to Nandini. I believe her family is very close to the Home Minister. They funded his election to the Lok Sabha when he was a nobody. If the Home Minister can put a call through to the governing body chairperson...'

'Sona...this makes me wonder why I am doing it anyway.'

'Yes, Geeti...why are you having a baby out of wedlock?'

'You are angry with us for not being more supportive...' Ranjana Malhotra was saying. 'But what could we have done?'

'I don't know, Ranjana Di,' I replied. 'You know I almost lost my job.'

'Nandini bailed you out, didn't she?'

'And Sona...'

'Well, Geeti...we would have taken a stand too, had anything happened. You received nothing in writing. The Principal was not doing anything untoward by writing to the governing body. He told Arundhati he would be posing it as a discipline problem, which it was. You told me you were not being able to hold any Pass classes because of the heckling.'

'And then?'

'We felt we would have to wait for the response of the governing body. After all, we just couldn't presume that they were going to be regressive. We couldn't start twisting the Principal's arm just because he was conveying a genuine problem to them.'

'Yet you chose to be blind to the fact that the Principal has never felt it necessary to convey the problem of the Commerce Department, where the Law paper has not been taught for the past three years.'

'Look Geeti, we have survived because we believe in procedure, in rules. There is a way of doing things… I am not criticizing you for using the strong-arm tactics that you did. You had a lot at stake. But as a department, we couldn't have participated in them.'

'I felt orphaned, Ranjana Di, because in a way, I felt I was doing what I did because of you…'

'Do you need some money?' asked Ranjana Di, abruptly changing the subject.

'No, I am going to sign a cheque.'

'Most of it is refundable,' she said briskly. 'This place is luckily covered by the university health scheme. I checked. It won't pay for the air-conditioned room, of course.'

'I didn't know…'

'That is not surprising,' she said grimly. 'You can stay at my place until you realize a few things…'

'No, no…'

'I can't leave you on the street like this. Heavens know what prompts you girls to take such risks…'

৭ Wolf ৡ

'This is a stupid condition, Geeti. How can you say stupid things like these?' Ratish had said violently.

'Ratish, I can't live like this. How can I live under the same roof with people who are trying their best to marry you off to somebody else?'

'They didn't know you... I didn't know you when this match came up...'

'But are you going to deny that they still want you to marry her?'

'So what? They know I am adamant.'

'And you feel these are ideal conditions for everyone to live together happily?'

'No, obviously not, but Geeti, for that matter, you have not made an effort to develop a relationship with them either. You have been so negative, refusing to do anything Mama tells you to do. Your Lakshmi and all have been a pretty bad influences on you, and then you get a job with so many giddy women.'

'Ratish, I object strongly to your calling them names. I love my job at Lajpat Rai. It is the first time in my life I am getting to know bright, committed academics.'

'You are getting carried away, as usual. You meet a bunch of so-called feminists and take their word as gospel truth. All of them with weird family lives—two divorcees and three spinsters in a department of twelve.'

'I think you are obnoxious.'

We were discussing the problems of feminine space in the department. Arundhati felt that women had been seen as a victim of patriarchy for far too long.

'We have to discuss women as aiders and abetters in their own exploitation now,' said Arundhati, rounding her 'o' sounds, as usual.

Sona Kapoor brought in the issue of economic disparity, warning Arundhati that the term 'women' could not be used unproblematically across disparities.

Nandini and I had looked at each other and grinned. 'Some are not quite women,' she had whispered in my ear.

Nevertheless, it had made me think. Arundhati always made me think. Wasn't I allowing a kind of victimization that would surely follow? The wedding that Ratish was insisting on... What would that be like? There would be a ceremony in which the Guptas would be wooden-faced, silent, pained...my parents anxious and accusing in turn. I would be dressed in a sari that Mrs Gupta would find too lower middle-class—hardly any jewellery, shameful!

Reshma would have tried and failed to organize my wardrobe for the event. There wouldn't even be a five-star hotel to save face. I would be tense, edgy, my make-up streaked with worry lines. Mr Gupta, in crisp white, would look slightly bored and make an obvious effort to be civil to my parents. Ratish would wonder what the fuss was all about—why wasn't I more relaxed, why didn't I coyly look up to my in-laws like most other girls would...

And after the wedding, there would be the inevitable censure of relatives and Mrs Gupta would look long-suffering, martyred by her greatness in accepting a bahu who came in with just a suitcase... After that... What would happen after that? According to Ratish, everything would settle down...like dust... We would be one family...but would there be a Geetika left?

Lakshmi had said, 'Come to Rochester if you want to remain who you are.'

What if I had gone away? There would have been no baby, nobody to feed every two hours.

Ranjana Di's house was so quiet, so peaceful; in a weird way, it reminded me of my home in Desertvadi. Like Mummy, she too was not particular about anything—things lay scattered on the floor everywhere. There were two bedrooms in the flat. She had put me in what must have been her children's room. Like her own room, this one also had bookcases reaching up almost to the ceiling.

There was a rickety ladder that went up to the uppermost shelf. Books were perhaps the only thing that didn't collect dust in this house. Ranjana Di would dust them herself every now and then, standing precariously on a ladder. The rest of the work was done by a woman called 'Raju ki Ma'. Every day I would ask her to tell me her real name and she would say she had forgotten it. A woman is known by her men, she would say.

'What are you if you only produce daughters?'

'You are lucky, memsahib, to get a son right away. I had to produce three daughters before I got Raju... Your husband will be very pleased. When is he coming back?'

I would point out to her that Ranjana Di was well-known in her own right and probably it was the son who got his identity from her. She would sigh and say, 'You don't know, memsahib, what a difficult life it is for her. She is a man in the way she works; she does everything, right from buying the vegetables to paying the electricity bill. She used to travel in buses till two years back. She would be out at eight in the morning and come back dog-tired at eight in the evening, after having stood in queues and been jostled in buses, and then she would study late into the night. It is only now that the children have started earning that she has begun to relax, only now that she has bought a car.'

This is what Ratish meant by quality of life. Quality meant having servants to pay the bills, having a car and a chauffeur; quality meant having time to paint one's nails and blow dry one's hair every single day of the week. Ratish was not prepared to stand in queues.

'What does your husband do, memsahib?' Raju ki ma asked me.

'He works in a company, a private company.'

'He should come back and see his son. You must call him back. Memsahib, it is absolutely necessary to keep your man with you when you are in this state. If you let them stay away, they start straying.'

'Really?'

'The lady I was working for before this…her husband had an affair. I told her not to stay with her parents for so long when she was having her baby, but she wouldn't listen. And your man, he is in Amrika. There, women have affairs quite easily…'

'That is all right, let him have affairs.'

Sex seemed so remote, so unreal, so frivolous; all that mattered was the demand of a hungry little stomach every two hours, the stretching of little limbs every now and then. The baby was so pink—Raju ki Ma said he had got my complexion. I couldn't stop looking at him. It seemed magical that he could open his eyes and move his little feet with their little toes. He had dark hair on his scalp even when he was born—soft, fur-like hair. Raju ki Ma said I was not to touch the scalp too much.

⊰ Mummy ⊱

'Have you taken your iron supplement today?' asked Ranjana Di.

What a strange relationship we had developed over the past week. She saw to my comforts efficiently, often anticipating my needs. Yet, she hardly seemed to spend much time with me. She would hold the baby in the morning while I bathed and readied myself for the day. She would talk to him in Marathi, even sing to him if he was restless. She was from Maharashtra but had retained her husband's Punjabi name after the divorce. Then she would go out for the day, leaving the caretaking to Raju ki Ma.

Raju ki Ma helped me with everything. She had even helped me stitch nappies out of an old torn sari.

In the evening, Ranjana Di would come back. That was when we would talk. We talked about the baby, Ratish, my dissertation, my plans for a PhD, her son who was a doctor and had decided to set up clinic in a small village, her daughter who had inexplicably become a fashion designer. She was finding it very difficult to come to terms with her daughter's decision, but I felt I understood. I understood why the daughter of a hardworking academic should choose something defined by glamour and fairy lights as a profession.

It made my heart ache for Mummy. There are many daughters who go the opposite way. Mummy...but you aren't here, you aren't here, Mummy, for me to explain.

Papa, Bhaiya, Swati...that's all I possessed for a family, and a cold, silent corpse... Mummy, Mummy, Mummy! I felt my heart break again...again and again, as it had broken for the past nine months. It was true, hearts could break; it felt like drowning. I could feel the blood flow out from every piece, I could feel the blood in my nose. It was impossible to shed any tears because of the blood...

Where was Mummy? Where was she? She had gone where it was impossible to seek her out. Yet the vacuum that was my broken heart had called out to her every minute for the past nine months... I couldn't even hear the baby grow in my womb because of the sobs... I had not heard him grow until the Principal of Lajpat Rai College asked, 'When will you be going on leave, Mrs Mehendiratta?'

At last, that phone call to Ratish and that too-familiar voice declaring, for the umpteenth time, its proprietorial rights. 'He has suffered enough...leave him alone...'

The receptionist at his office had been more helpful... 'In the States, somewhere... No, not work-related.'

He was somewhere in the US with Reshma, recuperating... How does one recuperate from life?

I had found myself incapable of putting it on paper—the impending motherhood...the loss of Mother. I had lost her even earlier, because of Ratish. She had become pale, very pale, wraith-

like. She had also become silent. She didn't reply to my letters,
she didn't fight with me anymore. I had told her about all the
difficulties I was having with Ratish. She just wrote back to say
that it was inevitable, we were so different.

I had wanted so much more from her... I was so angry...

One day, Papa wrote to say she was very ill. When I reached
Desertvadi, there was only a silent corpse. Only a corpse to be
angry with. I didn't know at that time that I was carrying a
baby... Even if I had known, it wouldn't have meant anything.
I just sat emptily, tracing the print on the fading curtains of the
Desertvadi house with my finger. I felt splintered glass at my
throat and behind my eyes. I slept sitting on the dilapidated sofa
and woke up crying many times.

I don't know who all came to pay their respects to the departed
soul. I saw a lot of faces I recognized. They all mouthed the same
words: 'Geetika should have been married. She should have lived
to see her daughter's wedding. Now she is your responsibility,'
they said to Bhaiya and Papa.

And I felt bitter laughter rise up like bile in me. How hard
she had tried to tell me that marriage wasn't all, and I had gone
on rebelling, trying men, trying Ratish...

⊰ Sister-in-Law ⊱

But I also lost the men because of you, Mummy. I lost Ratish...
I became too much your daughter. As you drew away from me,
I became you... I emulated your negations, the very negations
I had hated so much.

No, Ratish, I will not dress up in borrowed clothes.

No, I will not ask my parents to buy jewellery for me.

No, I will not ask them to come to Lutyenabad for an
engagement ceremony.

I became the Geetika who worked for a living; I became the
Geetika who was trying to write. I wrote incessantly, resolutely

turning Ratish away in the evenings. I was trying to create a place to live in.

I wrote home, desperately trying to reach you, Mummy. Why didn't you listen? You were so silent. You felt I had gone too far with Ratish to turn back. What did that mean to you? To you, I had become Booba and Sangeeta... Two bodies panting together... I should have saved that...like Vinita's trousseau... You couldn't face me with the knowledge of my excesses, could you? But you couldn't accept Ratish either...

Another time, another day... Reshma, Ratish's mother... Ratish's parents had organized a party at a five-star hotel to celebrate the birth of Reshma's son. That was when I realized what it meant—a birth, no...the birth of a son.

'Reshma's in-laws have given her a diamond necklace and earrings. He is the first grandson in the family. Her mother-in-law wrote to me to say how lucky Reshma is for their family. When she stepped into their home, her father-in-law got a posting abroad. Now she has produced the first grandson,' Ratish's mother said.

Mummy and Papa were in Lutyenabad at that time. They had come to meet the Guptas after receiving Ratish's invitation. They were at the party too. This was the first time they were meeting the Guptas. Mummy wore her maroon silk sari, which made her look paler, weaker. Papa wore his black suit. Ratish introduced them to his parents. His mother smiled a lot when they were introduced, but after Ratish left, her face became blank.

My parents stood uncertainly next to her. Mummy's skin, bereft of any make-up, looked very tired beside Mrs Gupta's. She was wearing a gorgeous Kanchipuram sari with a peacock-blue border. Reshma's mother-in-law strode up to talk to her; she at once turned her back towards my parents. None of us were introduced to Reshma's in-laws or to anybody else that evening.

I tried to talk to Reshma but, as usual, we got into an argument.

'It would have been nicer for you to have had the baby

here...' I said, just to make conversation.

'I had excellent medical attention there; besides, Rajan's parents wanted the baby to be able to get American citizenship...'

'But you said you don't want him to grow up there...'

'Well, I don't, but I want him to have the option.'

'It must have been difficult for you, at any rate, with your family so far away...'

'The wishes of my in-laws are very important to me. I think it is no skin off my nose to do what they ask me.'

Reshma never let go of an opportunity to lecture me on the duties of a daughter-in-law.

Her mother-in-law fawned over her. Has Reshma eaten? Has the baby had his milk? Has he been changed? Reshma beta, are you feeling all right? Don't exert yourself too much.

The in-laws' diamonds sparkled around Reshma's neck and in her ears. I had turned down her offer of lending me jewellery and a sari for the evening. I was wearing my Orissa sari and silver jewellery. Ratish's mother had been very angry seeing me dressed this way. She told me it wasn't even elegant.

Uniformed waiters made their rounds with trays serving drinks and snacks. Reshma sparkled around the hall, meeting people, accepting their presents. It was a very big hall with huge paintings in golden frames on the walls. I stared at the paintings, trying to control my tears all evening. It was a celebration of unbridgeable differences between Ratish and me.

I knew a large sum of money had been spent to host this party. I felt slightly sick when I saw the worried look on my parents' faces. I knew what they were thinking. I desperately wanted to reach out to Mummy, ask her, tell her, talk to her...

'Mummy, what are you thinking?'

'Nothing, beta.'

'I know you are unhappy about something.'

'You know I don't like these parties. The food nauseates me.'

'Mummy, do you like them...the Guptas?'

'How does it matter, beta? They are very rich.'

'Not very rich, Mummy. They are not really rich.'

I knew the bungalow they lived in belonged to the company. So did one of the two cars. But that made money all the more important to them. Losing out on the hardware daughter was that much more of a catastrophe. Reshma had married appropriately, but Ratish... Ratish would have to fend for himself—no security of a large bank balance for him.

Mrs Gupta would often tick him off for his extravagant ways in my presence.

'You will have to work harder, Ratish, to reach the standard you are taking for granted now. These are advantages you have because of your father. You could well have been staying in a small, pokey flat and saving hard to buy a car.'

'I have protected and cossetted my children all my life,' she would tell me. 'At times, I tremble to think what would happen to them if all this wasn't there.'

'They are richer than us. I can see that their value system is very different,' sighed Mummy and drew her pallav tightly around herself. I knew the air conditioning was bothering her.

'Let's go, Mummy.'

'All right, we will go and say goodbye to Mrs Gupta.'

I watched the frosty look on Mrs Gupta's face as she turned towards my parents. Ratish joined them at that point. He didn't look too happy either. In the taxi, I wanted to cling on to Mummy.

'Geeti, how are things between you and Ratish? Do you think he will go against his parents' wishes?' Papa asked me.

'Yes, Papa,' I answered. 'He will marry me.'

'Beta, I hope you realize that our standards are very different.'

'We can't afford parties like these,' added Mummy.

'Have I asked you to host one like this for me?' I asked angrily.

'Geeti, we realize that you have been growing in a different direction from us... You have chosen a family that is...different...' Mummy said.

'I didn't choose the family. I chose Ratish.'

'In India, beta, remember, one marries the family,' said Papa.

'Why, what about Swati and Sanju Bhaiya? Do you feel she has married the family?' I asked perversely.

'Sanjay is very different and we are very different, Geeti. All my life I have fought for certain principles and in a way, Sanjay has—'

'There you go, Mummy, defending Sanjay Bhaiya... In your scheme of things, he can do no wrong. I am the culprit, every time...'

I was sobbing, the humiliation of the evening pouring out of my eyes. Mummy cried too, averting her face from me. I knew that, for her, I was the cause of her humiliation. I loved her and hated her in turn.

The next day, we were all invited to the Gupta house for lunch. It was Ratish's doing. I rang up to tell him that we would not be able to make it.

'Geeti, this is amazing. Your parents have come all this distance and now they don't want to meet my parents.'

'They met yesterday.'

'Yesterday, my parents had no time to talk to them.'

'Nor the inclination...'

'What do you mean? Did you expect them to leave their guests and concentrate on your parents?'

'I expected them to acknowledge my parents. For that matter, acknowledge me, at least.'

'You mean Mama didn't do that?'

'She didn't.'

'This is amazing! If I remember right, she had told me to tell you to dress up properly as you would be introduced to everyone.'

'And perhaps I didn't meet her high standards... Reshma did offer me jewellery and clothes.'

'What was the harm in accepting them?'

'Why should I, Ratish? Why should I? I can't afford them…
Why should I wear them?'

'What do you mean by that? I can buy you whatever you like.'

'Not like this…not when we aren't married.'

'Geeti, why do you have these silly points of honour? Why
can't you be more relaxed about these things? I am sure Mama
didn't mean to insult you in any way. I will speak to her…'

❧ Combat ❧

He spoke to her. There was another storm. I didn't ask him what
happened because I knew. Delicate sobs, heartfelt grief…

With all the guests around, was it even possible for us to talk to
her parents? And really, they could have been more forthcoming…
Why did they keep standing in a corner? It is so like her to create
these scenes. Why is she so desperate to make you believe that
we are not accepting of her?

Or, Really, beta, why are you being so unreasonable? Reshma's
in-laws are conservative people… How could we introduce her as
a prospective bahu? Her parents seem to have strange expectations.
This is India—there has been no engagement ceremony, nothing…
And look at her. Did she even try to be one of the family? Did
she come and talk to us even once throughout the evening?

I could hear these words as Ratish charged me with omissions.

You have changed so much, Geeti… Have you found
somebody else? Of course, you don't want to go out with me…
Oh, you are working…nobody else in the world is working except
you. Nobody else is doing such a high-profile job like teaching in
Lajpat Rai… You are going to Nandini's. I am sure you have a lot
to talk about. She has had three husbands. That is true liberation,
isn't it? Why should you brother about the poor Guptas anymore!

I sobbed on Nandini's shoulder.

'What do I do, Nandini? What do I do?'

She didn't tell me. She just held my hand in her soft palm

when we took long walks around her garden. She just read my
stories and poems and we discussed them, sometimes with Raghu.
She wanted to know all about Desertvadi, about Mummy, about
Andy. I wanted to know about her too. Her children, Raghu,
her paranoid mother. We talked at night, watching the moon. I
had never talked like this before.

'Nandini, I am going to get rid of Ratish...'

'How?'

'I am going to say the final goodbye.'

'Well, Geeti...this is a major decision...'

'Yes, it is... I mean, it is like breaking up a marriage...'

'Oh, Geeti, marriage is a social institution... This is more
on the emotional level, isn't it?'

'Also, physical...'

'Were you going to save it up like your friend Vinita from
Desertvadi?'

We laughed. I had never laughed so much with anybody
before. 'I can't help feeling bound to him...'

'Why...why should you be bound to him in any way?'

'Perhaps because in his own way, he still wants me...'

'That is not enough, Geeti. You must want him too...'

I sought her out more and more after breaking off with
Ratish. I needed to. Ratish proved to be very difficult to shake
off. He followed me to college, to the women's hostel, once even
to Sona Kapoor's flat. I often felt embarrassed about myself those
days. I knew I was leaning on Nandini.

'Nandini, I can never do anything by myself. I need people
so much. I feel I am exploiting you by forcing you to partake
in what should have been my decision.'

'Geeti, this is your own decision. I am a part of it... You
have taken a decision to be friends with me. It means something
to me, too.'

I stayed with her for a few days, and then Mummy died.

❧ Honour ❧

'Oh, Geeti, why haven't you got rid of it? Come on...' said Nandini, when I told her I was expecting.

'Nandini, I can't...'

'Why can't you?'

'I feel I must have the baby. Everything will always be the same otherwise.'

'You can adopt a child later on. This is foolishness. One doesn't ruin one's life to change it. What will you do? How will you bring it up?'

'I don't know...'

'Look, I will take you to a doctor. It will be all right, Geeti.'

It wasn't. The doctor's clinic was white and cold. She said I was too far along and she would have to induce labour. It would be like childbirth, but there wouldn't be a child. I thought of the white sheet and a pale, dead beloved face...not again... I told Nandini I couldn't. I must have the baby because I must be different from Sangeeta, the girl who had had an abortion in Desertvadi. Mummy's debt...two bodies panting together... How could I let it be... The baby would give me Mummy, Mummy's paleness...

'Geeti, think about it. Contact me if you need help, any time. At least write to your awful Ratish, tell him...'

I couldn't heed Nandini's advice, couldn't do anything beyond going to Hari's beige-and-brown home to get Ratish's address. I was only half alive those days.

'Why do you want to write to him now?'

Hari lived in a plush flat in south Lutyenabad, which he had received in dowry from his father-in-law. His parents' flat in Greater Kailash had been spartan. This was anything but bare. The sofa looked overstuffed and had brown motifs on it. The curtains were brown too, the carpet beige. Hari was wearing shorts. I noticed he had put on a lot of weight.

'He really went through a lot for you, Geetika. I have never seen a man sit and wait by the phone for a call the way he did, day after day.'

I too waited, Hari, I too waited. But of course, feminine time is not worth as much.

'Is it fair to contact him again? I don't think you are the girl for him.'

'Why do you say that?'

'Ratish is traditional—we all are, to some extent. It seems you got rather carried away by the Jana experience.'

'What do you mean?'

'Well, what was that about The Anti-Man and that Bengali fellow you were seeing?'

'Ratish said all this to you?'

'You broke his heart, Geeti. He loved you so much. He was ready to go against his parents for you. Do you realize he was almost engaged to that girl from Calcutta before you came into the picture? And mind you, that girl is very nice. It's not for money that his parents were so interested in that match. And you just went on…'

'I just wanted us to have an independent life by staying separately. Is that so unreasonable?'

'It isn't…but where was the money? Did you expect Ratish's parents to finance you after the way you behaved with them?'

'It is possible to live independently on two salaries…'

'In some godforsaken place. Ratish is used to a certain standard of living. And his parents had accepted you in spite of everything, so why should he alienate them by staying separately?'

No reason, none at all… What a clear world you live in, Hari—black and white, beige and brown. You don't know what it would have meant for me to stay with them. But anyway, I don't matter. My father could never have afforded a flat like this to secure his daughter's future. I deserve what I am getting, Hari… I know.

How self-righteous he sounded after taking a fat dowry from his in-laws. What right did he have to be angry on Ratish's behalf? Why was I giving him that right, sitting here and listening to his nonsense while Ratish's baby grew inside me? He hadn't noticed the slight bulge under my salwar kameez.

'You had become far too egotistical, Geeti. Ratish is not a nobody to be treated like that. How can you lay terms and conditions for marriage? I am glad that you have seen reason now,' he said. 'You are a lucky girl, you know, to get somebody like Ratish...'

I noted Ratish's address quietly in my diary. But even then I knew I wasn't going to write to him.

'I think you have totally misread the situation,' I told Hari.

'What do you mean?'

'You won't understand...there is too big a gap between our understanding of marriage...'

He flushed, 'You may say what you like, Geetika; ultimately everybody is the same...'

'With honourable exceptions. For some of us, there are reasons other than material...'

'Then why don't you marry that Bengali chap?'

'I don't know who you mean.' A certain talking machine took over. 'I have not come to beg Ratish to marry me... It would be difficult to marry somebody who thinks like this, or whose friend can throw such things in my face.'

'I think you are being unreasonably sensitive. I have given you the address, tried to reason with you... I can't do more.'

'You have done well, Hari. Give my love to your wife.'

The baby yawned, showing his pink gums. Why was I thinking of such unsavoury things? I need not meet Hari again, need never see that flat with its beige carpet and brown curtains again, need never smell the shiny polish on the furniture.

⊰ Cows ⊱

Ranjana Di was by my side. 'Geetika, if you cry like this, you will be a wreck and the baby will be affected. You have taken a decision, now stand by it. This is what life is about.'

She sat close to me and ruffled my hair. 'I made a decision years ago to end my marriage. It has been hard bringing up two children on my own, but I won't say it wasn't worth it. They have left—I have made them leave me. I want them to be independent in the way I never was... I won't say it was an easy decision... I miss them like one would miss a part of one's body. You have years of togetherness with your baby, Geeti. Eighteen, twenty years, maybe even more... That's a lot. Don't cry.'

Togetherness...with this little bundle who sucks nourishment from me drop by drop... What about Ratish... Was there an option?

'You haven't told me what happened between you and...' She trailed off—'boyfriend' was too frivolous, 'husband' inappropriate. There is no word to describe a relationship in which bodies come together and create another one.

'We fought because I didn't want to live with his parents...'

The formidable one, as she was called by her students, cradled the baby in her arms... 'What was the reason for his not shifting out of the family house?'

'Emotional, financial... He said it was both.'

'Geeti, couldn't you have agreed? You must have been in love...'

The tyranny of love... Did I love Ratish at the end of it all? Accusations and counter-accusations, apportioning of blame.

You want to break the family... My parents won't be able to take this. They will die... As it is, Reshma is so far from them. What has Mama ever asked you to do—wear certain kind of clothes, behave in a certain kind of way? You can't change at all, can you? You feel you are perfect? You can't listen to people who are older and know better... I am telling you now, you will regret saying all this to me. You will realize that there is a lot of fraud in the world... You will be sorry.

'I did love him... There are certain things I still love about him,' I told Ranjana Di. 'It was easy for me to fall in love with him, you know, very, very easy...'

'Are his parents very unaccepting?'

'They frankly wanted him to marry somebody else... They want somebody very different for their son—somebody rich, well-dressed, somebody they can indulge and show off to the world...'

'I don't know, Geeti, perhaps life with disapproving in-laws is better than the one you are getting into as a single parent.'

'But don't you see how Ratish is involved in all this? He gives his parents the right to judge me. I feel I have lost that much of him ever since I met them... It will be ten times worse with the baby; they will probably say I blackmailed him into it...'

'That sounds bad,' she said. 'I have no right to ask you but why didn't you... Oh God, I can't say it with him looking at me like this...'

'I don't know... My mother had just died when I learnt about the baby... I couldn't do it then. I couldn't do anything with myself. Remember how I used to come to college those days?'

'Yes, with mismatched sandals on your feet and swollen, dark eyes. We all realized something was wrong. Nandini told us about your mother.'

'My father took it bad, real bad. He is with my brother in Bombay... They asked me to join them there but I didn't want to go. Also there was the job...'

'You haven't seen them since?'

'I write regularly, chatty lies about my job and my PhD. How I am too involved to even take a day off. How I will come for a long holiday soon... It is easy, they don't question anything. My father is still not well enough to pay attention. My brother is too busy with his own life. My aunt, who was here and who

I used to see once in six months, has shifted to her family home in Agra... There is nobody here, nobody...'

⊰ Elite ⊱

'Look, Nandini, isn't he beautiful?'

She blew her nose into a perfumed airline tissue. She had returned from her holiday in Europe just last night.

'I should have been here for the birth...'

'Not your fault, Nandini; he came fifteen days earlier.'

'How did you manage all alone?'

'I have not been alone. I have been here...'

'No, at the birth?'

'I did what your childbirth adviser asked me to do—deep breaths and earth imagery.'

Nandini had made me visit a grey-haired American lady who took childbirth classes. I had not gone for the classes but visited her a couple of times. Nandini had also seen to the practical details, like giving me her children's old baby things. I knew she felt awful about missing the birth—she came back a week earlier for it but had missed it anyway. Perhaps she should have been there; perhaps Ratish should have been there too, holding my hand, the way men did in the birth films the childbirth adviser had shown me. White-and-black American babies, nothing to do with me.

'Does he keep you awake at night... Oh, Geeti, I am asking all the conventional questions, which goes to show what a conventional creature I really am...'

'He sleeps through the night, Nandini. He is a great baby.'

'We have to name him... We can't keep calling him "the baby".'

'You name him...'

'Don't be silly... He is yours, all yours, Geeti.'

Nandini's eyes were filling again. I didn't want her to cry for me. She was holding the baby close to her heart; he seemed to like that.

'Vasant,' I said.

'I am so glad you have come, Nandini. We must talk,' said Ranjana Di.

'Yes, we must talk,' Nandini replied.

Ranjana Di looked very tired. The lines on her face looked deeper, especially in contrast to Nandini's fresh complexion. She seemed to be averting her eyes, as though she didn't want Nandini there.

'What is to be done now?' Ranjana Di asked.

'Well, Geeti has to look for a place to stay and she has to find a maid to look after the baby once her maternity leave ends...' Nandini replied in a matter-of-fact tone.

'The impossibility of the situation doesn't strike you, Nandini?' said the formidable one, getting into one of her famous rages.

'I don't know what you mean.'

'I am not surprised. You are, of course, delinking Geeti from this society, this country... Oh, Nandini, will you ever learn to see things in perspective?'

'I see her from the perspective of a woman... What do you propose to do now? Nothing can be done to wish away the situation...'

'Adoption,' said Ranjana Di, suddenly turning to me. She looked soft and hard, compassionate and cruel. 'Geeti, either go back to your boyfriend, marry him, live wherever he asks you to live—or give up the child.'

'I am amazed that you should find it fit to impose a decision on Geeti. She should make her own decisions,' Nandini said stubbornly.

'But not from the perspective of your class, Nandini... Remember, Geeti can't take holidays to Europe when the going gets too tough here...'

'Are you saying that the liberty of living one's own life belongs only to my class?' said Nandini, flushing in anger.

'The constraints are different for middle-class women.'

'Let her decide,' said Nandini, her voice rising. 'She has given birth, let her decide...'

'As long as her life is not ruined,' said Ranjana Di, getting up with difficulty to leave the room. Her joints troubled her these days.

Nandini sat as if made of stone. She turned to me slowly and said, 'Another skeleton in my cupboard as far as the department is concerned. They will never forgive me for this...'

'Nandini, I will talk to them; I will tell them that you are not responsible in any way.'

'I had access to your mind those days,' she said bitterly, 'and I filled it with elite tripe...'

'I wasn't aware of this, that you could be accused...'

'You were too busy idealizing the department, weren't you? Oh, Geeti, academics are as limited as anybody else. To date, they have not forgiven me for being who I am. They see no pain, no courage, no bloody justification in my situation... She was so angry when she came to know I had taken you to that childbirth adviser...just because she is an American... It doesn't matter,' Nandini paused, as if letting a cloud pass. 'Come, Geeti, we must plan your life...'

'How do I plan, Nandini? What do I do with my family... what's left of it, that is... What do I do?'

I knew Nandini had no answers. It was a bit like asking myself.

Nandini put her arms around me. 'Don't worry, Geeti; don't look so troubled. Why don't you stay with me for a while?'

'No, Nandini, I must make up my mind here,' I found myself saying. 'I must talk to someone, I must talk to myself.'

'You will also talk to me a bit. I will come tomorrow,' said Nandini with the stubbornness I liked so much. 'I will come tomorrow,' she repeated, daring the world.

◁ Plans ▷

Making sense, making sense of life. I must know where, I must know how. Time was running out. I must begin at the beginning and I must begin in the middle, the middle of life.

What are you, little Vasant? Calm now...crying? What are you to me? I will begin from your beginning...

The baby...the baby was escaped semen, a squirming being uniting with my body, just like that, just by chance.

Vasant was also Ratish's child... He could get Ratish's name, property... Ratish's son...his mother's grandson...

Why are you, Vasant? You aren't only because Ratish wouldn't let me take chemical risks with my body. You are also because a part of me had died and I couldn't kill any more of me.

I ran to Ranjana Di. 'I am not giving up Vasant.'

She looked up from the book she was reading. 'It is your life, Geetika...'

What am I? I asked myself... Not an academic. I am scared stiff of academia—all these scholars with fancy degrees from foreign universities...

You are what you are. You are a writer, Geetika. Perhaps you don't need to belong...perhaps you don't need an ideology—Arundhati's, Dipankar's... A feminist stand, an objective distance...

My writing is too middle-class. It has to be... Can we escape our origins? My origins... Desertvadi—I can never escape the value system of Desertvadi. I am Sangeeta, the girl who had an abortion. I am more brazen—I brought my shame into the world. I can never escape my guilt, never, never... But I know I have not committed a crime... Where was the crime? I had slept with a man and produced a child...

But Arundhati said my motives were far from innocent. What were my motives? To get back the dead... I had given birth to Mummy, paid back the debt.

Oh, Mummy, I don't feel guilty about you anymore. I can explain—will you let me explain?

Vasant rooted towards me…like this baby, such life as I make it, drop by drop.

⊰ Desertvadi ⊱

'It is very difficult to travel with a little baby,' said the woman on my right.

'What does your husband do?' asked the one on my left.

I was travelling second class in the small cubicle called the ladies' compartment. It was rather airless, but since it was December, it felt quite cosy and comfortable to travel in close proximity to so many women.

I was still nursing Vasant and had decided that women would make for better travelling companions.

'I don't have a husband,' I said.

'You shouldn't joke about these things. At times, Ma Saraswati sits on one's tongue and these things one says in jest come true,' said the first one, looking pointedly at my pink sari.

'I am not joking,' I said. 'His parents did not like me, so…'

'Oho, you poor thing! One must burn such in-laws. My niece's in-laws tried to burn her, you know. Oh, you are so young, what will you do? Where will you go?'

'I teach in a college,' I told them. 'I am going home to my father in Desertvadi for the holidays.'

'What about your husband?' she asked again.

'These men…' said the second one, 'always suckling at their mothers' breasts.'

Vasant, would you be like that too, to some nice woman? I smiled at him. He caught my hair and pulled. He must be missing Raju ki Ma.

I had become a paying guest at Ranjana Di's house. She had refused to let me go, saying that she needed to see Vasant everyday.

I had stayed and somehow, that had given me legitimacy in college. When I rejoined work last month, there was hardly any heckling in the Pass class.

The women were untying their bundles of food. I opened my tiffin too. The woman whose niece had been almost burnt stretched out her arms for Vasant.

'Haven't they seen him? Oh, the terrible people. If they can't accept *you*, they can at least accept their own flesh and blood.'

'He isn't their flesh and blood, he is mine... Look, he even gets his nourishment from me. What have they done to deserve him?'

'Arrey, give him to them...and you get married again. You are so fair, anybody will marry you,' she said. She was wearing wide gold bangles, undoubtedly the rewards of a judicious marriage.

'You are an idiot. Why should she give him up? Who will look after her in her old age then?' asked the second woman angrily.

'Who knows about sons these days? They get wives and keep hiding in their beds,' said the first, neatly reversing the imagery of suckling sons. 'My own brother, you should see him...he is like putty in the hands of his wife. Doesn't do a thing for his aged parents.'

'Did they beat you?' the first woman asked me.

'No...but they said a whole lot of hurtful things...'

'Arrey, then why did you run away? You should have stayed... In time, the in-laws would have died or become too old and you could have been happy.'

'I am happy now,' I said, suddenly discovering the fact. Yes, I was happy. I was happy to have Vasant smile at me, I was happy to teach, I was happy to write. I had started a story just yesterday.

'You are much too young,' said the second one, 'you must go back to your husband.'

'I don't want to go back to him... I don't want to see him ever again...'

They clucked disapprovingly and spread their beddings everywhere, on the floor, in the corridor. They even helped me unroll mine. I was sleepy, so was Vasant. We lay on the hard berth, his head on my arm. The gentle rocking of the train put him to sleep, much faster than usual. I slipped into a heavy, dreamless slumber too.

Early next morning, the train drew up at the Desertvadi station. I quickly put a blue sweater on Vasant. He was going to meet his family. Papa looked old and frail, standing in the misty, morning light. I was in his arms before anything could be said. His thin arms encircled both of us.

'Why?' asked Papa, and then kept quiet.

He knew why.

I had explained everything in my letter.

Everything…

What was left would take a lifetime to tell.

Acknowledgements

This new edition became possible thanks to Dibakar Ghosh, my perspicacious and ever-affable commissioning editor, and his team at Rupa. Finding Anupama Roy, a meticulous copy editor, was such a joy. For further editorial input, a big thanks to Smita Mathur.

At this special juncture, as I am given the privilege of witnessing the rebirth of my first literary baby, I must also acknowledge those without whose belief in *Geetika* I could not have reached this point: Manju Kapur, Partho Datta, Udit Khurana and Mukul Marwah—having you in my life is some karmic reward, perhaps!

Praise for the book

'[The writer] is witty, tackling an emotionally charged subject with just the right amount of melancholy. She's brooding, and she's full of questions just waiting to be answered.'

—*The Afternoon Despatch & Courier*

'[Anuradha Marwah] manages to invent a new language to convey the experience of growing up in a town such as Ajmer.'

—**Professor Makarand Paranjpe**

'[The book] exemplifies an average middle-class Third World woman's ceaseless intrapersonal and interpersonal struggle with the dominant phallocentric ideologies in her claim for equal gender rights.'

—**Dr Puja Chakraborty and Dr Krishanu Adhikari**

Praise for author's other books

'Anuradha Marwah is erudite, has a way with words and compels attention.'

—**Khushwant Singh**, *Hindustan Times*

'*Aunties of Vasant Kunj* is one of the funniest books I have read this year. [...] The core strength of her narrative is driven by her authentic dialogue-writing—the way she has been able to put in the character's mouths a unique localized twang, vernacular grammar, its intonation and speech patterns—truly reflecting the community she writes about.'

—**Sudeep Sen**, International Editor of *Ars Notoria*, Writer, Literary Editor, Translator

'Marwah's comical and sensitive writing offers an empathetic gaze that reclaims being an "aunty".'

—*The New Indian Express*

'Marwah turns the cultural/societal trope on its head in her rendition of three residents of Delhi's very bourgeois, very aspirational neighbourhood, Vasant Kunj. '

—*Biblio: A Review of Books*

'It is the story of women by women narrated with both humour and compassion, occupying a niche in popular literature between chick-lit and mature women's fiction, between popular and literary fiction.'

—*Borderless Literary Journal*

'Marwah masterfully weaves a relatable and hilarious narrative. [Her] storytelling is instilled with wit and sharp observations, highlighting the push and pull between tradition and modernity in Indian society.

—*The Times of India*

'Known for her sensitive exploration of contemporary issues, sharp observations, and rich characterizations, Anuradha continues to captivate readers with her unique voice and storytelling competence

—*Times Now*

'Indeed, Marwah's feminist vision explores women's lives, seeking empowerment and agency.'

—*The Tribune*

'It's [*Aunties of Vasant Kunj*] a perspective on women that few people in India write [...] it made me grin with unholy glee.

—*Deccan Herald*

'Anuradha Marwah has created a narrative that is both relatable and thought-provoking, offering a window into the complex lives of women who are often stereotyped or overlooked.

—*The Pioneer*

'Anuradha Marwah has established a distinctive presence in contemporary Indian literature, skilfully combining sharp societal critiques with a compassionate perspective on middle-class life.'

—*The Patriot*